MW01127618

Werewolf Academy Book 6

Vengeance

By Cheree L. Alsop

VENGEANCE

Copyright © 2015 by Cheree L. Alsop
All rights reserved. This book or any portion thereof may not be reproduced or used in any manner whatsoever without the express written permission of the author except for the use of brief quotations in a book review.
This is a work of fiction. Names, characters, places, and incidents are a product of the author's imagination. Any resemblance to actual persons, events, or locales is entirely coincidental.
ISBN1511953160
Cover Design by Andy Hair
Editing by Sue Player
www.ChereeAlsop.com

ALSO BY CHEREE ALSOP

The Silver Series-
Silver
Black
Crimson
Violet
Azure
Hunter
Silver Moon

The Werewolf Academy Series-
Book One: Strays
Book Two: Hunted
Book Three: Instinct
Book Four: Taken
Book Five: Lost
Book Six: Vengeance
Book Seven: Chosen

The Monster Asylum Series-
Book One: The Fangs of Bloodhaven
Book Two: The Scales of Drakenfall

Heart of the Wolf Part One
Heart of the Wolf Part Two

The Galdoni Series-
Galdoni
Galdoni 2: Into the Storm
Galdoni 3: Out of Darkness

The Small Town Superheroes Series- (Through

Stonehouse Ink)
Small Town Superhero
Small Town Superhero II
Small Town Superhero III

Keeper of the Wolves
Stolen
The Million Dollar Gift
Thief Prince

The Shadows Series- (soon to be released through
Stonehouse Ink)
Shadows- Book One in the World of Shadows
Mist- Book Two in the World of Shadows
Dusk- Book Three in the World of Shadows

PRAISE FOR CHEREE ALSOP

The Werewolf Academy Series

If you love werewolves, paranormal, and looking for a book like House of Night or Vampire Academy this is it! YA for sure.
—Reviewer for Sweets Books

I got this book from a giveaway, and it's one of the coolest books I have ever read. If you love Hogwarts, and Vampire Academy, or basically anything that has got to do with supernatural people studying, this is the book for you.
—Maryam Dinzly

This series is truly a work of art, sucked in immediately and permanently. The first line and you are in the book. Cheree Alsop is a gifted writer, all of her books are my complete favorites!! This series has to be my absolute favorite, Alex is truly a wonderful character who I so wish was real so I can meet him and thank him. Once you pick this book up you won't put it down till it's finished. A must read!!!!!
—BookWolf Brianna

Cheree does it again with the first in her new series Werewolf Academy. Once you start reading you can't put it down. Love the Heroes and Despise the Villains. Her details and your imagination puts you right in the action of the story. Download and Enjoy!!
—Doughgirl61- Amazon Reviewer

This new series follows young werewolves sent to a protected boarding school to keep them safe from werewolf hunters. Excellent worldbuilding, well-fleshed characters, and intricate plots - looking forward to more!
—Winged Wolf, Amazon Reviewer

Listed with Silver Moon as the top most emotional of Cheree's books, I loved Instinct for its raw truth about the pain, the heartbreak, and the guilt that Alex fights.
—Loren Weaver

Great story. Loaded with adventure at every turn. Can't wait till the next book. Very enjoyable, light reading. I would recommend to all young and old readers.
—Sharon Klein

The Silver Series

"Cheree Alsop has written *Silver* for the YA reader who enjoys both werewolves and coming-of-age tales. Although I don't fall into this demographic, I still found it an entertaining read on a long plane trip! The author has put a great deal of thought into balancing a tale that could apply to any teen (death of a parent, new school, trying to find one's place in the world) with the added spice of a youngster dealing with being exceptionally different from those around him, and knowing that puts him in danger."
—Robin Hobb, author of the Farseer Trilogy

"I honestly am amazed this isn't absolutely EVERYWHERE! Amazing book. Could NOT put it down! After reading this book, I purchased the entire series!"
—Josephine, Amazon Reviewer

"Great book, Cheree Alsop! The best of this kind I have read in a long time. I just hope there is more like this one."
—Tony Olsen

"I couldn't put the book down. I fell in love with the characters and how wonderfully they were written. Can't wait to read the 2nd!"
—Mary A. F. Hamilton

"A page-turner that kept me wide awake and wanting more. Great characters, well written, tenderly developed, and thrilling. I loved this book, and you will too."
—Valerie McGilvrey

"Super glad that I found this series! I am crushed that it is at its end. I am sure we will see some of the characters in the next series, but it just won't be the same. I am 41 years old, and am only a little embarrassed to say I was crying at 3 a.m. this morning while finishing the last book. Although this is a YA series, all ages will enjoy the Silver Series. Great job by Cheree Alsop. I am excited to see what she comes up with next."
—Jennc, Amazon Reviewer

The Galdoni Series

"This is absolutely one of the best books I have ever read in my life! I loved the characters and their personalities, the storyline and the way it was written. The bravery, courage and sacrifice that Kale showed was amazing and had me scolding myself to get a grip and stop crying! This book had adventure, romance and comedy all rolled into one terrific book I LOVED the lesson in this book, the struggles that the characters had to go through (especially the forbidden love)...I couldn't help wondering what it would be like to live among such strangely beautiful creatures that acted, at times, more caring and compassionate than the humans. Overall, I loved this book...I recommend it to ANYONE who fancies great books."

—iBook Reviewer

"I was pleasantly surprised by this book! The characters were so well written as if the words themselves became life. The sweet romance between hero and heroine made me root for the underdog more than I usually do! I definitely recommend this book!"

—Sara Phillipp

"Can't wait for the next book!! Original idea and great characters. Could not put the book down; read it in one sitting."

—StanlyDoo- Amazon Reviewer

"5 stars! Amazing read. The story was great- the plot flowed and kept throwing the unexpected at you. Wonderfully established setting in place; great character development, shown very well thru well placed dialogue- which in turn kept the story moving right along! No bog downs or boring parts in this book! Loved the originality that stemmed from ancient mysticism- bringing age old fiction into modern day reality. Recommend for teenage and older- action violence a little intense for preteen years, but overall this is a great action thriller slash mini romance novel."

—That Lisa Girl, Amazon Reviewer

"I was not expecting a free novel to beat anything that I have ever laid eyes upon. This book was touching and made me want more after each sentence."
—Sears1994, iBook Reviewer

"This book was simply heart wrenching. It was an amazing book with a great plot. I almost cried several times. All of the scenes were so real it felt like I was there witnessing everything."
—Jeanine Drake, iBook Reveiwer

"This book was absolutely amazing...It had me tearing at parts, cursing at others, and filled with adrenaline rushing along with the characters at the fights. It is a book for everyone, with themes of love, courage, hardship, good versus evil, humane and inhumane...All around, it is an amazing book!"
—Mkb312, iBook Reviewer

"Galdoni is an amazing book; it is the first to actually make me cry! It is a book that really touches your heart, a romance novel that might change the way you look at someone. It did that to me."
—Coralee2, Reviewer

"Wow. I simply have no words for this. I highly recommend it to anyone who stumbled across this masterpiece. In other words, READ IT!"
—Troublecat101, iBook Reviewer

Keeper of the Wolves

"This is without a doubt the VERY BEST paranormal romance/adventure I have ever read and I've been reading these types of books for over 45 years. Excellent plot, wonderful protagonists—even the evil villains were great. I read this in one sitting on a Saturday morning when there were so many other things I should have been doing. I COULD NOT put it down! I also appreciated the author's research and insights into the behavior of wolf packs. I will CERTAINLY read more by this author and put her on my 'favorites' list."

—N. Darisse

"This is a novel that will emotionally cripple you. Be sure to keep a box of tissues by your side. You will laugh, you will cry, and you will fall in love with Keeper. If you loved *Black Beauty* as a child, then you will truly love *Keeper of the Wolves* as an adult. Put this on your 'must read' list."

—Fortune Ringquist

"Cheree Alsop mastered the mind of a wolf and wrote the most amazing story I've read this year. Once I started, I couldn't stop reading. Personal needs no longer existed. I turned the last page with tears streaming down my face."

—Rachel Andersen, Amazon Reviewer

"I truly enjoyed this book very much. I've spent most of my life reading supernatural books, but this was the first time I've read one written in first person and done so well. I must admit that the last half of this book had me in tears from sorrow and pain for the main character and his dilemma as a man and an animal. . . Suffice it to say that this is one book

you REALLY need in your library. I won't ever regret purchasing this book, EVER! It was just that GOOD! I would also recommend you have a big box of tissues handy because you WILL NEED THEM! Get going, get the book..."
—Kathy I, Amazon Reviewer

"I just finished this book. Oh my goodness, did I get emotional in some spots. It was so good. The courage and love portrayed is amazing. I do recommend this book. Thought provoking."
—Candy, Amazon Reviewer

Thief Prince

"I absolutely loved this book! I could not put it down. . . The Thief Prince will whisk you away into a new world that you will not want to leave! I hope that Ms. Alsop has more about this story to write, because I would love more Kit and Andric! This is one of my favorite books so far this year! Five Stars!"
—Crystal, Book Blogger at Books are Sanity

". . . Once I started I couldn't put it down. The story is amazing. The plot is new and the action never stops. The characters are believable and the emotions presented are beautiful and real. If anyone wants a good, clean, fun, romantic read, look no further. I hope there will be more books set in Debria, or better yet, Antor."
—SH Writer, Amazon Reviewer

"This book was a roller coaster of emotions: tears, laughter, anger, and happiness. I absolutely fell in love with all of the characters placed throughout this story. This author knows how to paint a picture with words."

—Kathleen Vales

"Awesome book! It was so action packed, I could not put it down, and it left me wanting more! It was very well written, leaving me feeling like I had a connection with the characters."

—M. A., Amazon Reviewer

"I am a Cheree Alsop junkie and I have to admit, hands down, this is my FAVORITE of anything she has published. In a world separated by race, fear and power are forced to collide in order to save them all. Who better to free them of the prejudice than the loyal heart of a Duskie? Adventure, incredible amounts of imagination, and description go into this world! It is a 'buy now and don't leave the couch until the last chapter has reached an end' kind of read!"

—Malcay, Amazon Reviewer

"I absolutely loved this book! I could not put it down! Anything with a prince and a princess is usually a winner for me, but this book is even better! It has multiple princes and princesses on scene over the course of the book! I was completely drawn into Kit's world as she was faced with danger and new circumstances...Kit was a strong character, not a weak and simpering girl who couldn't do anything for herself. The Thief Prince (Andric) was a great character as well! I kept seeing glimpses of who he really was and I loved that the author gave us clues as to what he was like under the surface. The Thief Prince will whisk you away into a new world that you will not want to leave!"

—Bookworm, Book Reviewer

The Small Town Superhero Series

"A very human superhero- Cheree Alsop has written a great book for youth and adults alike. Kelson, the superhero, is battling his own demons plus bullies in this action packed narrative. Small Town Superhero had me from the first sentence through the end. I felt every sorrow, every pain and the delight of rushing through the dark on a motorcycle. Descriptions in Small Town Superhero are so well written the reader is immersed in the town and lives of its inhabitants."
—Rachel Andersen, Book Reviewer

"Anyone who grew up in a small town or around motorcycles will love this! It has great characters and flows well with martial arts fighting and conflicts involved."
—Karen, Amazon Reviewer

"Fantastic story...and I love motorcycles and heroes who don't like the limelight. Excellent character development. You'll like this series!"
—Michael, Amazon Reviewer

"Another great read; couldn't put it down. Would definitely recommend this book to friends and family. She has put out another great read. Looking forward to reading more!"
—Benton Garrison, Amazon Reviewer

"I enjoyed this book a lot. Good teen reading. Most books I read are adult contemporary; I needed a change and this was a good change. I do recommend reading this book! I will be looking out for more books from this author. Thank you!"

—Cass, Amazon Reviewer

Stolen

"This book will take your heart, make it a little bit bigger, and then fill it with love. I would recommend this book to anyone from 10-100. To put this book in words is like trying to describe love. I had just gotten it and I finished it the next day because I couldn't put it down. If you like action, thrilling fights, and/or romance, then this is the perfect book for you."

—Steven L. Jagerhorn

"Couldn't put this one down! Love Cheree's ability to create totally relatable characters and a story told so fluidly you actually believe it's real."

—Sue McMillin, Amazon Reviewer

"I enjoyed this book it was exciting and kept you interested. The characters were believable. And the teen romance was cute."

—Book Haven- Amazon Reviewer

"This book written by Cheree Alsop was written very well. It is set in the future and what it would be like for government control. The drama was great and the story was very well put together. If you want something different, then this is the book to get and it is a page turner for sure. You will love the main characters as well, and the events that

unfold during the story. It will leave you hanging and wanting more."
—Kathy Hallettsville, TX- Amazon Reviewer

"I really liked this book . . . I was pleasantly surprised to discover this well-written book. . .I'm looking forward to reading more from this author."
—Julie M. Peterson- Amazon Reviewer

"Great book! I enjoyed this book very much it keeps you wanting to know more! I couldn't put it down! Great read!"
—Meghan- Amazon Reviewer

"A great read with believable characters that hook you instantly. . . I was left wanting to read more when the book was finished."
—Katie- Goodreads Reviewer

Heart of the Wolf

"Absolutely breathtaking! This book is a roller coaster of emotions that will leave you exhausted!!! A beautiful fantasy filled with action and love. I recommend this book to all fantasy lovers and those who enjoy a heartbreaking love story that rivals that of Romeo and Juliet. I couldn't put this book down!"
—Amy May

"What an awesome book! A continual adventure, with surprises on every page. What a gifted author she is. You just can't put the book down. I read it in two days. Cheree has a way of developing relationships and pulling at your heart.

You find yourself identifying with the characters in her book...True life situations make this book come alive for you and gives you increased understanding of your own situation in life. Magnificent story and characters. I've read all of Cheree's books and recommend them all to you...especially if you love adventures."

—Michael, Amazon Reviewer

"You'll like this one and want to start part two as soon as you can! If you are in the mood for an adventure book in a faraway kingdom where there are rival kingdoms plotting and scheming to gain more power, you'll enjoy this novel. The characters are well developed, and of course with Cheree there is always a unique supernatural twist thrown into the story as well as romantic interests to make the pages fly by."

Karen, Amazon Reviewer

When Death Loved an Angel

"This style of book is quite a change for this author so I wasn't expecting this, but I found an interesting story of two very different souls who stepped outside of their "accepted roles" to find love and forgiveness, and what is truly of value in life and death."

—Karen, Amazon Reviewer

"When Death Loved an Angel by Cheree Alsop is a touching paranormal romance that cranks the readers' thinking mode into high gear."

—Rachel Andersen, Book Reviewer

"Loved this book. I would recommend this book to everyone. And be sure to check out the rest of her books, too!"
—Malcay, Book Reviewer

The Shadows Series

". . . This author has talent. I enjoyed her world, her very well developed characters, and an interesting, entertaining concept and story. Her introduction to her world was well done and concise. . . .Her characters were interesting enough that I became attached to several. I would certainly read a follow-up if only to check on the progress and evolution of the society she created. I recommend this for any age other than those overly sensitive to some graphic violence. The romance was heartfelt but pg. A good read."
—Mari, Amazon Reviewer

". . . I've fallen for the characters and their world. I've even gone on to share (this book) with my sister. . .So many moments made me smile as well as several which brought tears from the attachment; not sad tears, I might add. When I started Shadows, I didn't expect much because I assumed it was like most of the books I've read lately. But this book was one of the few books to make me happy I was wrong and find myself so far into the books that I lost track of time, ending up reading to the point that my body said I was too tired to continue reading! I can't wait to see what happens in the next book. . . Some of my new favorite quotes will be coming from this lovely novel. Thank you to Cheree Alsop for allowing the budding thoughts to come to life. I am a very hooked reader."
—Stephanie Roberts, Amazon Reviewer

"This was a heart-warming tale of rags to riches. It was also wonderfully described and the characters were vivid and vibrant; a story that teaches of love defying boundaries and of people finding acceptance."
—Sara Phillip, Book Reviewer

"This is the best book I have ever had the pleasure of reading. . . It literally has everything, drama, action, fighting, romance, adventure, & suspense. . . Nexa is one of the most incredible female protagonists ever written. . .It literally had me on pins & needles the ENTIRE time. . . I cannot recommend this book highly enough. Please give yourself a wonderful treat & read this book... you will NOT be disappointed!!!"
—Jess- Goodreads Reviewer

"Took my breath away; excitement, adventure and suspense. . . This author has extracted a tender subject and created a supernatural fantasy about seeing beyond the surface of an individual. . . Also the romantic scenes would make a girl swoon. . . The fights between allies and foes and blood lust would attract the male readers. . .The conclusion was so powerful and scary this reader was sitting on the edge of her seat."
—Susan Mahoney, Book Blogger

"Adventure, incredible amounts of imagination and description go into this world! It is a buy now, don't leave the couch until the last chapter has reached an end kind of read!"
—Malcay- Amazon Reviewer

"The high action tale with the underlying love story that unfolds makes you want to keep reading and not put it down. I can't wait until the next book in the Shadows Series comes out."
—Karen- Amazon Reviewer

"Really enjoyed this book. A modern fairy tale complete with Kings and Queens, Princesses and Princes, castles and the damsel is not quite in distress. LOVE IT."
—Brainc, Talk Supe- Book Blogger

". . . It's refreshing to see a female character portrayed without the girly cliches most writers fall into. She is someone I would like to meet in real life, and it is nice to read the first person POV of a character who is so well-round that she is brave, but still has the softer feminine side that defines her character. A definite must read."
—S. Teppen- Goodreads Reviewer

"I really enjoyed this book and had a hard time putting it down. . . This premise is interesting and the world building was intriguing. The author infused the tale with the feeling of suspicion and fear . . . The author does a great job with characterization and you grow to really feel for the characters throughout especially as they change and begin to see Nexa's point of view. . . I did enjoy the book and the originality. I would recommend this for young adult fantasy lovers. It's more of a mild dark fantasy, but it would definitely fall more in the traditional fantasy genre. "
—Jill- Goodreads Reviewer

To many, many more adventures with
My husband, Michael,
And with my children, Myree, Ashton, and Aiden.
Every day holds a new story;
I look forward to writing it together!

Chapter One

Alex walked up to Officer Dune. "I heard you wanted to talk to me?"

The officer turned at the sound of Alex's voice. He gave a small smile. Something hit Alex's chest so hard he stumbled backwards a few steps. The sound of a silenced gun being fired rebounded off the school. Alex looked down. A strange dart protruded from the front of his tuxedo. He glanced up and saw a gun in the officer's hand.

"Sorry, Alex. Money talks," Officer Dune said.

The man's voice was strangely muffled past the ringing that filled Alex's ears. He stumbled backwards against the rough brick of the school. His chest felt constricted and he had a hard time pulling in a breath. Alex fell to the ground. His last glimpse was of Officer Dune shoving the gun back behind his belt.

The officer lifted a cell phone to his ear. "I've got him."

***

Alex woke up feeling as though someone was standing on his chest. He held perfectly still, trying to remember where he was and why. Disjointed memories of the prom and talking to Officer Dune came to mind. His muscles tightened when he remembered being shot with the dart. Officer Dune had said something about money talking. He wondered who could offer the officer enough money to turn against a friend.

He had to know where he was. Alex pushed down the urge to open his eyes and instead used his other werewolf senses.

The scent of concrete matched the hard press of the floor that sent a chill through his clothes. He smelled blood, thick, gelatinous, and tinged with the overly coppery scent of werewolf that set his teeth on edge. Human smells came to his nose, but only a few were fresh as though wherever he was had been well used until recently.

His ears picked up the slight tapping of fingers on a keyboard, but it was faint as if the sound came from a few rooms away. The hum of several machines whirred in a corner. He could hear footsteps that echoed in a distant hallway. No voices reached his ears.

Alex listened harder, searching the space around him for the sound of breathing or a heartbeat. He had to know if there were people present before he opened his eyes.

He was alone. Only his own unsteady heartbeat and labored breathing met his ears. He opened his eyes slowly.

Whatever Officer Dune had shot him with made it hard to even force his eyelids to stay open. He couldn't move his head to the side; he could only stare up at the neon light on the ceiling that beat down mercilessly with its own persistent hum. From the corner of his eye, Alex made out where glass met at a metal corner. His heart fell. He was in a cage.

Footsteps drew closer. He closed his eyes, willing his breathing to slow. He wasn't fond of cages. The last one he had been captive in was in Drogan's helicopter and ended up with them crashing to the ground. Wolves weren't made to be locked in cages and werewolves even less so.

"We know you're awake." The voice was high pitched and nasal. "You might be a bit uncomfortable, but it should pass. Our new formula is a mite more powerful than we expected, but with your abilities, we didn't want to underestimate."

Alex kept perfectly still. Part of him had expected Drogan, but there was no smell of his half-brother in the room. Instead, the smell of humans and antiseptic permeated the air. He had no idea what they wanted, but the cage didn't bode well. Alex had no idea how long he had been out and knew Siale and the others would be worried sick. He had to get back to them somehow.

"Pretend to be asleep all you want," the woman continued. "We'll begin our work as soon as your companion shows up."

A phone rang. A button was pushed. "Dr. Kamala, they've arrived."

"Thank you," the woman replied.

Their footsteps faded from the room.

Adrenaline rushed through Alex. He concentrated on his fingers, willing them to move. He wondered what companion the woman was talking about. Given the situation, it didn't bode well for whoever they brought in. Fear for Cassie or Siale filled him. He had to get moving so he could defend who they had managed to catch.

His little finger on his left hand twitched. Alex gritted his teeth, concentrating on the slight movement. He forced every ounce of energy he had to his left hand. His other fingers began to respond. When his left hand closed, his focused on the right. The lethargy faded from it much more quickly.

Through sheer strength of determination, Alex was sitting up when the door opened again. Whatever they had shot him with was stronger than anything he had experienced before. He figured he had enough strength to stand, but barely. He could only hope it would be enough to get him out of the cage.

A smell rushed through the door as the woman entered. Alex's lips pulled back from his teeth in a silent snarl. He expected Drogan to walk through confident and cocky at having Alex captive. Instead, to Alex's shock, four guards were carrying the unconscious form of the Extremist leader between them.

Dr. Kamala pulled a strange key from the lanyard around her neck and inserted it in the door. When Alex pushed to his feet, she shook her head.

"Make one move and my guards will shoot you again. With a double dose of our concentrated liquid silver coursing through your body, I'm not sure you'll actually survive. Do you want to take that risk?" her voice hung in the air, the last word curled up high as though asked by a concerned parrot.

Alex leaned against the glass wall and made no move toward the door when it was pulled open. Drogan's still form was tossed inside and the guards moved quickly out again. Dr. Kamala put the circular key in the lock and turned it. The mechanics of several locking structures clicked into place behind a sheet of metal. Alex had no doubt by the smell that the lock was coated in silver.

"As soon as he wakes up, we'll begin," Dr. Kamala said with a satisfied nod. She turned and stalked away. The staccato click of her heels was a painful counterbalance to the heavy footsteps of the four guards who followed her back down the hall.

Alex dropped to his knees. He eyed Drogan, his chest heaving and heart pounding at the proximity to his enemy. Part of him debated whether he should just kill Drogan while the Extremist was unable to defend himself. The wolf side of him agreed wholeheartedly; his human side argued that it would be completely wrong.

As much as he wanted to tear Drogan's throat out, he also had no idea where they were or why they had been taken. Perhaps Drogan could be his key in escaping. If they were looking for a werewolf, he could throw the Extremist under the bus. He had to get out of there, and if killing Drogan defeated his chance of escaping, he figured he could practice a little self-control and wait until he knew exactly what they were up against.

Against the protest of his entire wolf side, Alex sat back against the wall as far as he could get from the Extremist and forced himself to use the patience that was the very least of his strengths.

"About time," Alex muttered when Drogan began to stir.

The Extremist leader lifted a hand and rubbed his eyes. Alex was reminded that Drogan was an Alpha by how quickly he appeared to be recovering from the concentrated silver. It set Alex's nerves on edge.

Drogan tipped his head to one side. His eyes narrowed when he saw Alex. "What are you doing here?" the Extremist growled.

Alex didn't move from his seat against the glass. "I could ask you the same thing," he answered levelly.

Drogan grunted and rolled over. He pushed up to a kneeling position. "I feel like I have a hangover."

"Am I supposed to feel sorry for you?" Alex asked.

Drogan shot him a look, his mismatched eyes filled with

aggression. "Want to fight it out right now?"

Alex snorted. "Like you're in a great position for a duel."

"I could say the same about you," Drogan replied, looking him over more carefully.

Alex sat up straight, pushing away all appearance of the headache the silver had left him with. "Better than you," he replied shortly.

Drogan sat against the opposite side of the glass cage. "So why are we here?" At Alex's silence, the Alpha hit the glass with the side of his fist as though to test it, not break it. "I've designed cages just like this. It's bulletproof. We're not going to shatter it."

"Great deduction, Sherlock," Alex replied dryly.

Drogan was about to respond when footsteps sounded down the hall. Both werewolves watched the door.

Dr. Kamala entered with her cronies close behind.

Drogan's eyes widened and he looked even angrier than he had upon waking up and finding himself in the same cage as Alex.

"Dr. Kamala, what are you doing here?"

Her eyes narrowed behind her green thin-framed glasses. "What's wrong, Drogan? Surprised I'm not dead."

Alex stared from one to the other, amazed that they knew each other. Whatever he had gotten in the middle of, perhaps he wasn't the focus. He chose to stay silent and watch in the hopes that he would find an out that could possibly still leave Drogan in the unbreakable cage.

Drogan rose, glaring at the doctor from the other side of the glass. "Yes. I thought I killed you and your little squirrely assistant." He made a show of looking at the skinny man to the doctor's right. "Still clinging to the good doctor's coattails, Steve? You'll be the first I disembowel when I get out of here."

The man's face paled and he looked away from Drogan.

Dr. Kamala lifted her lips in what was supposed to be a smile, but came out looking completely wrong on her face. "When my genetic testing revealed that you and Alex were related, it wasn't a far reach to deduct that you were also a werewolf. I should have expected the *Extremist Leader*," she said the title with a sneer, "To turn on his own to protect his hide. I hope you enjoy becoming the product of your own experimentation."

Drogan lifted his lips in a snarl, looking at that moment more like a wolf than a man. "Let me out of here."

Her eyes narrowed. "Not a chance. Time to see how it feels to be on the other side of the glass."

"Who helped you get me in here?" Drogan demanded.

Dr. Kamala smiled. "It wasn't hard to find allies ready to help me when I informed them that our beloved leader was in fact one of the beasts we've been hunting. Don't underestimate the power of betrayal." She turned to her men. "No time to waste," she said. "Get Alex out and hooked up."

"For what?" Drogan asked.

It appeared as though Dr. Kamala wouldn't answer. She toyed with her keys for a moment before sliding the round one into the lock. Before turning it, she gave them both an amused look and straightened her glasses. "I thought you would figure it out on your own. Apparently werewolves aren't as smart as I assumed."

Both Alex and Drogan bristled at the statement.

Dr. Kamala raised a hand. "Calm down, gentlemen, or should I say gentle dogs?" She chuckled at her joke. Steve, the skinny assistant, let out a little laugh he quickly smothered at a look from Drogan. The guards near the door acted as though they hadn't heard anything. Dr. Kamala ran a hand down her chin-length pencil-straight brown hair to smooth it.

"You are here because I need the Demon."

Ice ran through Alex's blood.

"He's the Demon." Drogan pointed to Alex with a touch of relief in his voice. "You've got him. Let me go."

Dr. Kamala gave a cold smile. "If only it was that easy. I need him in Demon form for the procedure to work."

Alex broke his silence. "What procedure?"

The doctor ignored him and kept her attention on Drogan. "If the procedure kills him, you have similar enough DNA to complete it."

"Why does he need to be the Demon?" Drogan asked, his relief gone entirely.

"Because of the endorphins emitted during the process," Dr. Kamala explained. "From what we've found in studying the areas where the Demon has been seen, he emits an adrenaline endorphin compound we have been unable to duplicate in our lab. We think it is the key to his ability to change into his Demon form. We need to harness it in order to recreate the Demon."

Drogan merely glared at her, leaving Alex to ask, "And by harness it, you mean?"

"Bleed you dry while you're in your morphed state," she replied calmly as though she hadn't just given Alex a death sentence.

"So what do you need me here for?" Drogan demanded, appearing completely unconcerned about Alex's fate.

"You share some of the same genetic material through your father, the General."

Drogan's eyes narrowed. "Curse the day I hired you."

"Don't worry," Dr. Kamala replied. "I do." She waved a hand at her guards and they approached the door. "The point is, if Alex dies before he morphs, we're hoping to be able to trigger the same response in you."

Alex and Drogan exchanged a look. Dread filled Alex at the thought that Drogan might be able to morph into the same powerful creature he was learning how to control. He couldn't imagine the devastation the Alpha would cause if that happened.

"Why do you need to harness the Demon's abilities?" Alex asked quietly.

The woman's eyes narrowed. "Just be a good Demon and change for us."

"No."

Everyone stared at Alex. He could feel Drogan's wide gaze, but refused to look away from Dr. Kamala. "I'm not some animal to be experimented on."

"Your situation proves otherwise," Dr. Kamala stated, her voice cold.

Alex crossed the short area to the door. "Just wait until I'm on the other side of this glass," he told her in a low growl.

"Shoot him," she replied, her gaze locked on his.

A small sliding panel on the side of the cage was opened and a guard aimed his gun at Alex's side. As much as he didn't want to comply with the doctor's wishes, getting shot again wouldn't get him closer to escaping.

Reason warred with his wolf instincts to fight back. Alex held up a hand. "Fine," he gave in. "I'll go where you want me to, but I won't morph."

"You'll do whatever I want you to," Dr. Kamala said.

Alex stood back for her to open the door. Four guns were immediately trained on him. He had no doubt the guards wouldn't hesitate to shoot if he tried anything. He stepped through the thick glass door and paused when one of the guards indicated for him to do so.

Alex glanced back to see Drogan watching him with an

unreadable expression. As soon as the door was locked, the woman walked away. At the guard's motion, Alex was forced to follow her.

Chapter Two

Alex had survived brutality before. He willed his heart to be calm while they strapped him to a table.

"Just morph or whatever you call it and we won't have to do this," Dr. Kamala said as though they were discussing changing a tire instead of torture.

"I'm used to pain," Alex replied.

A light of amusement gleamed in the doctor's eyes. "Not like this."

Steve cut Alex's shirt off, then attached electrodes to his chest. Dr. Kamala studied Alex's scars with an impassive expression.

"You should take better care of yourself," she noted.

Alex rolled his eyes. "Like not getting myself strapped to a table and tortured?"

"That would be a good idea," Dr. Kamala replied without a hint of humor.

Metal cuffs were fastened around Alex's wrists and ankles. He forced his face to remain expressionless when a cart with a dial and several knobs was pushed over by two of the doctor's assistants. One of them flipped a switch and the machine began to hum.

"I think I'm really going to enjoy this," Dr. Kamala said.

Alex clenched his jaw, refusing to emit a sound when wires were attached to the electrodes.

"You might want a mouth guard," the doctor told him. She lifted a white object. "It'll keep you from breaking your teeth." When Alex glared at her and refused to open his mouth, she shrugged. "Have it your way." She tossed it back on the cart as though she couldn't care less.

"Start with level two," she told the assistant who stood ready near the machine.

The young woman nodded and turned the dial.

Electricity rushed from the electrodes and coursed through Alex's entire body. His back arched and he gritted his teeth so hard in an effort to keep from crying out that he thought they would break. Every nerve, muscle fiber, and cell felt like it was ignited with electric fire until Alex felt like he was burning from the inside out. His hands clenched into fists and his arms shook with the strain. He had never felt such pain before.

Blue pulsed through his vision in time to the surges of electricity. Alex channeled all of his focus into keeping the Demon at bay. He wouldn't let Dr. Kamala win.

"Kate, raise it to level three," the doctor intoned in her high-pitched, monotone voice.

When the electricity increased, so did the pain. A hum sounded in Alex's mind. The wolf instinct to survive fought to break free. It took everything he had to keep the Demon from forcing its way through. He wanted to phase to wolf form and tear them apart, but he knew if he let his body do anything, the Demon would take over and all would be lost.

"Level five."

Alex's head slammed back against the table. His body shook as he fought to keep from yelling out in pain. He shut his eyes and saw Siale's face. She danced with the grace of a bird, floating across the floor of the prom at Greyton High School. Her dress accentuated her gray eyes, and they twinkled as she laughed at something he said. The pain became a cloud of brilliant red, unbearable, unbreakable, and all-consuming.

"That's enough," Alex heard Dr. Kamala say above the hum in his mind.

The electricity immediately shut off. Alex had no idea how long he had been strapped to the table. Small jolts raced through his body. He felt as though ever nerve was fried and overly sensitive; even the pressure of the table against his back hurt. The silence that filled his ears was too loud, and each breath made his heart skip a beat.

"Get him to the cage. We'll continue tomorrow," Dr. Kamala's impassive voice intoned.

Alex couldn't find the strength to move, let alone fight, when he was unstrapped and carried roughly by four men back to the glass cage. Their grips on his arms and legs felt like they burned through his skin, but he couldn't force himself to break free. Alex was tossed inside the cell unceremoniously as though he was a piece of garbage. The door was shut and locked, then the guards walked away.

"Have a nice time?"

Adrenaline surged through Alex's frayed nerves at the sound of the Extremist's voice. He tipped his head to see Drogan sitting against the far wall, his legs crossed at the ankles and his hands resting casually in his lap.

Instincts made Alex hide his pain and warned him to face his enemy at all times. He gritted his teeth and pushed up to a sitting position. A grunt escaped his lips when he leaned against the glass near the door. The cool surface sent sharp tingles through his worn body.

He felt Drogan's gaze and looked up. The Alpha's attention was on the scars that lined his bare torso.

"Werewolves generally heal better than that," Drogan said, his voice expressionless.

Alex tipped his head against the glass. "Silver tends to interfere with the healing process."

"I recall a few instances of you being injured with silver weapons."

Alex glared at his half-brother. "You should try it sometime."

The barest hint of a smile touched Drogan's lips. His mismatched eyes narrowed. "Maybe you'll be the one to serve up such a dish."

"I will," Alex said with as much conviction as he could muster.

All he wanted to do was sleep, but with Drogan in the same cage, his instincts wouldn't allow him to let down his guard. He closed his eyes, keeping the rest of his senses tuned onto the werewolf's position.

"Why not just give them the Demon?"

Alex snorted without looking at Drogan. "You'd like that, wouldn't you? If I give in, they can drain the life out of me, get my blood with the adrenaline and whatever it is she called it, and they can make their own Demon or infuse someone with my blood or whatever they plan to do. I'd be dead and you can continue with your screwed up plans if you ever get out of here."

"That's not what I meant."

When Alex refused to be baited by his brother's impassive tone, Drogan sighed. Alex heard him shift against the glass, but the Alpha made no move to draw closer.

"If you become the Demon, you can break free. I've seen your strength." There was a hint of longing in Drogan's voice he couldn't hide. "You can tear these walls down the way you destroyed my curs that attacked your precious Academy's forest. With power like that, nobody could stop you."

"Nothing is unstoppable," Alex told him. He opened his eyes and looked at the Extremist. "They have enough guards and silver in that room to destroy an army of werewolves. The machines are already set up. Your doctor plans to inject me the moment I morph. I wouldn't have a chance."

"What about now?" Drogan asked. "Break the glass. Get us out of here."

Alex closed his eyes and tried to find the blue-tinged strength that came from the Demon. He finally shook his head. "I can't. The electricity took too much out of me. It won't listen."

Drogan's eyebrows rose as though the information was new. "You mean you don't control it?"

Alex gave himself a mental kick for giving Drogan any sort of information. He had to admit, "Not all the time. I'm working on it."

"I'll be you are," Drogan said, crossing his hands behind his head.

"What's that supposed to mean?" Alex demanded.

Drogan shrugged. "That you're the protector of your beloved Academy, the students, your sister," he grimaced, "Meredith. You don't care about much more than that."

"They're my pack."

Drogan rolled his eyes. "Yeah, whatever. Werewolves protect their packs and all that. It's pretty lame, don't you think?"

Alex couldn't tell if the Alpha was baiting him or truly curious. He was careful to watch his words. "It's family. That's what this is all about, protecting my family and making the world a safer place for them to live."

"Do you hear yourself?" Drogan asked with a hint of amusement in his voice. "'A safer place for *them* to live.' You already don't expect to survive to see your new world where everyone lives in peace and happiness with pink fluffy clouds and rainbows." His tone was dry when he said, "What kind of family instincts could you have if you're ready to throw your life away at any given moment? How is that living for your pack?"

"I'm protecting them," Alex said, his voice almost a growl. "If I have to die to do it, then so be it."

"I've seen you fight, Alex. It's like you want to die. I think you're looking for an excuse to get away from your precious pack. You already did that in Greyton, didn't you? You abandoned them. Perhaps I can help you by destroying them all. I don't know how you showed up in time to stop my last attack on the Academy, but it was a close thing. You won't be so lucky next time, Little Brother."

Alex's hands clenched into fists and he spoke through gritted teeth. "There won't be a next time. You're not getting out of here alive, Drogan. Brother or no brother, you're a threat to my pack and I won't let you hurt the people I care about."

"People," Drogan replied with a scoff. "You mean beasts."

Alex ignored the barb. The Extremist's comment made him think of something else. "What are the mutants?"

Drogan gave a little huff of dry laughter. "You mean the curs? They're ironic, really, considering that they were made in our attempt to create something like your Demon. Now I'm in the same boat as the werewolves we experimented on."

Anger filled Alex at Drogan's words. "You kill people with them."

Drogan nodded. "They're happy to do anything I ask them. I was the first werewolf to command them, so I have their loyalty. I'm the only one Lucian will listen to."

"Lucian?"

"The biggest cur, with the scar down his face. He's a brute, that one. I gave him that scar pulling him off one of our other doctors, but the man had already been mauled to death."

"You're their Alpha." The thought of the mutated, hulking beasts following Drogan as the leader of their pack sent a shudder down Alex's spine. "They're your pack."

"I guess a pack *is* good for something," Drogan said with a hint of amusement.

The conversation had exhausted Alex enough that against his will, he felt himself falling into a sort of restless slumber. Unable to fight it, Alex kept his back to the door so that he would feel it open if anyone tried to come in.

"Move one inch and I'll show you what the Demon can do," he growled.

The last thing he saw was Drogan raising his hands with an entertained expression. "I wouldn't want that, even if I believed you could try. Save the Demon for Kamala. I want to see her expression when she realizes what she's up against."

***

"Come on, Alex. Stop fighting."

Dr. Kamala's high voice sounded like a buzzing mosquito above the hum that filled Alex's mind. She had started him straight at five. The pain felt even more intense than he remembered. The Demon fought to get free. It wanted to tear the doctor and the entire room apart, to kill everyone who tortured and caged him. The Demon fought to bring revenge to his captors.

But she wanted that. Dr. Kamala wanted him to lose control and let the Demon free. She was ready for it. She would paralyze him with her silver and drain him dry. She would use his blood to make more beasts like Drogan's curs, but with the Demon's power. They would kill anyone she told them to. Alex's loved ones would be in danger. Nobody would be safe if the Demon broke free.

"No."

The single word spoken through Alex's clenched teeth changed something. He heard the doctor arguing with him, telling him that the pain would stop, but he didn't let the words sink in. Instead, he was concentrating inwardly to where the Demon resided in every beat of his ragged heart and each breath he took. It was a part of him as much as his wolf side.

He could feel it there, but it had changed. It was almost as if in refusing to give in to Dr. Kamala's coaxing, he had taken control. It no longer fought to break free, but waited as though biding the time he called for it. He was stronger than the Demon. She would never get him to give in.

A smile crossed Alex's face, chasing away the rictus of pain. He opened his eyes to see rage fill Dr. Kamala's features as she realized what she was looking at.

"You'll give me the Demon if it kills you!" she screamed.

She reached over him and spun the dial.

"Ten will kill him!" Kate, her assistant, protested.

Dr. Kamala ignored her. The pain that surged through Alex's body was so intense his back arched to the point that he felt it would snap in two. A yell ripped from Alex's lips. His limbs pulled of their own accord against the bonds that held him to the table. His body shook. He couldn't take the fire that raced beneath his skin as though cooking him from the inside out. He closed his eyes, hoping to see Siale's face, but all he could see was red and white, pulsing and burning. His heart skipped a beat, then another. The pain was too intense. He couldn't breathe.

Something snapped. There was an explosion of white in Alex's mind, and everything went dark.

Chapter Three

Alex was dancing. He felt himself swaying from side to side as he and Siale made their way across the floor, but something was wrong, his feet didn't touch the ground. Siale spoke to someone behind him. When he turned to see who it was, there was nobody there. Panic filled him. He looked back and Siale was gone. He stood alone on the dance floor. The lights went out one at a time until he stood in a single pool of light amid darkness so deep his werewolf vision couldn't pierce it.

Something hit him hard, throwing him across the room. Pain exploded in his ribcage. He struggled to breathe. The last light faded. The pain flooded through him again. He couldn't see his attacker. He couldn't fight. He wanted to find Siale. She shouldn't be alone in the darkness. She needed him.

The next burst of pain was so sharp Alex opened his eyes. Light flooded against his retinas. He saw Drogan's form leaning over him. The werewolf had both hands gripped together in a club, ready to slam down on Alex's chest again.

Alex put up his hands, catching Drogan's arms before he could complete the attack. In his current state, he shouldn't have been able to best the Alpha, but Drogan rocked back on his heels, watching Alex with an unreadable expression.

Every breath hurt. Alex had experienced enough broken ribs to know that he was dealing with several. He put a hand to his chest as he pushed up, unwilling to stay in such a defenseless position any longer. He moved back to sit against the glass with a considerable amount of effort.

"Pretty good for someone who just died."

Alex studied Drogan. "What are you talking about?" He was amazed how painful it was to talk.

"You were dead," Drogan said. "They threw you in here

like a pile of junk. Your heart wasn't beating."

Alex tried to understand what the werewolf was saying. "So you hit me?"

Drogan's eyes narrowed; whether in humor or disgust, Alex couldn't decide.

"I guess you could call it that. I slammed your chest with my fists until your heart started again."

Alex didn't know what to say. His enemy, the one who was responsible for his parents' death and his constant fear of losing his loved ones, had just brought him back to life.

Drogan must have read his confused expression because he lifted a hand. "Don't go reading too much into it. If you die without giving them the Demon or breaking us out of here, I'm screwed. I'm just protecting my hide."

"Noble," Alex muttered.

"Yeah," Drogan replied. "And breaking as many of your ribs as I could in the process was just a bonus."

Alex fought back a reply. No matter how he felt, the werewolf had just saved his life. His chest ached. He set a hand on it. Even touching the skin hurt, whether from the electricity or Drogan's animalistic version of CPR he didn't know. Bruises were already spreading dark and angry across his chest. He longed for the healing touch of moonlight. As it was, he could feel himself healing, his body grudgingly settling into the restorative cadence that kept him alive.

A strange silence settled between them. There wasn't tension, really, or camaraderie. That was impossible after all they had gone through. Instead, it was as if going through the things they were experiencing beneath Dr. Kamala's hand put them on a level playing field. Alex wasn't sure how he felt about that.

After a few minutes of silence, he asked a question that had been bothering him. "How did your mom die?"

The question hung in the air, thick and tangible as though the words were made of smoke that refused to dissipate.

"I told you werewolves killed her," Drogan said finally.

"But why?" Alex replied. He opened his eyes to look at the Alpha. "It doesn't make sense."

Drogan's eyes narrowed. "It's pretty easy to understand," he said with a tone that reminded Alex that the hatred was still very much there. "I was four years old. Dad's brothers were trying to help rehabilitate some werewolves, they got out and tore my mother apart in front of me. What doesn't make sense about that?" he spat, glaring at the wall across from him.

Alex was quiet for a few minutes before he said, "You're a werewolf."

"Brilliant deduction, Sherlock," Drogan said, throwing his words back at him.

Alex thought as he spoke aloud. "Hear me out. If you're a werewolf, you got the genes from someone, and we both know it wasn't your father." He ignored Drogan's glare that threatened death and continued, "So your mother must have been the werewolf. If that's the case, why did the other werewolves attack her? It doesn't make any sense. Unless..."

"If you make me ask 'Unless what', I'm going to kill you," Drogan growled.

Alex spoke the thought he knew would anger the Alpha even further. "Unless our father was setting you up for a lifetime of hatred of werewolves."

Drogan pushed up to his knees, anger twisting his face.

Alex held up a hand in an attempt to buy himself more time. "Hear me out. We both know the General wouldn't hesitate to stoop to such levels if he was afraid his son would turn out to be a werewolf. What better way to keep the beast at bay than to instill such a hatred of werewolves that the instincts would die completely?"

Drogan rose and crossed the cage, towering over Alex. "Are you suggesting that my father had my mother killed as a setup?"

"He left mine to die in a gutter," Alex pointed out.

Drogan's mismatched eyes narrowed in rage. "He loved my mom. He loved her!" the werewolf shouted.

"Mine, too," Alex replied quietly.

Drogan grabbed him by the throat and slammed him against the side of the cage. Alex grabbed his hand, trying to pry his fingers away.

"You know I'm right," he spoke through his tight throat. "It makes sense. You phased after your dad died. Your sorrow at losing him was stronger than your hatred of our race."

"You're the one that killed him," Drogan shouted. "He would be here if it wasn't for you."

Footsteps thundered down the hallway.

Alex kneed Drogan in the stomach. "The same goes for my parents," he said when the werewolf dropped him.

"They weren't your parents," Drogan pointed out, circling.

The doors flew open behind them.

"They were my parents," Alex shouted. He dove at Drogan, grabbing him by the knees and tackling him to the ground. He grabbed the Alpha by the throat. "They raised us with love, something you know nothing about. The General used my mother and threw her away, just like he did to your mom."

Drogan chopped his arms and rolled, throwing Alex onto his back. He punched at Alex's face. Alex blocked the blows with his forearms.

"You know I'm right," Alex realized with a start. He

grunted when a punch hit home. "You knew when you phased for the first time."

"You're wrong," Drogan replied, but his tone carried panic as though Alex's guess hit too close to home.

Alex let the next punch connect and grabbed the werewolf's arm when Drogan pulled back. Alex swung a leg up and hooked it around Drogan's neck. He used his momentum to swing up to Drogan's back and locked an arm around the werewolf's neck. "Your father could never love a werewolf," Alex said. "He used them and threw them away like garbage."

Drogan rose to his feet and slammed Alex's back against the glass.

"Stop it!" Dr. Kamala shouted from outside of the cage.

Both werewolves ignored her. Alex continued, "But what if one of the werewolves gave him a son, a successor for the Extremist battle he was so passionate about? He could love the son as long as he stayed human, and what better way than—"

"Don't say it," Drogan barked. He grabbed Alex's arm and ducked, throwing Alex to the ground.

The blow knocked the wind out of Alex's bruised lungs. He tried to rise, but Drogan grabbed his throat. Alex met the werewolf's gaze, reading the pain in them when he said, "Than to get werewolves to kill his mother in front of him and scar him for life against his own kind."

"I'll kill you," Drogan roared. His hands tightened around Alex's neck.

Alex's survival instincts forced their way to the forefront. He kicked out so hard the Alpha flew across the cage. Drogan slammed into the door with such force that a crack spider webbed out from the locking mechanism.

"I'll kill everyone you love," Drogan growled. He ran at

Alex.

"He's the one who killed her," Alex said, dodging to the side so that the Alpha in his mad rush slammed against the glass.

Drogan turned with the speed of an Alpha and rushed again. He grabbed Alex around the waist and rammed him against the door. The glass shattered around them.

"Shoot the werewolves!" Dr. Kamala called.

Alex rose. A dart hit his back, propelling him to the floor again. Drogan grabbed a large shard of glass and drove it down toward Alex's eye. Alex moved his head at the last moment and the glass shattered against the cement floor.

"You're one of us," Alex said. "Stop fighting it."

Drogan's hand was streaming blood as he grappled for another piece of glass. A dart hit him in the shoulder, slowing him.

"I'll never be one of you," the Alpha snarled. He reached for Alex. With the effects of the liquid silver streaming through his veins, Alex couldn't move away. Drogan would kill him.

Another dart slammed into Drogan's shoulder, spinning him to the right. He collapsed to the floor.

"Finally," Dr. Kamala said. She stared at them both with her hands on her hips. Instead of living, breathing creatures, she watched them as if they were merely experiments that had gotten out of hand. She smoothed her hair and picked up her clipboard from the ground. "If we let them kill each other, we'll never get the results we need. Strap them to the compound tables."

Alex was hoisted into the air and carried back into the experimentation room. He could see Drogan being transported the same way. Alex was brought past the electricity table to another one against the far wall. It was upright and had indents formed to fit a body. Thick cuffs were fastened around his arms and legs, waist, and neck, pinning him effectively to the cold metal. Out of the corner of his eye, he could see Drogan being locked onto a similar table.

Dr. Kamala didn't bother to hide her frustration when she said, "It'll take hours for the silver to get out of their systems. That's too much precious time wasted."

"I'm sure the chemical trials will be successful," Kate replied. "You'll get the Demon for sure."

"We'll experiment on both of them at the same time," Dr. Kamala said, her tone firm with the conclusion. "I'll not wait any longer than it takes for the silver to leave their systems."

The door shut and the sound of locks being fastened echoed through the big room.

"Ridiculous," Dr. Kamala exclaimed. "Absolutely ridiculous."

Their voices died away with their footsteps.

Alex couldn't move. Claustrophobia-tinged panic rushed through him. He had to escape. He couldn't imagine what the doctor had planned next. Chemical experimentation sounded even worse than the electricity. He had already died once.

As hard as he fought, Alex couldn't force himself to move with the effects of the silver dart in his veins. He didn't know how long he struggled before he was able to calm down enough to think. Last time, he had focused on one part at a time. He closed his eyes and concentrated on a finger. It took a considerable amount of effect, but a few minutes later, the pinky finger on his left hand twitched.

Alex breathed through his teeth. It wasn't enough progress. He had to get out before the doctor came back, but if he panicked, he lost the ability to move altogether. He sucked in a breath and let it out, focusing his attention on his finger once more.

***

A single set of footsteps sounded down the hall. It was too soon. Alex could move both hands and wiggle his toes, but any shows of strength would be completely past him for a while longer. If whoever was coming was supposed to begin the tests, he would have no chance.

The door opened. Kate, the assistant, poked her head in. She looked past both werewolves, searching the room.

Alex held perfectly still, hoping that if she was checking on their progress, she would conclude that they weren't close to ready.

Kate shut the door behind her. She drew something from the pocket of her scrubs.

Alarm filled Alex at the sight of the gun. Kate lifted the weapon and aimed. Confused at the line of her trajectory, Alex willed his hands not to clench into fists and give him away. The hum of a silenced bullet buzzed past him and hit something out of the range of his periphery. She aimed past Drogan and did the same. Turning, Kate fired two more times, taking out the cameras on either side of the door.

She hurried across to Alex, her expression showing something close to alarm. Alex had no idea what she was up to. He flinched when her hand touched his wrist. Her palm was cold and clammy.

"Good, you can move," she said, her voice toned more for herself than for Alex. She put a key into the cuff on his arm and turned it. The cuff opened.

Realizing he had already given himself away, Alex decided he couldn't do any worse by speaking. "What are you doing?"

"Getting you out of here," she replied without looking at him.

Chapter Four

Surprised, Alex asked, "Why?"

"Because she'll kill you." Kate gave him a searching look. "She already did, actually. I don't know how you're still here. I wanted to get you out before, but I couldn't without them seeing."

She unlocked the other cuff. Alex flexed his fingers. "Why are you helping me? Aren't you one of them?"

"An Extremist intent on sucking the blood out of every werewolf we catch so we can make some super creature that will listen to the league's every whim?" she asked, looking up at him with her hand paused on the cuff at his right ankle.

"Yes," Alex replied; he watched her closely.

Kate shook her head. "I can't see anyone else die." Moisture filled her eyes and her jaw tightened as though she forced herself to stop talking.

She unlocked both cuffs on his legs and moved to his waist. It was a moment before she said, "She killed my fiancé two and a half years ago with the help of your comrade over there."

"He's not my comrade," Alex muttered.

"Good," she said. "If you were with Drogan, there's no way I would let you out. He can burn with the concoctions Dr. Kamala had so much fun creating. It would serve him right. Thorpe didn't deserve to die." Her voice caught. She unlocked Alex's waist, then hesitated at his neck. She met his gaze. "Will you kill me after I unlocked this one?"

Alex kept his voice firm and calm when he replied, "No. I won't hurt you. You have my word."

She watched him a moment, then reached up and unlocked the final cuff.

Alex fell forward. His legs gave out and his landed on his

knees on the tile floor.

"Get me out," Drogan demanded.

Alex rose to his feet before Kate could help him and crossed to the Alpha. Drogan's threats swirled in his memory as he looked up at the Extremist. "You've taken so much from me," he told the werewolf. "You won't take anymore."

Drogan's eyes widened with the realization that he was going to be left. "Don't do this, Alex."

"We've got to go," Kate said. "They should be investigating the downed cameras by now."

"You're through hurting werewolves," Alex said. He turned away from Drogan.

"Alex!" Drogan shouted. "I'll hunt you down, Alex, and when I do, I'll kill you!"

Alex ducked out the door behind Kate. He let it shut against Drogan's enraged screams.

Kate led him down one side hall, then another before she asked, "Isn't he your brother?"

Alex was silent for a moment. He finally shook his head. "He's no brother of mine."

The place was quiet. Alex guessed it was late at night by the silence. He followed Kate down a flight of stairs. They were almost to the bottom when a sound caught Alex's ears. Fire filled him at the familiarity of the claws on tile.

"Hold on," he whispered, catching Kate's arm. The human hesitated.

As if on cue, the door below them flew open. Two of Drogan's curs entered the stairwell.

"What is that?" Kate asked, her voice tinged with fear.

"Looks like Drogan brought his own backup," Alex replied.

The creatures climbed up the stairs; their heavy footsteps shook the ground.

Kate let out a little shriek of fear.

"Stay behind me," Alex told her.

With the remains of the silver still in his veins, he wasn't sure he could take the curs on. He tried to find the will to morph, but the strength avoided his command.

Alex backed up so that Kate was sheltered behind him in the corner of the landing. He could hear her little whimpers of fear as the curs drew near. The one on the right was huge. It was the scarred one, Lucian, that Drogan had told him about. The curs growled with each breath and their massive heads swung from side to side. When they reached the landing Alex and Kate were on, both sets of eyes locked on Alex.

Kate had risked everything to save his life. Alex was prepared to do the same for her. He bent his legs and held up his hands in a fighting stance, ready to protect her with whatever he had available.

To Alex's surprise, Drogan's curs glared at him and continued on up the stairs. He watched them cautiously, prepared for the moment they would turn and attack. That moment never came.

"They left," Kate said, her voice shaky.

Alex stepped away, letting her free from the corner. "They're going to free Drogan. I should stop them." He set a foot on the stairs leading up.

Kate grabbed his arm. "Don't be ridiculous. You can barely stand upright, let alone take those things on. They would tear you apart. Why don't you live and defeat him another day."

Alex cracked a smile. "You and my sister would get along great."

Kate led the way down the stairs. Her steps were slow as if she expected more curs to appear in the doorway at any moment. Alex pushed the door open and checked the small parking garage. He could smell more curs, but there were no others in sight.

"It's clear," he told Kate.

"Let's get out of here," Kate replied. She led the way to a little blue car near the end of the garage. "You should probably lie down in the back until we get out of here."

As strange as it felt to follow a human's orders, Alex did as she said. Kate grabbed a blanket from the trunk and spread it over him. Alex listened tensely as Kate gave one of the security guards at the exit her card.

"Leaving late," a man noted.

"Yeah, you know Dr. Kamala. She likes to squeeze out every hour of daylight she can."

"Tell me about it," the guard replied. "I should be getting overtime for this shift, but I won't."

"You and me, both," Kate said with a little laugh.

Alex had to give her credit for the small talk she was able to make. There was only the slightest hint of a tremor in her voice that the other human probably couldn't detect.

After what felt like an eternity, the guard said, "You're clear. See you tomorrow."

"Thanks, Gerald," she replied.

The car moved over a bump and the sound of the tires changed from the higher hum of cement to the lower vibration of asphalt.

"Thank goodness," she exclaimed.

Alex threw the blanket back, filled with relief that he was away from that nightmarish place.

She glanced at him in her rearview mirror. "You should probably rest. You look horrible."

Alex gave her a small smile. "You're assuming I don't always look like this."

Kate gave a real smile in return. "I've seen you on the news, Alex Davies. Why else do you think I broke you out? You can bring down Drogan and Kamala. There're rumors that you have a whole werewolf army at your command." She paused, then asked, "Do you?"

There was a hint of urgency in her voice as if his answer was the most important thing in the world. He thought of the Academy and of the humans from Greyton who rallied to save the students. She had taken quite the risk to save him. Her family might be in danger, too. She deserved his reassurance.

"I do," Alex replied quietly.

Kate gave a satisfied nod. "Good; then you can bring down the Extremists. Thorpe will finally be avenged."

"I'm sorry about your fiancé," Alex said.

"Me, too," she replied. "We were young," she smiled. "At least younger than I am now. I loved him all through high school. I was working when Drogan's men captured him. It took a long time to find the trail to Dr. Kamala. By then, he had been killed and they were on to other werewolves with their experiments. I got them to hire me in the hopes that I could fight back." She met his gaze in the mirror. "It's taken two years for someone like you to get there."

"I'm grateful for you," Alex told her. His eyes kept closing of their own accord.

"Just make sure it was worth it," she replied.

"I will," he promised. He forced his thoughts to focus. "Where are you going?"

Kate's reply was soft at first as though the word was unfamiliar. "Home," she said. A slight smile touched her lips. "I'm going home," she repeated. "I haven't been there since Thorpe was taken." Her voice tightened. "I'll bet Mom thinks I'm dead or something."

"She'll be glad to have you back," Alex told her.

Kate gave a damp smile at the thought. "She will." She glanced back at Alex. "Where should I take you?"

"Anywhere," Alex replied. "My friends will pick me up. With Drogan getting out, the further you get away from me, the better."

She nodded. "I'll take you to a city where you can hide out until they can get to you."

A thought occurred to Alex. "Any chance you know where Greyton is?"

Kate nodded with a hint of surprise. "Yes. We pass by it on the way to my mom's. Do you have friends there?"

"Yes." The thought of going back to the Academy filled him with relief. "That would be a great place to get dropped off."

"Good," Kate said with a firm nod. "Get some sleep. We have a ways to go."

Alex's eyes were already closed. He couldn't think of a place more comfortable than the backseat of the little blue car with the moonlight streaming through the windows and the last remnants of silver fading from his veins.

***

"Alex?"

He opened his eyes with the realization that the car had stopped. His first thought was that Drogan or Dr. Kamala had found them. Alex grabbed the tire iron from the floor and sat upright, prepared to fight them off.

Kate stood outside the door. She lifted a hand with an understanding expression. "It's okay. I know exactly how you feel. But we're safe." She glanced behind her. "We've made it to Greyton."

Alex's gaze shifted to their surroundings. The sight of the familiar buildings and the streets for which he had bled to keep safe chased away the tension. He pushed the door open and rose.

"How do you feel?" Kate asked, eyeing him uncertainly.

"Good," Alex replied with surprise. He rolled his shoulders and took a deep breath. His ribs had healed and the last effects of the silver had seeped away during his sleep. The moon was almost a complete circle and he could feel the pull reminding him that it would be full the next night. He smiled. "Thank you very much."

"Just make sure that was worth it," Kate replied, shaking his hand.

"It will be," Alex promised. "I'll make sure Drogan and Dr. Kamala get the justice they deserve."

"Glad to hear it," Kate said. She reached for the car door, but hesitated. "Are you going to be okay?" she asked. "You had a rough couple of days."

Alex gave her a reassuring smile. "I'll be fine, thanks to you." On a whim, he reached back into the car and grabbed one of the sticky notes from her console along with a pen. He quickly wrote Trent's phone number on it. "If you ever get into trouble, you can reach me at this number."

"Thanks," she replied. She grabbed some coins from the cup holder and set them in his hand. "So you can call your friends."

"I appreciate it," Alex told her. He shoved the money into his pocket with the realization that he was only wearing pants. His shirt had been destroyed by Kamala's assistants, and he had no idea where his shoes had gone. The rough gravel under his feet felt cool and reassuring.

Kate climbed back into the car and gave a little wave. Alex waved back and watched her drive toward the rising sun.

Chapter Five

Alex walked to the gas station at the corner, taking care to keep to the shadows so that nobody would call the police about a teenager running half-naked around the city. Things had sure changed since he went on his personal vendetta against the gangs of Greyton. Instead of hiding indoors after the sun went down, citizens were proactive now. He could hear the sounds of kids playing night games in the park. The weather was perfect for it and now parents weren't so afraid to let their children have fun after dark.

Grateful the payphones were on the side of the gas station without windows, Alex slid the coins Kate had given him into the pay slot. He punched the number he had written down on the piece of paper.

"Hello?"

Alex smiled at Trent's suspicious voice. He knew the werewolf was already no doubt plugging the unknown number into his system, tracing the call to find out who knew one of the Wolf Den's phone numbers.

"Hey, Trent."

"Alex? Alex!" Trent sputtered. "I can't believe it's you! Are you okay? We've searched everywhere! You disappeared into thin air! There was no trace at all, but we didn't stop looking. We were thinking Drogan found you or maybe other Extremists, or some of the gangs. You have quite a few enemies out there. Where are you? Wait, my computer says Greyton. How on earth are you in Greyton?"

"Trent?"

"I mean, one minute you went out the door to say hi to Officer Dune, and the next you were gone, completely vanished, like you were blown off the face of the earth! Not blown as in blown up by a bomb or anything, but like the wind, you know, like dust in the wind. Isn't there a song about that?"

"Trent!"

"Uh, sorry, Alex." Trent sounded embarrassed at his babbling. "I'm so happy to hear your voice I can't even think straight right now."

"I'm okay," Alex reassured him. "It wasn't a pleasant experience, but I'm back. Any chance you could pick me up?"

"Definitely," Trent replied. "Siale will be so happy! She's been scouring the news, working with the Greyton City Police and with Jaze and the Black Team, and she won't give me a chance to breathe with all her—"

"What about the police?" Alex asked, cutting him off.

"Well," Trent said, sounding baffled. "They're just as anxious as we are to get you back. We've kept things on the down-low, but they know you disappeared. They've been combing the city, shutting down more gangs in the process. They were hoping to find you in one of the hideouts, but as you probably know, they weren't successful. Officer Dune has been our biggest advocate toward getting you home."

"Officer Dune?" Alex asked, surprised.

"Of course," Trent replied, his confusion deepening. "He's been beside himself. The man won't rest. I get at least two dozen phone calls from him day and night. He's desperate to find you. It makes sense. His department was responsible for the safety of the students at the prom, and you guys are friends."

"Yeah," Alex said, keeping his voice level. "I might need a bit of time before you pick me up here. I'll call you back."

"Can I tell everyone you're okay?" Trent asked with a hint of desperation in his voice.

Alex could tell trying to reassure everyone while searching for him had worn out his friend. "Yes, please."

CHEREE ALSOP

"Um, what should I tell them?"

Alex leaned against the wall and looked up at the moon. "Tell them I was kidnapped by Extremists who tried to make me morph into the Demon."

"Make you?" Trent asked. "Alex, what did they do?"

"I'll tell you later. All that matters now is that Drogan was kidnapped, too. They thought they could make him morph into the Demon also, since we share similar genes. I need you to find out if that's true."

"I'll do what I can," Trent replied. "Is he still there?"

Thoughts of the Extremist werewolf filled Alex with regret that he hadn't gone back to finish him when he had the chance. It would have been worth getting caught again to wipe out the threat from his half-brother. "No. He got out. How's our security at the Academy?"

"Solid," Trent answered. "Brock and Mouse have had us on lockdown since everyone got back from the prom."

"Good. Keep it that way," Alex told him. "Drogan has a vendetta."

"He always has."

Alex rubbed his forehead. "I have a feeling it'll be more so now."

"We'll be ready," Trent promised.

Alex said goodbye and hung up the phone feeling torn. The fact that Officer Dune was at least acting adamant about getting him back even though the man was the reason he had been tortured by the Extremists was troubling. He had to find out what the officer was up to.

Alex kept to the shadows as he made his way to the Greyton City Police headquarters. Officer Dune had to pay for his betrayal. Alex didn't know exactly what he would do. He hoped something would come to him when he saw the officer.

Officer Dune's familiar form appeared at the door to the headquarters about a half hour later. He ran a tired hand along his short beard and walked down the steps.

Instead of confronting him, Alex followed the officer through the streets of Greyton. Officer Dune walked three blocks before turning north. Alex soon found himself taking a tour of the more docile neighborhoods he hadn't visited. Officer Dune glanced back once, but Alex was careful to keep to the shadows thrown by the streetlights and the slowly rising sun. After a few more blocks, Officer Dune led him to a small house at the corner of a cul-de-sac.

Alex silently jumped the back fence and crept through the yard in time to hear the officer thank someone. A glance around the house showed a middle-aged woman talking to him on the doorstep.

"She kept the applesauce down," the woman said, "And she said she felt stronger. She wanted to wait up for you, but I told her it would be better if she got her rest."

"I appreciate it, Marigold. I have the same shift tomorrow night."

"I'll be here," she promised, crossing the sidewalk to her car.

Officer Dune watched her drive away before shutting the door. Alex ducked back around the side of the house and followed the officer's progress through the windows.

Officer Dune paused in the first bedroom to put away his weapon and badge before continuing down the hall. Alex lost him for a moment, then a door pushed open and the light from the hallway spilled into the room at the end of the small house.

"Daddy?" Alex heard a girl say.

"I didn't mean to wake you," Officer Dune replied, his voice gentle.

Jamie sat up in the bed. Alex's wolf eyesight made out the fact that she had no hair. There were dark circles under her eyes and her cheekbones stood out as she hugged her father.

"Marigold said you're feeling better."

Jamie nodded. "I think I'll be able to go back to school soon."

Officer Dune smiled even as his eyes filled with tears. He blinked them away before he sat back so that she wouldn't see. "Yes, you will." He motioned for her to lie down and he tucked her into the bed once more. "As long as you get good sleep and your dad doesn't keep waking you up."

"Oh, Dad," she said with an answering smile.

"Goodnight, my Jamie," he told her, crossing to the door.

"Goodnight, my Daddy," she replied.

He pulled the door shut and darkness closed in once more.

Alex slipped the latch on the sliding kitchen door and crossed silently to the door to the officer's room.

"You betrayed me," he growled.

Officer Dune dropped the cup he had just filled from the pitcher by his bed. His face turned as white as his pillow at the sight of Alex standing there.

The officer's eyes flickered to his gun hanging just inside the cracked closet door.

Alex reached him before Office Dune could even move. He picked the officer up by the neck and shoved him against the wall.

Officer Dune struggled in his grip. "I was wrong," he forced out through his constricted throat. "You didn't deserve that."

"They would have killed me!" Alex said. His hands shook with the effort it took to not break the officer's neck. The thought of the little girl in the next room was barely enough to keep the Demon in check.

"I was desperate," Officer Dune said. Tears rolled down his cheeks. "I was wrong."

Alex brought him closer and said, "You took an oath to serve and protect." He swallowed past his own tight throat. "I trusted you."

He couldn't blame Officer Dune for wanting to protect his daughter, but they had been friends, once. Werewolves didn't betray each other. The friendship he thought he had with the officer made it hard to comprehend such deceit. He had almost died. Siale would have never known what had happened to him. Pain gripped his heart at the thought.

Officer Dune pulled weakly at Alex's hands. Alex realized the officer's face was bright red. He released his grip. Officer Dune fell gasping to the floor. Alex turned away.

After a few minutes of ragged breathing, Officer Dune rose and stumbled over to sit on the bed, though it was more like collapsing as if his legs gave out. "I was so wrong," he said, burying his face in his hands. "So very, very wrong."

Alex remained by the door and kept his face carefully expressionless. "You gave me to them."

Officer Dune nodded without looking up at him. "I didn't have a choice."

"There's always a choice," Alex replied coldly.

The officer's shoulders shook. "I made the choice of a father instead of the choice of an officer and the friend you deserved."

Alex tried not to be moved by the pain in the officer's voice. Sorrow wafted from him. Alex knew he was looking at a man filled with true regret. He clenched his hands into fists, trying to keep his stalwart front. "They wanted to kill me."

Officer Dune lowered his hands, but kept his gaze on the floor. Tears fell where he looked, pattering on the carpet in soft splashes that filled Alex's ears. "I shouldn't have done it. I didn't want to. It killed me when they took you away."

Alex asked the question that had eaten at him since he felt the dart hit his chest. "Then why did you do it?"

Officer Dune opened a hand in the direction of Jamie's room. "My daughter has leukemia."

Alex leaned against the doorframe. He didn't know what it meant to be a father, but he had seen Jaze sacrifice so much to protect the children at the Academy as if they were his own. Now with little William, he saw the same look in the dean's eyes that he saw in Officer Dune's. A father would sacrifice everything to save his child.

"You needed the money," Alex said quietly.

"I thought I did," Officer Dune replied, his voice soft. "Jamie's medical bills were so high we were going to lose this house. It's the house..." His voice choked off. He swallowed, then continued, "It's the house my wife and I lived in when she died." He took a shuddering breath. "I couldn't bear to lose it, and I couldn't afford to pay more medical bills, especially if Jamie needed another round of treatment. With Jamie sick, I was about to lose everything."

His jaw clenched for a moment, and he looked up at Alex. "The second you were gone, I realized my mistake, my terrible, horrible mistake. I had just killed my friend, someone who trusted me and who saved my life and the life of my partner. I gave him away for money." He said the last word with disgust as though even the syllables tasted bad.

"Maybe it was the right decision." Alex spoke the words quietly, trying to understand despite everything he had gone through.

"It wasn't," Officer Dune replied. "It could never be."

"You were trying to save your daughter."

The officer's voice broke when he said, "She is in

remission; we just found out yesterday. We made it through." He tried to smile, but failed. "I betrayed you and it wasn't even necessary."

Alex didn't know what to say or do. Nothing was what he had expected it to be. The angry confrontation he had expected had instead turned into the heartbroken confession of a lost father trying to fight for his daughter. He would rather Jamie live than himself. She was young and innocent. The voice in the back of his mind said that he had been the same way, once.

Officer Dune finally broke the silence. "What will you do?"

Alex stared at him. There was an acceptance to the man's expression as if he expected the werewolf to kill him for his betrayal and he knew he deserved it.

Officer Dune lowered his eyes once more to the floor. "At least don't let Jamie find me, please."

When Alex spoke again, it took so much work to voice what he needed to say that his words came out raspy. "Do you not know me by now?" He swallowed and continued in a voice barely above a whisper. "What kind of an animal do you think I am?"

He left the room. His mind reeled; questions and memories flooded through him, swarming him with conflicting emotions.

"Alex, wait!"

Alex barely heard the officer's request. He slid the kitchen door open and stepped into the backyard. He didn't stop until his bare feet stood on the grass still cool from the night. The warmth of the rising sun fell on his shoulders. He lowered his head, unable to look around him.

"Alex, I sent you away to die." Officer Dune said, stopping a few feet behind him. "I deserve death in return."

Alex glanced back at him. "Nobody deserves death. They deserve life. That's what we fought for in the Saa. That's what I gave back to this city. People deserve to live." He lowered his voice. "Werewolves deserve to live, too. But that doesn't mean I'm going to shoot you down or tear you apart because you were thinking of the little girl in there who needs you."

Alex gestured toward Jamie's window. He blinked back the tears that burned in his eyes, refusing to let them fall. "Of anyone in Greyton, you should know my character by now. I would never leave a child fatherless, especially your child." His voice dropped. "And I'm not a murderer."

Officer Dune watched him with tears flowing unabashedly down his face.

Alex turned away from the sight and said with his shoulders bowed, "I just needed to know why."

Officer Dune crossed to him without a word. The officer put a hand on Alex's shoulder. The touch of the man's hand felt different than it had before. They weren't comrades or friends any longer. Alex had trusted him, and to werewolves, trust was everything. He had almost died, and the man next to him was to blame.

The wolf part of him said to end the threat, and the Demon surged with agreement. However, Alex's human side warned him that they might need an officer in Dune's position. As much as he wanted his own revenge, the sorrow and regret he had heard in the officer's voice said he would do what he could to try and repair the damage he had done.

Alex took a steeling breath and turned toward him. Officer Dune threw his arms around Alex and gave him a tight, fatherly hug.

"I am so sorry," the officer said.

Alex stepped back when the officer was through. "I know."

"I'm so glad you're here."

Alex nodded without speaking.

Officer Dune looked him up and down critically. "You need clothes and food. Come on. It's the least I can do."

Alex shook his head. "I'm fine. Take care of Jamie."

He walked through the darkness and turned into the nearest alley away from the officer's gaze. He leaned against the wall and let the emotions hit.

Officer Dune had been a friend, a close one. He had saved the officer's life, and they had worked together to free the city from the gangs that held it hostage. The betrayal he felt was worse than even his loathing for Drogan, because his half-brother had never pretended to be anything he wasn't. Alex vowed to be more careful who he trusted. It was a painful lesson, and one that had almost cost him his life.

Chapter Six

Jaze was out of the jet the instant it touched the ground. The walk from the officer's house to the small airport on the edge of Greyton City had given Alex time to push past his frustration with Officer Dune and embrace the fact that he was going to see Siale, Jaze, and the others again. Alex couldn't stop smiling when the dean hit the tarmac running.

Jaze caught him up in a tight hug. "I can't believe you're here," he said, holding Alex so tight he could barely breathe.

"I'm okay," Alex reassured him.

Jaze stepped back and looked him over. "You didn't tell Trent everything that happened."

Alex shook his head. "Some things are better off not being told."

Jaze put an arm around his shoulders and walked him to the jet. "Everyone wanted to come." A smile spread across the dean's face, telling Alex just exactly how many werewolves he had forced to wait at the Academy. "I told them I needed to debrief you." They climbed up the short steps. "Trent insisted on flying, though."

Trent was already out of the pilot seat and charging at Alex. "I thought I was dreaming when you called."

Alex chuckled, stepping back out of his friend's tight hug. "You know you're the first I'd get ahold of."

Trent nodded proudly. "And I'm glad. You should have seen it when I told everyone you were alright. There was laughing and crying." His smile faltered. "I think everyone was worried that this time you wouldn't be coming home."

Alex forced a smile. "I'm too stubborn to kill. You know that."

"Thank goodness," Trent replied with an answering smile. He hurried back to the pilot's seat and slipped on his earphones.

"Good to have you back," Mouse said, waving from the copilot seat.

"I can't believe you let him fly the jet."

"He's very stubborn," the professor told Alex with a wry smile. "But he's picking it up fast. If I'm not careful, I'll be out of a job."

Trent shrugged. "Or we can get another jet."

A debate started about why another jet would be useful. By the sound of it, they had undergone the same argument before.

"I'd recommend buckling up," Jaze said, motioning for Alex to take a seat toward the back. "It gets a bit bumpy."

Alex watched Greyton City fade away outside his window. The sun was overhead and bright, washing the city in shades of gold and yellow that reflected from the sky rise windows.

"Were you in Greyton the whole time?" Jaze finally asked, his tone level as if he was trying to be careful with his questioning. "We found mutant tracks around the school when we were searching for you, but nothing connected. We couldn't find a way to follow where you had gone."

Alex sat back in the seat, debating how much to tell the dean. Jaze had been there for him ever since his parents were killed. The dean had never steered him wrong. He let out a slow breath. "I was betrayed by a friend."

Jaze watched him closely. "Who?"

Alex studied his hands. "Officer Dune."

Jaze rose from the seat. "He denied ever seeing you that night. I'm going to make him wish he'd never set—"

Alex grabbed the dean's arm before he actually succeeded in making it to the door. It didn't matter that the plane was already in the sky. The dean appeared ready to jump right out to exact his vengeance on the officer. The fact that Jaze looked ready to tear Officer Dune apart gave Alex a sort of feeling of relief. It matched how he had felt coming back from the Extremists, and let him know that it was okay.

"We've cleared it up."

Jaze stared down at him, his chest heaving. "You cleared up the fact that Officer Dune betrayed you to the Extremists? How on earth do you clear up something like that? You trusted him! We both did!"

Alex nodded, accepting the dean's anger because he knew it was directed more at the officer and the situation than at him. "I did trust him. That's why it hurt and why I had to see him when I got back to Greyton."

Jaze slumped in the seat next to Alex. He leaned his head against the seat in front of them and turned to glance at the younger werewolf. "So tell me why I shouldn't make him pay for what he did to you."

Alex thought of the man's daughter, of her sickness and all Officer Dune had been through watching her battle leukemia. The officer hadn't told him everything, but it had been there in his voice and his eyes. No man should have to fear his daughter's death, and after losing his wife, Jamie was the last person Officer Dune had. He couldn't blame the man for trying to do everything he could to save her.

"His daughter's sick." Alex said quietly. "He's been through enough. We'll keep him as a contact because he's a valuable asset in our efforts towards werewolf acceptance, but I won't ever trust him again."

His answer deflated a bit of the fire in the dean's dark brown eyes. He held Alex's gaze, searching his face. "You're sure?"

"I'm positive. And I'll be more careful who I place my trust in." Alex's response was hard to say, but it had the effect of calming the dean further.

Jaze nodded. "I trust you in this. We'll bug his house and track his movements, and I don't know if I'll be able to practice as much self-control if I see him again..."

Alex smiled at what the dean left unsaid. "Thanks for caring. I really am okay."

Jaze sat back. "Then let's talk about what happened after you were betrayed."

Alex kept his voice low so Trent wouldn't overhear as he told the dean about Dr. Kamala, the Extremist stronghold, and Drogan's surprise capture.

"His own men turned on him?"

Alex nodded at Jaze's question. "I guess finding out their leader was one of the werewolves they despised shook his standing. It didn't sound like all of them were on Dr. Kamala's side, but he was in the cage."

"Which says a whole lot," Jaze replied.

Alex told Jaze about the torture with electricity, keeping his voice level when he talked about his heart stopping. Jaze's conflicted expression deepened when Alex described waking up with Drogan hitting his chest.

"He said if I died then he would be next, so it was in his best interest."

"He saved your life," Jaze said, his tone unreadable.

"Yeah," Alex replied, thinking of their conversation and Drogan's threats. "But it changes nothing."

Jaze nodded without speaking.

A though occurred to Alex. "It hasn't skipped since."

"What do you mean?"

Alex put a hand to his chest, realizing the truth. "Since Drogan got it beating again, my heart hasn't skipped." He was quiet a moment, feeling the rhythm of his heart that was more regular than it had been since he lost his parents. "What do you think that means?" he asked quietly.

Jaze shook his head. "I'm not sure." He smiled at Alex, reassuring him with the look. "But I'm glad. Maybe when it stopped it was able to heal correctly, fixing the problem."

"Maybe it wasn't Drogan at all," Alex replied, but doubt touched him at the statement.

Jaze must have read his need to move past the topic, because he said, "So how did you get out?"

Alex told the dean about his conversation with Drogan and how the Extremist attacked him when they were talking about his mother. He told about being shot with the silver dart and strapped to the table. Kate's bravery struck him again when he told about her freeing him, reminding him how lucky he had been that she was there. He made sure to repeat Drogan's threats so Jaze would know that the Academy could be in danger. The dean's gaze tightened when Alex mentioned the curs they had passed in the stairwell.

"Mouse and Brock have added new security measures. The term is almost over and the students will be going home next week."

Alex could tell there was something else the dean wanted to tell him. "What is it?"

Jaze shifted in his seat to face the student. "Red's invited you to stay at his place for the summer."

"Siale's dad?" Alex asked in surprise.

Jaze nodded. "When Trent told us you were safe, he also mentioned that you wanted to take extra precautions in case Drogan attacked. I made a few phone calls. Red invited you, Cassie, and Tennison to spend the summer with him and Siale. He said he has some things he could use help on. I feel that getting you away from the Academy for the break would protect you and also the students there while we work on locating Drogan. What do you think?"

Alex usually looked forward to summers at the Academy and the ability to enjoy it as they used to before it was flooded with students, but after falling for Siale, he had dreaded the months apart. The thought of an entire summer with Siale, Cassie, and Tennison was a welcome one.

"What about rescues? Will you need me on your team?" he asked, trying to think it through.

"We took care of things before you joined us. If it gets too crazy, we could send the jet."

Alex was quiet for a moment. He finally nodded. "I think it's a good idea."

Jaze smiled. "I figured you'd say that."

Trent's landing on the tarmac at Haroldsburg's tiny airport was bumpy, but Mouse reassured Alex that it was far better than their landing at Greyton City.

"It's true," Trent said, walking Alex to the waiting SUV while Jaze and Mouse covered the jet with a tarp. "I think my teeth almost rattled out the first time I landed. I'm getting a lot better. Maybe next time Mouse will let me fly it alone."

"Maybe," Alex said, trying to keep his tone positive even though he doubted whether giving Trent all of the reins so soon would be a good idea.

"Thanks," Trent replied, slapping him on the back. "I'm glad you're on my side."

They climbed inside the SUV. Silence filled the vehicle.

"If you do that again, I think I'm going to retire as your best friend."

Alex glanced at Trent. "You mean if I disappear."

Trent nodded. "Yeah. I probably lost ten years in the last couple of days. Stress is bad on the heart, you know? Jordan thought I was going to have a nervous breakdown."

Alex kept his attention on the threads lining the seat in front of him. "Were you?" he finally asked his friend.

After a few moments of silence, Trent answered, "Yeah. Probably."

Alex glanced at his friend. "The moment I knew I could call you and come home was when I realized I had really escaped."

Trent nodded. "I knew you'd call. I kept my phone with me everywhere. Jordan said if I carried it much longer, it'd be imprinted in my hand, but she always took it for me if I needed her to." Trent let out a shaky sigh and threw Alex a smile. "Having the girl of my dreams has definitely given me some perspective on life."

Alex nodded. "Me, too. It's like we're growing up or something."

Trent laughed. "Yeah, something like that."

The ride to the Academy was over quickly. Any thoughts Alex had about sneaking from the garage to Pack Torin's quarters vanished the second he climbed out of the vehicle.

"Alex!" Cassie shouted.

Siale reached him first, throwing her arms around his neck and kissing him firmly. She then stepped back, looking up into his eyes. "You're okay?" she asked, her eyebrows pulled together with worry.

Alex smiled at her. "I am now."

She hugged him again and this time he was the one to kiss her. It took him a minute before he realized everyone was watching them. His lips creased in a smile, and Siale's answered. Alex glanced up at the students and professors around them.

"Uh, sorry about that," he apologized.

Laughter flooded through his friends.

"You can't even go to a dance without getting into trouble," his twin sister said. Cassie hugged him. "I'm so glad you're home. I think a trip to Red's is what we all need." Her eyes widened and she looked at Jaze as if worried she had given something away. "Did I just spoil the news?"

The dean shook his head with a warm smile. "I already told him. Alex thinks it's a good idea."

"Yes!" Cassie exclaimed. She pushed her brother's shoulder. "Maybe we can get through the summer without worrying about your life."

"You might be asking too much," Alex told her.

"We'll have fun," Siale said. "Dad's getting things ready."

"Glad you're back," Tennison said, shaking Alex's hand. "And I'm glad you're not leaving me there with just the girls."

"Hey!" Cassie said in a mock hurt tone.

Tennison gave her an apologetic smile. "Can you blame me? Werewolf girls are crazy."

"You mean *can be* crazy," Cassie corrected.

"Sure," Tennison said with an innocent shrug.

Alex followed them through the tunnel to the main school halls. Word of his escape, or what the students thought of as a near escape, spread through the school. Alex didn't correct the rumors that he had been forced to go into hiding to avoid capture by the Extremists. He felt that the less the werewolf students feared angry humans intent on destroying them all, the better. He just wished he could feel the same way.

Chapter Seven

Drogan's threats hung in the back of Alex's mind as he waited by the window. The fading light would give way to the full moon soon enough. Tingles ran through his skin, beckoning to him, reminding him that he would have no choice to give into the form of the wolf as soon as night fell. He wanted to phase, but the thought of everyone at the Academy except for the few humans turning into wolves left him feeling as though the place was defenseless. He wanted to talk to Brock and go over the new security measures, but there wouldn't be time.

Alex made his way outside. He couldn't wait any longer for the moon. The thought of becoming a wolf and putting aside his restless worries was a welcome one.

The door opened and Alex turned at the sound of footsteps.

"I think we had the same idea," Siale said, her smile growing at the sight of him. "I can never wait."

The door opened again, revealing Cassie and Tennison.

"Really? Everyone's anxious?" Cassie asked.

"Maybe the moonlight's getting stronger," Terith said, rounding the corner of the Academy with Von at her side.

Trent and Jordan followed closely behind. "There may be something to that," Trent replied. "I'll do some checking when we get done to see if there has been a lessening of atmospheric interference for the moonlight to get through."

"Is that supposed to make sense?" Jericho asked, joining them from the steps.

"Either way, we're here," Tennison said. "What should we do?"

Everyone looked at Alex. He shrugged. "Anyone up for wolf tag?"

The wolves ghosted through the trees. Alex's paws hit the ground in a near silent cadence, eating up the forest floor as he pushed himself to run faster. The trees sped by in a blur that contained more scent than sight, the sharp aroma of sap warmed by the summer sun, the musky odor of the chipmunks that scolded the wolves from the safety of the canopy, and the earthy, rich smell of pine needles decaying in the shadows of the widespread branches that blocked out most of the descending sunlight.

A gray and white form caught up to Alex's right side. He gave Siale a wolfish grin and glanced forward again in time to see the trees give way to the wide-swept meadows below them. It was one of his favorite places, the point where the forest thinned and the valley coasted down in a blanket of wildflowers lit by the light of the full moon.

He and Siale stopped at the edge of the trees to catch their breath. They had run all night, enjoying the quiet of the forest while held in wolf form by the full moon.

Cassie and Tennison trotted up to Alex's left side while Trent and Jordan stopped near Siale's right. Terith and Von had stopped to catch fish in the stream. Jericho stood behind Alex, his black coat blending with the shadows. The wind danced through the leaves of the small bushes and grass high enough to brush a stag's belly. The clover and dew scent of rabbits tickled Alex's nose. He wanted to jump into the grass and start a hunt for the spirited creatures, but they didn't have much time until the sun rose, and Alex was anxious to get back.

A glance at the lightening horizon said they were pushing it as it was. Alex couldn't fight the thought of danger that whispered in the back of his mind. He didn't want to keep his pack of friends out any later than they needed to be. Jericho gave a small huff. Alex nodded in agreement. He turned away from the beckoning meadows.

As if she read his concern and wanted to lighten the mood, Siale gave Alex's shoulder a soft nip and darted away, beckoning him to join in the chase. Soon, all of the wolves were dashing through the trees playing tag as they made their way back to the Academy.

Nobody stood a chance when Jericho was it. Only Tennison could best him in speed, but the Alpha was faster and older, cutting past trees and leaping bushes with a strength only those with a black coat had.

Alex ran with the Alpha at his heels. Despite the other werewolves running around them, Jericho was intent on catching Alex in the final tag of the game. Alex lowered his head, determined to make it through the Academy gate before Jericho caught him. He ducked under a low-sweeping branch and juked to the left, then right, dodging trees with a skill he had achieved through much practice, yet Jericho persisted.

The thick rock walls and the iron gate loomed into sight past the trees. Alex could feel as much as hear Jericho's pursuit. He had only one more chance to throw the Alpha off and make it through without being tagged, but it was a long shot.

When Alex jumped, he felt the minute brush of air as Jericho's teeth barely missed his ankle. Alex landed on the lowest branch of the thick, ancient oak tree that sprawled near the Academy wall. He teetered back and forth, reminded why wolves don't climb trees. Several feet of empty space followed before the wall. Alex glanced back and gave a wolfish grin at the look of surprise on Jericho's face before he leaped to the wall. He gave a bark of triumph, and the Alpha answered with his own toothy grin. Alex jumped off the other side.

He yelped when he landed on the bushes he had completely forgotten about. He scrambled through the scratchy branches and managed to right himself with some dignity still intact when the wolves burst through the gate. They greeted Alex with snorts and huffs of laughter which he returned. Siale reached out with her muzzle and withdrew something from the top of his head. Alex had to grin at the sight of the branch of leaves from one of the bushes.

The werewolf students phased behind the trees and pulled on the clothes they had left there.

"Did you forget about the bushes?" Cassie asked.

"Completely," Alex told his sister.

"We practically lived in them growing up," she reminded him.

Siale slipped her arm through Alex's. "It's okay. I thought it was hilarious."

Alex grinned at Cassie. "See? There are benefits to being a klutz once in a while." He gave Siale a light kiss. "I'll be your idiot."

Siale laughed. "That's the most romantic thing you've ever said to me."

"I have a lot more where that came from," Alex told her, pulling her close as they walked up the stairs. "I can also be your fool, your dope, or your moron."

"My Prince Charming?"

Alex shook his head. "Way too much pressure."

Siale's smile made his breath catch in his throat. "At least I know where the line is."

Alex couldn't help himself. He pulled her close and kissed her. She stepped back with a laugh, glancing behind them. "You're going to get us in trouble."

"Don't worry. Everyone else is still running around. We started early and they're getting back late."

78

"Not everyone," Trent reminded him. "We're still here watching you guys make out."

Alex rolled his eyes. "It was just a kiss," he said with a laugh.

He opened the door to the Academy.

"Where are you going?" Siale asked.

"I need to run up to Pack Torin's quarters for a sec."

"Going to clean the toilets?" Jericho questioned.

Alex grinned. "Something like that. What are you guys up to?"

"I want to watch the sunrise from the courtyard," Siale said. "We'll meet you by Jet's statue?"

"It's a date," Alex replied.

She smiled at him and he ducked inside.

Alex hurried up the stairs. As much as he hated to admit it, he really was going to clean the toilets. Torin had given him the job when he chose Alex as his Second. It was a punishment, but it kept the peace between them. With everything he had done to ruin relationships between him and the Alphas at the Academy, he owed it to Torin to do something for being kept around. If he hurried, he would still be able to catch the sunrise before the rest of the werewolves showed up.

Alex reached the top of the stairs only to stop short at the sight of the entire Pack Boris waiting for him at the end of the hallway.

"Hey, Alex," Boris said.

Alex turned to leave, but two more members of Pack Boris jogged up the stairs behind him.

"What is this, Boris?" Alex asked levelly.

Boris gave a humorless smile. "I saw you leave early and took a chance on the fact that you'd come back early, too." Hatred filled his icy blue eyes that used to match his sister

Kalia's exactly. "It's time for you to stop getting away with everything. Why can't you just die, Alex?" he asked, his voice thick with anger. "We're going to make you wish you'd stayed gone."

"I've beaten you before," Alex reminded him.

"Because you're a mutant freak," Boris replied, his tone cold. "But I have a pack for a reason."

"Why?" Alex asked, forcing his tone to remain light. "So they can do your dirty work for you?"

Boris' eyes narrowed. "So we can deal out a little payback."

Alex bent his knees, his hands ready. "Bring it, Boris. I'm not afraid of any werewolf who would follow you."

It might have been foolish to say, but Alex was angry enough that he was past caring. Ambushing him outside of his room was as much of an impingement of territory as a wolf could stand, and the wolf inside of him was gnashing its teeth for payback of its own.

Nate attacked first. Alex flipped him onto his back and turned to the right in time to catch Daniel's fist and use the momentum of his punch to throw him into two other Grays. Alex blocked a kick, but caught Boris' punch directly on his left ear. The impact made him stagger. Two punches to the kidneys forced him turn to defend himself. He slammed a haymaker into Mitch's jaw, dropping him, and ducked in time to avoid an identical punch to his face. He followed with two blows to his attacker's stomach along with an elbow to the back when the werewolf bent over.

He was about to throw Ken into his pack mates when a sound caught Alex's ear.

"Did you hear that?" he asked, rising.

"I heard the sound of your bones breaking," Daniel said.

Alex rolled his eyes at Pack Boris' Second. "Did you work

on that comeback all night?"

Daniel growled and tackled Alex around the waist. He fell backwards and kicked out, sending Daniel flying over his head. He jumped back to his feet only to be grabbed from behind.

"Enough," Boris yelled. He stood with his back to the stairs and his full attention on Alex. "You deserve to suffer for Kalia. She's dead because of you!"

Alex didn't struggle. The guilt he carried made the Alpha's words ring true. He couldn't blame Boris for hating him. Kalia would still be alive if it wasn't for the fact that she liked Alex and the General found out about it.

"Fine," Alex said quietly. He stopped struggling against the arms that held him.

"What was that?" Boris asked, his tone suspicious.

"Do what you want. Maybe it'll help you feel better."

Boris' eyes narrowed. He stalked forward, watching Alex as though he expected him to fight free.

"Breaking your face will make me feel better," the Alpha said.

Alex didn't flinch from Boris' fist when it hit his face. The impact of the Alpha's knuckles turned him halfway around. Alex gritted his teeth and straightened back up. Hands grabbed his shoulders. The Alpha hit him again.

Alex stood up again with the taste of blood in his mouth. The voice in the back of his mind said that the fact that the taste was familiar wasn't a good thing. Alex ignored it.

Boris slammed a fist into his stomach.

Alex doubled over with a gasp that he tried to stifle.

"Good one," Daniel said.

"Shut up," Boris snapped.

"Quiet."

Everyone stared at Alex in surprise. He tipped his head to

the side, trying to hear the sound again. There it was. A scream called faintly up the stairs.

"Don't you dare tell Boris to—"

"Quiet," Alex and Boris repeated.

Boris walked toward the stairs. Alex took a step forward, but members of Pack Boris pulled him back.

A scraping sound came up the stairs. Alex was about to ask Boris what he saw when the werewolf turned around with wide eyes. Before he could move, a cur leaped up the last few feet of steps and tackled the Alpha.

The hulking, misshapen wolf creature pinned Boris to the ground. Its human-like head bared teeth that jutted out in all directions. Boris struggled, but the cur's sharp black claws dug into his shoulders. The Alpha gave a yell of pain.

Several members of Pack Boris screamed.

"What is that?" Daniel demanded, his voice high with panic.

Alex crossed the hallway in two strides and dove into the creature, throwing it off of Boris and down the stairs. It scrambled back to its feet and ran up the stairs again, its claws gouging huge chunks out of the wood.

Boris and Alex met the cur's headlong rush. Boris grunted when one of its claws slammed into his stomach. The creature was huge and strong. Alex knew they couldn't beat it with sheer strength. It shoved them backwards as though they weighed nothing. He needed to morph. He tried to force it to happen.

"Attack!" Boris yelled.

Chapter Eight

Pack Boris obeyed. The dozen werewolves ran to them, charging into the creature with the force of a battering ram. They forced it back toward the stairs. Daniel reached Alex's side. Boris crouched, tearing the claws from his stomach and getting better leverage with his shoulder. Nate caught its paw before it could wreck more havoc on the Alpha.

They were almost to the stairs. The cur's claws gouged the carpet and wood. It fought, pushing them back. Mitch yelled when the claws slashed across his chest. Alex knew the cur would tear all of them apart. They were students who deserved to live, not be slain by some experiment gone wrong.

Alex felt the change. Blue touched his vision. His muscles lengthened. He could feel the strength surge through his limbs.

With a growl, Alex shoved back. The other werewolves fell to either side. Alex caught the cur in a bear hug and leaped, throwing them both off the stairs.

They hit about halfway down. Alex landed hard on top of the creature. It gave a strangled yelp and its neck twisted beneath Alex. He felt as much as heard it snap. They rolled a few more feet, but the cur was deadweight. Alex kicked free and climbed back to his feet. The morph faded, leaving him human once more.

"What was that?" Mitch asked, clutching his bleeding chest.

"I don't know," Boris replied. His shoulder and stomach bled, but he didn't appear to notice.

More screams sounded from below. Alex took off down the stairs four at a time. The second his foot touched the bottom, three curs looked over from the students they were terrorizing. They turned away from their prey and stalked toward him.

Ice ran through Alex's veins. It was obvious by their actions that they had come to the Academy to find him. Students were being hurt and possibly killed. He had to stop it.

"I'm over here," he yelled.

"Alex, be quiet!" Pip said from where he cowered in a corner near the Great Hall. "They'll kill you!"

"I've got to get them out of here," Alex replied.

The three curs stalked closer. Two more appeared from the Great Hall. Alex fell back toward the doors. If he could get all of them to follow him, the students might be safe.

"Come get me," he yelled again.

"Get me, too," Pip called, standing up.

Alex stared at the little werewolf with big ears who had almost gotten both him and Cassic killed a few years back. "Stay there," he ordered.

Pip nodded, his eyes wide as if he had just realized the consequences of gaining the curs' attention.

More screams came from down the professors' hall.

"Come on," Alex yelled. "This way, you cowards!"

Two more curs appeared from that hallway. Growls filled the air as the beasts pursued Alex. He backed toward the doors that led outside. As soon as his back touched the glass, he shoved the doors open and ran outside. The seven curs took off after him.

They were fast, faster than Alex could run in human form. Fear raced through him at the thought of being torn apart by their lethal black claws. He had no doubt Drogan had given them his scent. The Extremist had vowed to kill him. Alex knew it was his fault the curs were at the Academy. He had to get them away from the students.

Claws tore down his back. Alex let out a yell and spun around. The adrenaline surged through his body, forcing him to morph. He blinked and blue filled his vision. The curs attacked as his body changed. Alex was buried beneath a pile of writhing, angry creatures caught between being human and werewolf. They were so heavy. Teeth tore into his shoulder and his thigh. The pain made him morph faster. Strength poured through him. He heaved upward, shoving the bodies away.

As soon as they were clear, Alex took off between the trees. The curs crashed through the forest after him. Their snarls and angry roars filled the air, driving him to run faster. He might have been strong in rage mode, but he knew better than to think he could take them all on.

Alex didn't know where to go. The curs were gaining on him. Claws reached out and snagged his ankle. Alex tripped and rolled, coming to a stop against the trunk of a tree with enough force that the branches shook and leaves rained down. He ducked and a set of claws scored the tree trunk where his head had been. Alex lashed out, catching the creature across the face. It reared up with a cry of pain, clawing at its damaged eyes. Alex scrambled out from beneath it and took off running again.

Unable to think of anywhere else to go, Alex made for the cliff. He reached the boulders and took them two at a time. He could feel the hot breath of the closest cur as he climbed. He didn't dare look back. There were so many of them. Alex refused to call for help. Any who came would surely be killed by Drogan's mutated beasts. Alex was sure he would die in the forest he loved so much.

He reached the cliff top and wavered near the edge above the lake. The six curs who had made it reached the top and advanced toward him. Their snarls left no doubt that they had been sent to kill him. Drogan was no longer playing around. Alex was about to be shredded to pieces by his half-brother's creations.

After they were finished with him, Alex knew they would attack the Academy again. He wouldn't be able to protect the students, Siale, or his mother. Cassie and Tennison would be in danger. He couldn't keep them away from Trent.

The thoughts filled him with desperation. He looked around quickly. There was one more chance. It was a slim one, he knew, but if he could face them one at a time, perhaps he could take a few down with him and minimize the damage they would wreck on the Academy.

The curs were almost to him. Alex backed up to the edge of the cliff. He felt the blood streaming down his back. His ankle didn't want to hold his weight. He could imagine what it would feel like to be torn apart by the serrated claws and jagged teeth in front of him. He wouldn't let it happen to the other students.

Alex grabbed the first cur by the head. Before it could move, he lunged backwards, pulling it over the cliff edge with him. Everything slowed. The creature's teeth grabbed his shoulder, grounding down against his collar bone. Alex yelled as its claws tore at his chest. Remembering the cur on the stairs, he wrapped his arms around its head and neck, holding tight. He jerked his body to the right, managing to turn them just before they hit the water.

The icy cold of the lake enveloped him. The creature struggled as they were pulled down to the bottom, deeper than Alex had ever been. He felt it panic and push to get free. Its claws raked his sides, but he didn't let go. The cur's struggles became stronger. Alex heard the repercussions of other curs hitting the water. His lungs burned, but he still held on.

A moment later, the cur's struggling ceased. Alex pushed away from the body, his lungs screaming. He fought back the impulse to breathe and kicked for the surface.

As soon as Alex's head broke through to air, he gasped, pulling in huge breaths. He looked around quickly. He could see huge rings in the water where the other curs had landed, but they hadn't broken the surface yet. Alex swam quickly to the closest one.

Beneath the water, the beast was struggling. It kicked with its massive limbs, but was fighting to get high enough to reach the surface. Alex took a deep breath and dove. His arms encircled the creature's head. His muscles tightened as the cur struggled. Alex gave a hard jerk. The creature twitched, then went still.

Alex reached the surface again just as two of the curs surfaced as well. He swam to the first one. There was panic in the beast's eyes. Alex ducked under the water, missing a swipe of its claws when it attempted to climb on him to stay up. Alex came up behind the creature and latched onto its neck. The cur clawed at his arms, but he didn't let go. As its struggles slowed, it sank beneath the water. Alex held on until he was sure it was dead.

The other cur had just reached shore when Alex broke through the water again. It lay gasping in the grass. Alex wondered if Drogan had thought about his beasts swimming. There was no sign of the other two that had followed him to the cliff. He forced himself toward the shore.

The cur there was trying to rise. Its massive limbs shook as it struggled to hold its weight. The cur smelled like blood. Alex wondered how many students it had hurt. He spotted a broken branch near the creature's head. He grabbed it in his clawed hand and shoved down, using his morphed strength to stab the branch through the cur's eye. It shuddered, then held still.

Alex could only stare at the creatures around him. The attack hadn't given him time to think about what was happening. He had just killed five of Drogan's curs and maimed another. He knew two others lay at the bottom of the lake, victims to their massive bodies. A pit formed in his stomach at the thought of how many others there could be. He started toward the school.

"Alex!"

He knew the voice by heart. It reached his sensitive ears with a fear and pain that tore through him sharper than any cur's claws. Alex took off running. He pushed his morphed body, running far faster than any werewolf could. He crashed through the trees and reached the gate within seconds. He yanked it open so hard he ripped it off the iron hinges. Throwing the gate aside, Alex ran around the Academy to the courtyard.

He reached the corner and froze.

Siale was lying on the top step. Blood colored the cement around her and injured students cowered away from the scene.

Above Siale stood the massive cur, Lucian. He met Alex's gaze and the corner of his lip lifted in a toothy smile that pulled at the scar running through his eye. Alex's heart skipped a beat. The cur bent his head toward Siale, intent on finishing the job he had started.

Alex ran across the courtyard. The cur's fangs opened, dripping blood-tinged drool. There was no way he would reach Siale in time. He passed Jet's statue. The cur's jagged teeth were about to close on Siale's neck. Alex ran faster, but was too far away. The cur would kill her.

Siale's hand lifted at the last second and she drove a knife into its throat.

Lucian jerked back with a roar of pain. Blood streamed from the wound. Alex hit the first step and leaped. He dove into the cur, barreling him away from Siale. They slammed into the side of the Academy. The stone cracked under the impact of the cur's body. Lucian snarled and shoved Alex away. He ducked under the huge cur's sweeping claws and drove his own into Lucian's side.

The cur gave another roar and jerked back, tearing Alex's claws out of its flesh. Alex pummeled him again and again, fueled with rage. His hands slicked with blood as he forced the cur away from Siale. They reached the stairs and Lucian stumbled down. The beast hit the bottom and rose to his feet. He scrambled away with a bellow of wrath that rebounded off the Academy walls. Two other curs appeared from the side of the school and joined Lucian. They raced to the wall and their claws gouged the stone when they climbed over.

Alex wanted to pursue them. Instinct demanded for him to slay the curs who had attacked his home. He needed to see Lucian dead for attacking Siale.

Siale.

Alex turned. All thoughts of revenge or fighting fled at the sight of his love lying on the cement.

Blood poured from gouges across her stomach. Her head lolled back and he couldn't tell if she was breathing. Alex fell to his knees next to her. His morphed form faded as he stared at her torn and broken on the steps of the Academy.

"Siale?" he asked, his voice shaking.

Memories flashed to Kalia, of holding her in the snow. He felt the sticky cold of the flakes that landed on his blood-soaked hands. He watched the way the blood puddled beneath her, melting the snow until she had nothing left to bleed. Kalia had called his name, begging him to help her. He had failed, and watched her be lowered into the ground.

Tears clouded his vision. He couldn't do it, not again. He couldn't sit there as the life blood of another person he loved seeped away. Siale was his one. She completed him in every way, and he hadn't gotten to her in time. She had called for him with fear in her voice like Kalia's. He was undone, empty. He had failed her completely.

A sound caught his ear. He looked down. Siale gave a shallow breath, but didn't open her eyes. Hope fluttered faintly in his chest like a butterfly with broken wings. She was broken, but she had been so before. Her blood was his blood. Alex slid his hands beneath her and stood. The doors to the Academy had been smashed by the curs. He walked through the mess of broken glass and twisted metal.

The Academy was filled with scared students. Even though the curs were gone, the sour, animal scent of them lingered in the air along with blood and fear. Carnage coated the floors along with deep gouges from the creatures' claws. Students huddled together, some working to patch up their friends. Alex glimpsed a body lying still on the floor. He turned away, intent on the medical wing.

"Alex!" Cassie exclaimed. "Oh thank goodness!" She ran down the stairs two at a time. "They said you led the curs away through the forest..." Her voice died at the sight of Siale's body in his arms. "Oh no."

"She needs help," Alex said, stumbling toward the medical wing. Cassie grabbed his elbow, guiding him there. She carried most of Siale's weight, helping Alex make it through.

Chapter Nine

"Mom!" Alex called as soon as he reached the doors. He shoved them open with his shoulder, aware of how difficult it was. He knew he was losing blood, but he didn't care. Siale was still alive. He had to save her.

"Alex?" Meredith's voice came from further down the hall.

"Mom, Siale needs help. She's bleeding..." Cassie looked down at her arms covered in blood. "A lot."

Meredith and Lyra appeared. Alex's mother's face washed white when she saw Siale's condition. "This way," she directed them.

Both members of the medical team at the Academy looked as though they had been hard pressed already to care for the students who had been injured. Alex glanced in a room they passed and saw someone working on a student.

"Brock and Mouse are helping, along with Jaze and Nikki. More students keep flooding in. We're trying to keep up," Meredith said, leading them to the next empty room.

At Meredith's motion, Alex set Siale gently on the bed. Siale gasped despite how careful he tried to be and curled around her injured stomach. The sheets immediately soaked red with blood.

"You have to help her," Alex said with panic in his voice. "She's lost so much blood. You have to save her!"

"We'll do everything we can," Meredith replied. She gave Cassie a look.

Alex's sister set a hand on his arm. "Come on, Alex. We need to wait outside."

"No," Alex protested. "I have to be here for her."

When he refused to leave, Cassie brought him a chair. He sat in the corner and watched Lyra and Meredith work on

Siale. They cut away what remained of her shirt, exposing her shredded stomach.

"Get Mouse and Jaze," Meredith commanded quickly.

Lyra left the room at a run.

Alex buried his face in his hands. Cassie rubbed his back. Tennison appeared at the door; he and Cassie spoke quietly for a moment, but Alex didn't hear what they said. A deep sound filled his ears like the rushing of the ocean. It ebbed and flowed, covering everything that was happening around him, the beeping of machines that had been hooked up to Siale, the scuff of sneakers on the tile floor, and the whirlwind of activity as they tried to save the life of the girl he loved.

After what felt like hours later, a hand touched his shoulder. He looked up to see Meredith watching him, her brow creased in concern. Jaze, Lyra, and Mouse waited near the door. Someone had pushed open the curtains near Siale's bed, bathing her in healing moonlight. Every room in the medical wing at the Academy had a huge window and beds that could be moved to the best position to be blanketed by the moon. Sometimes it made all the difference between living and dying.

"We've done what we can. Only time will tell now," his mother said. "You need to let me clean your wounds so they'll heal."

Alex rose. He limped to the bed. Siale stomach was covered and her other wounds bandaged. Her face was pale and eyes closed. She looked worse than when they pulled her from the body pit.

"She has to have more help. There's got to be more we can do." Alex knew he was babbling, but he couldn't stop himself. He had never felt so helpless in his life. "She needs a blood transfusion. She lost so much blood." He pushed up what was left of his sleeve. He barely noticed the blood that covered his arm from the cur bites. "Take my blood. Give it to her. Anything to save her."

Meredith shook her head. "You're not a match. We already have—"

"No!" Alex said, surprising himself with the strength he still had left. "She needs help. She can't just lay there and die. I have to do something, anything!"

Meredith put a hand on his chest and pushed him back down to sit in the chair. "You listen to me, Alex," she said in a voice that left no room for argument. It was the first time she had ever used such a tone with him. "You're bleeding and about to fall over at any minute. You are my son and you will let me take care of you. Now. You can't help Siale if you bleed out."

Shocked by his mother's demand, Alex looked from Meredith to Cassie. His sister appeared just as worried as his mom.

"Come on, Alex. You need to get bandaged. Look at you," Cassie pleaded.

For the first time, Alex glanced down at himself. His shirt was in tatters. If he remembered correctly, it used to be green. Now, what remained of the material was dark brown where the blood had dried and almost black where it continued to flow. His chest was a patchwork of claw marks, his shoulder was chewed opened to the bone in parts, and he could feel the stickiness where his shirt clung to his back.

He didn't remember any of it, getting bitten, clawed, anything. All he could think of was seeing Siale on the top step with Lucian hovering over her. The cur's crooked smile was seared into his brain.

"Alex?" Cassie asked gently.

Alex took a breath. It hurt more than he remembered

breathing should. He nodded.

Meredith and Cassie helped him to his feet. Jaze held open the door. Alex stepped on his right foot and winced. The dean ducked under his arm and helped him to the next room.

"Can I go back to Siale's room when we're done?" Alex asked quietly while Meredith cut away what remained of his shirt.

"Yes, you can," his mother replied, her tone gentle. She reached up and cupped his cheek. "I love you, Alex."

"I know, Mom," he replied, touched by her gesture. "I'm sorry I put you through this."

"This isn't your fault."

"It is," Alex replied. He glanced up at Jaze and winced when Lyra began to dab at the claw marks down his back. "Drogan said he was going to kill me. I just didn't realize he would come after me the second I got home."

"You couldn't have known," Jaze said. "None of us did. The way those mutants attacked destroyed our defenses with the first wave. They threw themselves into the guns and anything else we used, shielding the bullets with their bodies. Those beasts were nearly unstoppable. We have students in critical condition and parents on their way in as fast as they can get here. Drogan has a vendetta against this school that he developed from his father. That's been obvious since his first attempt."

"I was the one the curs were after." Alex rubbed his forehead in an attempt to clear his thoughts.

"Curs?" Jaze asked.

Alex nodded. "That's what Drogan called them. He must have sent them after me. I only had to call for them and they started to chase me. I led them to the cliff." He closed his eyes, remembering. "They jumped off after me."

His mother's gentle fingers slowed. He could feel the attention of everyone in the room. He kept his eyes closed, feeling the throb of his wounds with every beat of his heart.

"I thought it would be a good way to pick them off, or at least a few of them. I knew I couldn't take them all."

His mother's ministrations stopped altogether.

Alex opened his eyes. "I pulled one down with me and when it hit the water I realized they couldn't swim, at least not well. I held the cur down until it drowned. I broke another's neck, and killed two more." Alex figured he could spare his mom and sister the details. "The water slowed them enough that I could handle them. I thought I had them all, then I heard Siale call my name."

He swallowed, the memory of her cry for help echoing with another. "When I got there, Lucian had her."

"Who's Lucian?" Jaze asked, his voice forcibly calm. "Is he one of the mutants, I mean curs?" he corrected himself. It was obvious how much the attack on his students had affected him. The dean looked ready to throttle something. His hands opened and shut in a gesture Alex recognized.

"He's the leader of the curs. He was the one who freed Drogan from the Extremists." Alex didn't let himself think of what had happened there. "Siale stabbed him with a knife and it gave me enough time to chase him away, but she was already hurt..." his voice faded.

"She's strong, Alex," Cassie reassured him, coming to the side of the bed. She took his hand. "You know what Siale's gone through. She can make it through this."

Lyra pressed bandages to Alex's shoulder to slow the bleeding so it could heal. He gritted his teeth at the pain. "She shouldn't have to be strong."

"Neither should you," Meredith said, wrapping his ankle. "But you're the strongest boy I know."

"And the craziest," Cassie said.

Alex gave her a small smile. "That's why I'm still here."

She nodded. "Definitely."

Alex settled back on the bed.

"The curs have no instinct for self-preservation," Mouse said from Jaze's side.

"What do you mean?" Alex asked, glancing at him.

The small professor explained, "That's how they broke through our security. They swarmed our weapons systems. At least a dozen died in the process, but their bodies blocked the guns that line the perimeter, allowing the curs to enter through the forest. That's probably why they jumped off the cliff after you. They don't fear death."

"That makes them all the more dangerous," Alex said.

Jaze nodded. "But also beatable. We can use that as a weakness against them. No fear of death can also mean no recognition of the things that lead to death, as you've described. It might give us the means to beat them."

That gave Alex something to think about. Jaze and Mouse left them to tend to the many needs of the other students. Alex couldn't imagine how they felt. The Academy had been washed in blood when he carried Siale through it. So many had been hurt.

"Alex?"

He opened his eyes, only at that moment aware that he had nodded off. His wounds were bandaged and everyone else had left besides his mother.

"Is Siale okay?" he asked immediately.

"She's sleeping," Meredith answered. She smoothed Alex's hair back from his forehead. "How are you feeling?"

"Better," Alex answered. He sat up.

"Maybe you should rest a bit longer," she told him, her voice filled with motherly concern.

Alex took the time to look at her, really look at her. There were circles under her eyes and her face was pale.

"You're the one who needs to rest."

She blinked at his caring observation and gave him a smile. "Thank you, son. I will make time for it later. Right now, there are students who need my attention."

"Do you mind if I rest in Siale's room?" Alex asked.

Surprise crossed her face that he took the time to ask. She nodded. "Of course." She helped him rise to his feet.

Alex put his weight on his ankle and was glad to find that it would hold him. He walked carefully to the door with Meredith at his side. He paused in the hallway.

The scent of blood filled the air. When he took a breath through his mouth, he could taste it.

"How many were hurt?" he asked quietly.

"Twenty-seven," Meredith replied. "Three students were killed, five are critical along with Siale. Trent is holding on by a thread."

Alex felt as though his feet were suddenly glued to the floor. He stared at his mom. "Trent?"

She nodded, her eyebrows pulled together as though she realized he hadn't known. "He's three rooms down. They found him by the Great Hall..."

Alex was already to Trent's room. He pushed the door open with his shoulder, forgetting until the pain flooded through him that it wasn't a good idea. Jordan looked up from where she sat at the side of the bed. Tear tracks showed on her cheeks.

"Oh, Alex," she said; fresh tears welled in her eyes.

He crossed to her. Jordan hugged him gently and turned her attention back to Trent.

The small werewolf had a thick bandage across his throat. His eyes were shut. It looked like he was grimacing in pain even though he was unconscious.

"What happened?" Alex asked quietly.

"We were in the Great Hall when they attacked," Jordan told him. "Trent went running out to see if he could help, and one of them clawed him. It continued on its way as though he didn't matter." Her voice tightened. "I held his throat until your sister found us."

Her fingers shook. She linked them together in her lap to still them.

It killed Alex to see his friend in such bad shape. The steady beeping of the monitor near Trent's head gave only minimal reassurance. Alex wished the moonlight that fell across the bed would work faster.

"He's going to be okay," he told Jordan, hoping the words were true. "Trent's strong. He has to be to put up with me."

She nodded with a grateful smile. "Thank you, Alex."

"How is Siale doing?" she asked after a couple of minutes of silence had passed.

Alex shook his head. "Not well. I need to get back to her." He gave Jordan what he hoped was a reassuring smile. "Will you let me know when Trent is up?"

She nodded. "I will. Thank you, Alex."

He made his way back up to Siale's room. He was grateful to see Meredith there.

"Is Trent going to be okay?" he asked her. He eased into the chair. She took a step forward to help him, but he shook his head. "I'm fine."

"I'll believe that when I see it," she replied, giving him a motherly smile. She leaned against the counter. "Trent lost a lot of blood. Terith donated for a transfusion. If he can pull through tonight, I think he'll be okay. It's been touch and go." She looked at Siale. She didn't have to say anything. Alex knew what she was thinking. As bad as Trent was, Siale was worse.

"Drogan will pay for this."

"There will always be people who want to kill werewolves," Meredith said quietly.

Alex looked up at her. "Not like this. Drogan used animals to hunt us like we're animals. He sent them into our home. Students are hurt and," he swallowed, "Dead. Nobody should have that kind of hatred for another person. He will pay."

The surge of energy from his anger left him drained. He bent with his elbows on his knees and buried his face in his hands. He could feel the tiny pulses of his blood against the bandages. There would be more scars to add to his tattered body. He felt like they were holding him together. He knew it wouldn't take much to fall completely apart.

"I'll have a cot brought in," Meredith said, her voice gentle.

"I can sleep on the chair," he replied without looking up at her.

Her hand touched his shoulder. "Alex." When he finally glanced up, he could see the hint of steel in her gaze again. "I am your mother, and I say you will sleep in the cot. You're trying to get better yourself."

He nodded, forcing back a small smile. As much as he hated being told what to do, it was nice to have a mother who cared.

When she left, he moved the chair next to Siale's bed. It ate at him to watch her lying there, so still and withdrawn as though her soul had already left. He brushed her cheek with the backs of his fingers just to remind himself what it felt like to touch her. Her skin was cool, but not cold. He sat back, hoping beyond hope never to feel cold skin beneath his fingers again.

He loved her. Sitting there next to the bed, uncertain of whether she would awaken again or not, he realized how very much that was true. He couldn't breathe without thinking about her, couldn't see the color gray without picturing her eyes. Her laughter was the best sound he had ever heard, and the sight of her hurt and unconscious was enough to send him after Drogan with nothing but his bare hands, except that he was afraid to be away from her side in case she awoke.

Chapter Ten

Footsteps were heard up and down the hallway all day as the staff cared for the students who had been injured. A familiar voice awoke Alex from a dazed sleep. He sat up at the sound of the door opening.

"Hello, Alex."

"Hi, Dr. Benjamin."

The human doctor gave a small smile. "We have to stop meeting like this."

Alex nodded, but couldn't muster a smile back. He turned his attention to Siale. Dr. Benjamin crossed to the bed. He checked her bandages and recorded her vitals on the chart he held.

"Do you know the hardest thing about treating werewolves?" the doctor said after his pen had stopped scratching across the paper.

"What?" Alex asked.

The doctor gave him a straight look. "They often survive wounds that would kill a human." He nodded at Siale. "That type of a trauma would be fatal for someone like me. But for her?" He lifted his shoulders a tiny bit. "We won't know until tomorrow. It's the waiting that the hardest."

Alex nodded in agreement. "How's Trent?"

"Rushton?" At Alex's answering nod, Dr. Benjamin said, "As good as can be expected. They gave him blood right away, and his vitals, though lower than I like, are at least promising. I think he's going to pull through."

Relief flooded Alex. He didn't know if he could handle losing two pack mates right then.

At his expression, the doctor gave a wry smile. "Sometimes caring is the toughest part. As much as I try to avoid you werewolves, I keep finding myself getting caught up in saving you. Do you know why?" At Alex's questioning look, Dr. Benjamin gave a true smile. "Because I really do care."

"I'm glad you're here," Alex said, holding out a hand.

"I got here as soon as I could. I wish it had been sooner." He shook Alex's hand. "We'll do what we can to save her."

"Thank you."

Dr. Benjamin turned to leave, then paused. "How about you?"

"What about me?"

"Your chart says you were cut up pretty good."

"I have a chart?" Alex asked, more surprised that the doctor had cared to go through it.

Dr. Benjamin crossed to him. "It's a thick one, believe me." He didn't wait for Alex's permission to pull back the werewolf's gown so that his shoulder was exposed. Alex kept from showing the pain as the doctor prodded and poked. He bit back an exclamation when the doctor peeled back the bandages in one area and investigated with his gloves.

"You have a good medical team here," the doctor finally noted. He pressed the bandages back into place and tossed his gloves in the garbage can.

Relieved that the man was finished with his examination, Alex sat back gingerly in the chair. "I'm still here because of them."

Dr. Benjamin patted him on his good shoulder. "Hang in there, Alex. We'll do what we can to help your friends pull through."

"I'm going to propose to her."

Dr. Benjamin paused with his hand on the doorknob. "What was that?" he asked, glancing back.

"I'm going to propose to Siale. I decided that today, sitting here wondering if she'll ever wake up." Alex sat up straighter even though it hurt to do so. "I want her to know she'll never be alone. She's my soulmate."

"She's your one," Dr. Benjamin said with understanding in his voice.

Alex nodded. "My only one. I almost lost her before. It would kill me to lose her now."

Dr. Benjamin gave him a warm smile. "I'm glad you found your one."

"Bring her back to me," Alex said; pleading crept into his voice.

Dr. Benjamin gave a firm nod. "I will. I promise."

"Where is she?"

Alex stood up at the sound of Red's voice. Two seconds later, Siale's father burst into the room.

"My little girl," he exclaimed. The man dropped to his knees beside the bed. He looked up at the doctor. "How is she?"

Dr. Benjamin's tone became purely professional. "She has experienced severe trauma to her stomach. My colleagues tended to her wounds and gave her a blood transfusion. Time is now our ally."

"Is there anything else you can do?" Red pleaded.

It broke Alex's heart to watch Siale's father beg the doctor to save his daughter.

Dr. Benjamin shook his head. "We've done everything we can," he said, his tone gentle. "Siale has survived life-threatening wounds before. She's very strong; I feel like she's going to pull through."

Red turned his attention back to his daughter. Dr. Benjamin took it as a dismissal. He nodded at Alex and left the room to check on the other patients.

"She fought hard," Alex said quietly.

Red looked up. His eyes, colored green and blue, softened

at the sight of Alex. "Were you here?" he asked.

Alex nodded. He lowered his gaze. "I tried to save her, but I found her after she had already been attacked. She stabbed the cur with a knife."

Red's lips lifted in the smallest smile. "She's always been feisty." His smile faded when he looked at his daughter.

Siale's face was as pale as the pillow case. Alex wanted to touch her cheek to make sure that she was still warm, but he didn't dare in her father's presence. Lyra brought in another chair and the two sat in silence, watching Siale and hoping beyond hope for her to open her eyes again.

Alex awoke with a start and found Mr. Andrews standing in front of him.

"Sorry, son," Red said with an apologetic expression. "I asked if you wanted me to grab something from the lunchroom. Jaze stopped in and said it was open to the parents."

"I'm okay," Alex told him, touched by his concern. "Take your time. I'll watch over her."

"Thank you," Siale's father replied.

Mr. Andrews crossed to the door.

"Uh, sir?" Alex asked. When Red turned, he said, "If you hear about Trent, he's a friend of mine who got hurt. I need to know he's going to pull through. The not knowing is killing me."

Mr. Andrews nodded with an understanding smile. "I'll find out how your friend is doing."

As soon as his footsteps disappeared down the hall, Alex was at Siale's side. Her breathing was so shallow it scared him. He touched her arm, brushing her skin with the backs of his fingers as gently as a breath.

To his surprise, Siale stirred. "Alex?" she asked. Her eyes partially opened, but didn't focus on him.

"I'm here, Siale," he replied. He wanted to touch her, to reassure her, but didn't know what to do to keep from causing her more pain.

She shook her head. "It's not right. Something's not right." Panic touched her voice and she began to claw at her stomach, trying to pull off the bandages beneath her hospital gown. "Alex, they've got me! They won't let go!"

Afraid that she was going to hurt herself further, Alex grabbed her hands. "You're safe," he tried to reassure her. "Nobody has you."

"Yes, they do!" she replied. Tears streamed down her cheeks. "The bodies. They won't let go. They're pulling me down!"

Nausea rushed over Alex at the memory. "You mean the body pit?"

"Yes," Siale said, her voice barely a whisper of fear. She grabbed his arm, her grip weak. "They won't let go. Hold me, Alex. Keep me from them."

Alex climbed on her bed and had her in his arms in a heartbeat. The moonlight from the window fell on his shoulders and back; he felt the soothing effects of the healing light. Alex held Siale to him the way he had in the body pit. "I've got you, Siale. I won't let you go," he promised.

She nodded, pressing her face against his chest as if she couldn't stand the sight of the memories washing over her. "They keep holding on, Alex. What do I do?" Her hands shook as she clutched his arms.

Alex was afraid all of the movement had reopened her wounds. He held her close, remembering again the feeling of bodies beneath him, the stench clogging his nose and mouth, clinging to the memory. Her mother had been one of the bodies. He hadn't found that out until later, and knew the horrors of the long hours they had spent there together had scarred Siale even deeper than himself.

"I can feel them looking at me, Alex," Siale sobbed. "I'm supposed to be one of them. They want me to be one of them."

"No," Alex replied, his voice strong and filled with possessiveness. He put his forehead against hers. "They can't have you. You're my Siale. I'll keep you safe."

"You promise?" she asked, her voice feeble.

"I promise," he replied.

She let out a shuddering breath and fell quiet, her body shivering with weakness. He didn't know if she slept or if she was too weak to talk any longer. He couldn't let her slip away to join the dead they had fought so hard to survive. His eyes burned at the thought of losing his love. He couldn't say goodbye. He wouldn't.

Thoughts of the body pit reminded him of what had helped her to pull through. She had asked him to talk, to do anything to distract her from the horror of their situation.

"When we're out of the Academy, you know what we'll do?" He paused, then forced a smile when he said, "We'll go to college in a world where we won't have to hide what we are. We'll make it safe for the younger ones like William. He won't have to grow up in fear." He felt Siale's shivering calm. He swallowed past the knot in his throat and continued, "We'll be able to be whatever we want, doctors, scientists. Maybe I can finally find something I'm good at." He could picture the smile she would have given him at the statement and hear her telling him that he was selling himself short.

Alex talked until his throat was so dry he couldn't swallow, but he didn't dare leave her alone. He rested his head back against the window and listened to the sound of her breathing. The steady rush soothed his thoughts. As long as she breathed, she fought to survive.

"Alex?"

He opened his eyes and found Red in the doorway. He realized his situation wasn't ideal for Siale's father. "She woke up," he said, wondering if he should get up. "She was afraid..."

Alex moved to ease Siale down to rest on the bed, but Red shook his head. "You should stay there. She looks a bit better. I think she needs you." He touched her forehead. "She's not as pale as she was before."

Alex looked at Siale, hoping her father's words were true.

Red gave him a small smile. "Thank you for taking care of her." He held out a cup of water. "You looked like you could use a drink, so I brought one back for you."

Alex shifted Siale carefully so that he wouldn't jostle her and reached for the cup. "Thank you very much."

"Healing takes a lot out of you," Siale's father said, sitting back down in his chair. "Take it easy so you don't get sick."

Alex nodded, forcing himself to sip at the water instead of gulping it down like he wanted to.

"I asked Jaze about your friend Trent," Mr. Andrews said.

"How is he?" Alex asked anxiously.

Red smiled. "He's awake and talking. Jaze said someone named Jordan wouldn't leave his side. He said she pretty much pulled the boy through with her strength of will."

Alex smiled back, tension easing from his shoulders. "Good," he replied. "That's really good. Good for him."

Silence settled between them.

Red eventually ran a hand through his brown hair. He let out a small sigh. "It's all regrets."

"What is?" Alex asked after a moment of silence.

Red shook his head. "It's so easy to regret simple decisions, like letting Siale come here, or leaving Siale and her mother and going to work the night the General stole them away. I always wonder what would have happened if I had stayed home that night." He waved his hand to indicate Siale's condition. "What if I never let her come here? She might not be in this bed."

"She'd be safe," Alex replied quietly. He was the one who had begged Siale to come to the Academy. So much had happened that he blamed himself for. He felt like he couldn't take anything else at the moment and still stay sane.

"It's easy to regret," Red continued, his voice understanding, "But eventually we have to realize that there will be consequences to whatever actions we take. Life happens. Siale wanted to be here, to be with you." He gave Alex a small smile. "Every time we spoke on the phone or she sent me letters, you're all she talked about. I couldn't have kept her away from you."

Alex asked the question swirling through his head. "What if she's safer without me?"

"Sometimes safer isn't always the right choice." At Alex's uncertain expression, Siale's father gave an understanding smile. "I see it in your face, son. You carry the weight of all of this, but you're just a boy." Red sat back. "Why do you think I invited you and your friends to our place for the summer?"

Caught off guard by the change of topic, Alex said, "I'm not sure."

Red smiled at him. "So you can be a teenager. After what I've seen on the news and heard from Jaze, you guys need a chance to just be kids, to make stupid mistakes, to stay up so late that you watch the sunrise the next morning. I saw it when you first came to the warehouse. You're too young to carry so much weight on your back. You're going to snap before you've had a chance to even live."

Alex was quiet before he asked, "Are you sure you still want us there?"

Red replied in a wry tone, "What? You think the fact that having Extremists out to kill you no matter where you are might deter your welcome in my werewolf safe haven?"

"Yes," Alex replied.

Red picked up the blanket at the end of Siale's bed and set it around both of them. "I'm willing to take the risk. If Drogan finds you, he finds you, but we'll be ready. At least you won't be here in a school full of kids."

The silence that settled over them was comfortable. Alex could feel Siale's heartbeat strengthening. The scent of blood lessened as the night faded into dawn. Red leaned one elbow against the counter and fell asleep with his head at what looked like a very uncomfortable angle. Healing and everything else Alex had gone through had taken a lot out of him. He leaned his head back and let himself sleep knowing that he would awaken if Siale needed him for anything.

Chapter Eleven

"Rough night?"

A smile touched Alex's lips before he even opened his eyes to see Siale watching him. Though she still looked pale, the brightness of fever had left her eyes and she gave a smile that was so welcome he wanted to cry. Forcing himself to keep his machismo intact, Alex returned her smile.

"Nothing we couldn't handle," he replied. He nodded and Siale followed his gaze.

"Dad!"

Red awoke and sat up so fast he fell off his chair. He scrambled to his feet and was at his daughter's side in a blur.

"Siale, you're awake!"

She gave a little laugh that was music to Alex's ears. He climbed off the bed, aware of how much he already missed holding her in his arms.

"I'll give you guys some time to catch up," he said.

"You don't have to go," her father replied.

Siale's warm smile filled Alex with happiness. He returned the smile. "I'm going to check on Trent. Do you want anything?"

Siale shook her head. "Just you back here with the news that Trent's okay."

"I'll bring it," Alex replied.

He walked down the hall feeling as though he floated. Knowing Siale was going to be alright banished the last of the darkness that had filled him through the long night. His aches and pains were gone to the point that he barely felt them; one more day and he would never know he had been injured.

"Well, don't you look like a new person," Meredith said when Alex poked his head in the nurses' lounge.

He surprised his mother by crossing straight to her and

giving her a big hug. "Thank you for saving Siale."

"She's awake?" Meredith asked, returning his hug.

Alex nodded and stepped back. "She's going to be just fine, thanks to you and Lyra. I don't know how to thank you."

"Your smile's enough," his mother replied fondly. "I've missed it."

Alex leaned against the table. "Did you get any rest?" A closer look at his mother revealed the same dark circles under her eyes and weariness in her gaze even though she tried to hide it. "I'm guessing not."

Meredith shook her head. "Not really, but it doesn't matter. Sleep can wait when our students' lives are on the line. Fortunately, I can say we saved everyone we could, including Trent."

Alex nodded. "Red told me. I'm on my way to visit him." He asked the question he didn't want to. "Mom, how many students did the curs kill?"

Meredith hesitated as if she didn't want to tell him. She finally gave him. "Four. Three Termers and Kayce."

Alex rubbed his forehead. Kayce was one of the younger Lifers. He hadn't known the werewolf well, but the redhead had been a regular on Raynen's pack. "Which Termers?" he asked.

Meredith's eyes studied the floor, letting Alex know just how much it hurt her to lose them. "We lost Daniel Adamson."

"Boris' Second?"

His mother nodded.

Alex let out a slow breath. Boris had taken quite a few blows. While Daniel wasn't Boris' usual Second, having been chosen just for the shakeup term, the pair had seemed to get along and work well together. Alex knew Boris wouldn't take the loss well.

"We also lost James Duncan and Pip Jones," Meredith said quietly.

Alex paused. He looked at his mother. "Pip? He died?" At her nod, regret rushed over Alex. Pip had almost gotten him and Cassie killed a few years back, but the little werewolf with the big ears had only been trying to protect his family. Since then, Pip had become an integral part of Pack Jericho. The thought of the pack's quarters without the enthusiastic werewolf was an empty one.

"His parents took his body back for burial," Meredith said, her voice soft as if she knew Alex was hurting. "They asked for a private funeral. With everyone going home tomorrow, Jaze felt it would be best."

Alex nodded. He inhaled a shuddering breath and let it out. "What do you do?" he asked quietly, more to himself then his mother. He looked at her. "What should I do?"

"What do you mean?"

"Drogan's curs were looking for me. Maybe I shouldn't go with Red when the Termers leave tomorrow. I should be helping Jaze hunt them down so they can't hurt anyone else."

His mother watched him closely, understanding him as only a mother could. "You need to go."

Alex shook his head, but Meredith spoke before he could. "I want you to leave this place."

Alex pushed away the small pang of hurt at her words.

"This may be home," his mother continued, "But there is pain here and unrest. You're not safe. You need to go and give Mouse and the others a chance to make it safer for you and the other students. You shouldn't have to live in fear, Alex. I don't know how many of the other parents are going to let their children come back. And maybe they're right."

The unspoken concern hung in the air. Alex set a hand on

Meredith's arm. "Mom, this is my home and my family is here. I want it to be safe as much as anyone else."

"Then give them a chance to make it that way," his mom replied with a touch of pleading in her voice. She covered his hand with her own. "Go with Red. Take Cassie and Tennison, and have some fun where Drogan can't find you. Experience what you're supposed to at your age."

"I'm going to propose to Siale."

Alex's words hung in the air for a moment. Meredith stared at him, her eyes bright with surprise. Her mouth turned up in a smile so huge that when her eyes filled with tears, Alex didn't know what was wrong.

"Mom?"

"I'm so happy!" she said, her tears breaking free. She threw her arms around his neck and sobbed, "My little boy is getting engaged."

Alex chuckled and patted her back. "It's okay, Mom."

"I know," she replied with a half-sob, half-laugh. "I'm just so proud of you I don't know what to do!"

"Come with me to pick out the ring," Alex offered, trying to keep from his voice how anxious he really was about the task.

Meredith took a step back so she could look at him. "Really?"

Alex nodded with another chuckle at the hopeful shock on her face. "Of course. You're my mother." He gave her a warm smile. "I need your input in these things."

Meredith went into planning mode. "We'll bring Cassie, for sure," she said, looking at Alex for confirmation.

"Definitely," Alex told her. "She'd kill me if I left her out."

"Maybe we can get Jaze to fly you guys to Red's a day later."

"That's a great idea," Alex said with relief. He had been worried trying to figure out how to look at rings without Siale being there. The extra day with her father would no doubt be welcome for both of them. Telling her Jaze needed him to finish a few things at the Academy wouldn't be a far stretch. He was highly interested in the changes Mouse and Brock would be making, and wanted to do what he could to ensure the safety of the Lifers who would be staying at the Academy during the summer.

"Go check on Trent," Meredith told him with a warm smile. "I'll work out the details."

Alex gave her another hug. "Thanks, Mom. I knew I could count on you."

He made his way down the hall to Trent's room. Instead of finding Jordan waiting worriedly by the side of her love's bed, he found Trent and Jordan sitting on the bed holding hands and talking.

Alex tapped on the open door with his knuckles. "This is a much better way to find you," he said with a smile. "I hope I'm not interrupting."

"Come in, Alex!" Trent said. His voice was scratchy, but he looked so much better Alex knew the werewolf would be completely healed by the next evening.

Alex crossed to his friend's bed. "I came by before, but..."

Trent nodded. "Jordan told me. She said Siale was in bad shape, too."

"She's going to be fine," Alex told him, taking the chair by the bed. "She's tough, like you."

Trent shook his head. "I'm not that tough." He touched the bandages around his throat. "If it wasn't for Jordan, I wouldn't be here."

"I'm more grateful for that then you know," Alex said, smiling at Jordan. "You're my right-hand man, Trent. What would I do without you?"

"Get into more trouble," Trent confirmed. "I wouldn't be nagging in your ear for you to take care of yourself."

"At least you make me consider it," Alex answered.

Trent chuckled. The sound was a bit rough and he put a hand to his neck as if it bothered him a bit.

"I'll go get you a drink," Jordan said, excusing herself. She patted Alex's shoulder on her way past. "Dr. Benjamin said he needs more sleep."

"I won't keep him for too long," Alex promised.

They watched Jordan leave. "You have a good girlfriend there," Alex said. "I don't think a dozen werewolves could have pulled her from your side."

Trent nodded, his eyes on the doorway as though Jordan couldn't return soon enough. "She's my reason to breathe." He glanced at Alex. "I hear you took care of most of those curs."

Alex sat back in his chair. "A few of them. Not enough." He indicated Trent's throat. "They caused a lot of pain, and students died."

Trent swallowed and winced. "I heard about Pip," he said quietly.

Alex nodded. There wasn't anything to say. They had known the small werewolf for the same amount of time. Both knew how much he would be missed.

"Are you leaving tomorrow?" Trent asked.

Alex hesitated, thinking of his conversation with his mother. "I feel like I shouldn't."

"But you are," Trent guessed. At Alex's nod, Trent sat up straighter. "Good. You should."

"I feel like I'm abandoning everyone," Alex admitted.

"Just me," Trent told him. At Alex's concerned look, the scrawny werewolf grinned. "Kidding, Alex. Geesh. You take everything so seriously. You need to get out of here."

"That's what my mom said."

"She's a smart woman," Trent replied. "And I'm not just saying that because I got an A in her class. She knows what's best for you. Listen to her."

Alex voiced what was bothering him. "What if the curs attack again? I won't be here to help fight them."

"Jordan said they found seven bodies, six in and around the lake, and one in the forest with its eyes gouged out. It apparently ran into a forked tree trunk, strangling itself after it was blinded. A bunch more were shot at the perimeter." Trent watched Alex, his eyes searching his friend's face. "How many more do you think Drogan has?"

"I don't know," Alex admitted. "But the way he talked made it sound like they had a lot. They're strong. I couldn't have beaten them if I didn't jump in that lake."

"They were looking for you?" Trent guessed.

"Yeah, for sure. The way they followed me when I ran was obvious."

"So we'll make it obvious that you left," Trent replied, already thinking ahead. "If they know you're gone, it'll protect the Academy. Drogan can waste his time looking for you, and the students and staff will be safe." He smiled. "I know you. Thinking Drogan's after you instead of anyone else is the only way you can relax."

Alex was amazed at his friend. After everything Trent had gone through, the werewolf was still watching over him. He heard Jordan's footsteps and stood. "You're amazing, Trent. Hang in there, okay?"

"You too," Trent said.

Alex hesitated beside the chair. "Seriously, though. You almost died. I don't know what I would have done."

Trent smiled at him. "Now you know how I've felt nearly

a dozen times, and why I keep telling you to take care of yourself."

"Friends are hard to come by." Alex put a hand on Trent's shoulder. "Brothers are a whole lot harder. Take care of yourself, brother."

Trent's smile stayed with him as he made his way back up the hallway. He entered Siale's room filled with resolve. Life was going to change again, but he was ready for it. The warm smile that melted his soul when he walked through Siale's door let him know he made the right decision. He crossed to Siale's side, ready to make his life what he wanted it to be.

Chapter Twelve

To Alex's surprise, most of the professors went with them to pick out the ring. Apparently the news that one of their students planned to propose made everyone excited. The moment they stepped into the jewelry store, Alex felt the eyes of every salesperson lock on him.

"I, uh, would like to pick out an engagement ring," he said to the closest person.

The man's eyes flicked to Jaze and Nikki, then back to Alex. "We're more than happy to oblige, Mr. Davies."

Alex's attention, which had strayed to the display boxes nearest the man, immediately locked on him again. "You know who I am?"

"Is there a problem?" Vance asked, coming up behind Alex.

The salesman shook his head quickly. "Not at all. We're happy to accommodate any of our customers." He gave Alex a searching look. "We've seen you on the news. It's just that we seldom have werewolves in here."

At the word werewolves, silence settled over the store. Despite Greyton City's steps in werewolf acceptance, there were still conflicts regarding werewolf approval with the rest of the nation. It was a tense subject.

"Perhaps you would like something in our white gold settings," a girl said from further in the store.

Alex nodded. "I think she would like that," he replied carefully.

The man in front of him smiled and the tension dissipated. "Splendid. We have a new selection of princess cut diamonds that might be of interest."

Alex glanced back at Cassie. His sister shook her head, her expression one of relief. She followed Alex and the others to the back. "You've become a celebrity," she whispered.

Alex ran a hand through his hair. It was getting longer than he usually wore it. "Maybe I should get a haircut before we leave."

"Might not be a bad idea," Tennison answered from Cassie's other side. "Change your appearance. It'll give you a break from hordes of adoring fans."

Cassie pushed Tennison's shoulder and he laughed.

"But still, it's not a bad idea," she agreed. "Gem does a great job."

"I'd be happy to!" the little werewolf with neon green hair said from across the store, reminding Alex that every werewolf could hear their quiet conversation.

"Thank you," Alex told her.

Gem grabbed Dray's hand and skipped beside him to another counter. Kaynan and Grace fell in next them. Alex could hear Kaynan describing the different settings and diamond cuts to his blind wife. The exactness of the werewolf's descriptions made Alex feel completely lost when it came to selecting the right ring. Gratitude filled him when Nikki and Meredith started trying on the rings he picked out so he could see what they looked like.

"I think you should get this one," Cassie exclaimed, holding up a ring with several smaller diamonds on an intricately worked silver leaf-shaped setting. She lifted her hand, admiring the ring in the light.

"It's pretty," Alex acknowledged. "It's just not the right one for Siale."

"What if she likes my tastes instead of yours?" Cassie challenged.

Alex grinned. "Then she'd be after Tennison instead of me."

Cassie laughed. "Good point." She turned back to the

ring on her finger, leaving Alex to his decision.

"I do like that one." Alex studied the ring his mother held.

"It's beautiful; I like the simple design," Meredith replied.

Uncertain which ring he should pick and worried about choosing one Siale might not like, Alex excused himself and wandered around the store again.

Tennison fell in beside him. "Having a hard time?"

Alex sighed. "Yes. Who would've thought it'd be this hard? There are so many rings here they all start to look the same. What if I pick the wrong one?"

Tennison tipped his head back toward Cassie. "I know which one I'm getting."

Alex stared at him. "What?"

Tennison winked and continued down the aisle. Alex stared after his sister's boyfriend. He tried to picture her getting engaged. They felt so young, but after everything, living to see seventeen felt like an accomplishment. He knew Cassie would be happy with Tennison. The tall, lanky werewolf leaned over a display close to the end of the store.

"Hey, how about one of these?" he asked.

Curious, Alex made his way to the werewolf's side. He peered down into the case of what turned out to be vintage rings that were definitely of an older make than the others in the store. They were beautiful and had their own style.

One in particular stood out. It had a diamond in the middle with seven small light purple stones around it that reminded Alex of the dress Siale had worn to the prom. Purple set off her gray eyes so beautifully and was her favorite color.

"Did you find another ring that strikes your interest?" the young saleswoman asked.

"Can I see that one?"

She lifted it out with a warm smile and set it in his palm. Alex knew immediately that he had found the right one. The white gold setting was the perfect accent for the simple diamond.

"I like that one, too," the saleswoman said. "The purple gemstones are amethyst. European soldiers believed amethyst protected them in battle back in medieval times." At Alex's curious look, a blush ran across her cheeks. "Sorry. I love mythology behind gemstones. It's fascinating."

"It is," Alex agreed. He studied the ring, picturing it on Siale's finger. It was perfect. Even the thought of the amethyst providing protection was a reassuring one, even if it was just a myth. The world used to think werewolves were myths, too. He nodded. "This is the one."

"Do you know her size?" the woman asked.

Alex stared at her. He hadn't stopped to think about things like finger size. Of course girls had different sized fingers. He hadn't planned on being asked the question.

"Here," Cassie said, showing up at his elbow. "This should help."

She held a silver band with a little green stone in the middle that Alex had seen Siale wear on occasion.

"Where did you get that?" he asked, amazed.

Cassie shrugged, her eyes twinkling. "When Mom told me your plans, I figured I'd better have your back."

"Thanks," Alex told her with relief.

The saleswoman took the ring and compared the two. "I don't think this is going to need any sizing." She smiled at Alex. "You have an exact match."

Alex waited at the front of the store while Jaze, Nikki, and Meredith took care of the purchasing part. He had offered to earn the money doing jobs around the school to pay for the ring himself, but Jaze had told him that instead, he would pay him for the hours he had spent freeing werewolves.

"You trained for it and you're improving the quality of the lives of those you free. You should get paid for it," Jaze explained.

"But I didn't do it for money," Alex protested.

Jaze nodded. "That's why you're getting paid. Consider this a first installment."

Alex wandered outside. He leaned against the building and took a deep breath of the warm summer air.

"When are you due?" Gem's excited voice carried from the parking lot behind the jewelry store.

"We're about three months along," Grace answered. "I'm thinking the middle of November."

"December for us," Gem told her.

"I'm so happy for you!" Grace exclaimed.

"Yeah, congratulations," Dray told them.

Kaynan chuckled. "Look at us. Turning into old married couples soon to have kids of our own. Did you hear that Jaze and Nikki are expecting again?"

Alex's heart skipped a beat. He put a hand to it. It didn't hurt like it used to. He was amazed how normal it felt after Drogan had revived him. The thought that his insane half-brother had saved his life settled over him uneasily. He turned his attention back to the professors' discussion as much to get away from his own thoughts as to hear what they were talking about.

"Yes, and Colleen and Rafe are going to have their own little one in September. They've got us all beat," Kaynan said with pride in his voice for his sister. "I wouldn't be surprised if Lyra and Mouse are close behind. It's about time to start settling down."

"I'd love a quiet home with a little yard and a white picket fence," Gem said with a small sigh. "It'd be a great place to raise a little one."

"We should all set up in the same neighborhood," Grace said.

"We're forgetting one thing." Dray's voice was quiet and grounding. He paused, then said, "Jaze."

The silence that fell over the group was short-lived.

"Of course," Kaynan replied. "We'll stay at the Academy for as long as Jaze and Nikki need us. There's no way we'd abandon him with everything that's going on."

"Yes," Grace agreed. "As nice as it would be to settle down in homes of our own, we're there for the school."

"We owe it to Jaze and Vicki. That amazing woman gave us a home when we had nowhere else to go," Gem said. Alex could hear the smile in her voice. "It's nice to do our part to give back."

"It really is," Dray said.

The rest of the werewolves left the store. Alex fell in beside them, accepting the small velvet box Meredith held out to him.

"Are you okay?" his mother asked.

Alex nodded, chasing away the feeling of sadness that had settled over him. "I'm fine," he said. "A bit nervous, I guess."

Meredith smiled. "You're going to do great. Siale will love the ring. It's perfect."

Alex slipped the ring box into his pocket. "Thank you for your help." He tried to keep in the conversation during the trip back to the Academy, but he couldn't help thinking of the professors and their want for a normal life. He had never thought of the fact that the Academy was also keeping them from having their own homes and raising their families. Being in charge of so many students, a lot of them year round, had to take its toll.

"Are you okay, Alex?" Gem asked a few hours later while she cut his hair.

"Yeah, you're pretty quiet," Cassie noted from her seat in the corner.

Alex tried not to move his head as he glanced at his sister. "Is my haircut the most entertaining thing going on right now?"

Cassie gave a dramatic sigh. "Unfortunately. I'm all packed for tomorrow morning and Tennison fell asleep after helping Dray in the greenhouse all afternoon. His clothes smell like fertilizer; it's pretty bad. Have you smelled it in there?"

Gem laughed from behind Alex. "Dray's in his element. I think he misses the farm sometimes."

Alex saw an opening to ask her what was on his mind. "Do you miss it, too?"

Gem's scissors paused in their rhythmic snipping. "I do, a bit," she admitted. She drew the comb through Alex's hair and cut it again. "When we moved to farm country, it felt like the middle of nowhere. The town was so small and there were fields as far as the eye could see."

"You sound like you learned to love it," Cassie noted.

"I did," Gem replied. "I met Dray, and he taught me that the fields were full of wheat, alfalfa, and corn. I learned how to swath hay and flood irrigate." She crossed in front of Alex and combed through his hair, checking the length of the ends as she smiled and said, "I even learned to like fertilizing."

Cassie made a face in the corner.

Gem laughed. "I know, right? I guess that's when you know you belong somewhere."

"Do you want to go back?" Alex asked.

Gem looked at him as if realizing how serious he was about the questioning. "Maybe eventually," she finally answered. "When I'm not needed here." She took a step back and gave Alex's hair a critical look. Her hand strayed unconsciously to her stomach as she studied him. "I think that'll help with everyone being so star-struck around you, Mr. Davies."

Alex chuckled and rose from the chair. He accepted the hand mirror she held out. His black hair was shorter than he was used to, and made him look older.

"It's a good look for you," Cassie told him. "Siale's going to wonder where her scruffy werewolf went."

"Scruffy?" Alex repeated with mock indignity.

Gem laughed. "I don't know if I would go with scruffy, but you were looking a bit shaggy. Now you're ready for city life."

Alex smiled. "Thank you, professor."

"Any time," she replied, twirling her scissors around her finger. "Let me know if you want me to dye your hair. You'd look good with red tips."

Alex laughed. "I think I'll pass this time."

Gem shrugged, her blue eyes twinkling. "Your loss."

Cassie caught up to Alex on his way down the hall. "Alex, guess what?"

"What?" he asked.

"I think Gem's pregnant! Did you see all the signs? She's definitely expecting," his sister exclaimed, trying to say it quietly while practically shouting in her excitement.

Alex nodded. "I know."

Cassie stopped dead in the hallway. "You saw it, too? I didn't think you were paying attention. You seemed detached and—"

Alex cut her off before she asked him what he had been thinking about. "I knew back at the ring store. I overheard the professors talking. Kaynan and Grace are expecting, too, and Colleen and Rafe. I think Jaze and Nikki are going to have another baby, as well."

Cassie's hand flew to her mouth. Her eyes were so wide it looked like she was about to explode.

"Cassie?" Alex asked with a hint of worry.

She shook her head with her hand still over her mouth. "I know it's supposed to be a secret," she said, her voice muffled behind her fingers. "But I want to tell everyone."

Alex put his hands on her shoulders and gave her a serious look. "You can't tell anyone. If they choose to keep it a secret, that's their choice. Let them tell when they're ready."

Cassie nodded without taking her hand away.

"Can I trust you?" Alex asked.

Cassie nodded again. "I won't tell anyone. I promise."

Alex rolled his eyes and pulled her hand away. "Seriously, Cass. They deserve their privacy. It's got to be hard trying to raise a family at this school."

Cassie nodded. She followed Alex to the stairs. He started up.

"Hey, Alex?"

He paused halfway to the top and turned. "Yeah?"

"I never realized you cared so much."

Her words hurt. Alex pushed the feeling down and watched her, wondering what she was getting at. "Of course I care. Why wouldn't I?"

Cassie took two hesitant steps up the stairs as if she realized her words had been a bit harsh. "I mean, you're so busy trying to get Drogan and protecting everyone, sometimes it's like you don't see who's in front of you."

Alex eased down to sit on the steps. He linked his hands together, studying them. "I get so caught up with trying to stop him from hurting those I love that I forget to pay attention to my loved ones." He looked down at his sister.

"Which do you think is worse?"

Cassie leaned against the wall and gave her brother a fond look. "You don't have to worry so much, Alex. We know why you do what you do. You care. Sometimes you're just busy saving the world." Her smile deepened. "Do you think Superman ever forgot to have breakfast with his sister like we used to?"

Alex couldn't help but smile back. "I don't think Superman had a sister. Or maybe he did. I don't remember. The point is, we'll have breakfast together."

"Promise?"

Alex nodded. "In fact." He headed back down the stairs.

"Where are you going?" Cassie asked when he passed her.

"Come on," Alex called over his shoulder. "You're going to miss it!"

She jogged to catch up to him. "Miss what?" she asked when she reached his side.

Alex pushed one of the doors open to the Great Hall and made his way to the kitchen. A quick peek inside showed that it was empty.

"Cook Jerald must be asleep."

"Yeah," Cassie agreed. "Like most decent werewolves."

Alex grinned. "Good thing we're not decent." He crossed to the refrigerator and opened it. A glance inside showed exactly what he was looking for.

"Alex, what are you..." Cassie's voice died away at the sight of the egg and cheese quiche Alex withdrew.

"Why wait for breakfast?" Alex asked.

"Seriously?" Cassie exclaimed. "We could get in trouble."

Alex winked at her. "By the time Cook Jerald finds out, we'll be halfway across the country."

Cassie laughed. "Fine, but if you get me in trouble..."

"You know it'll be worth it," Alex concluded.

Cassie gave the quiche a long look. Alex knew it was her favorite food. Luckily, Cook Jerald usually kept a pie or two in the fridge in case the professors got hungry or if Jaze's team got back at an early hour from one of their missions. There was no way Cassie could say no.

"Yes, it will," she finally agreed. She grabbed two forks from the tray and joined him at one of the tables.

Chapter Thirteen

Siale rushed out as soon as the car reached the warehouse. Red followed after her at a more sedate pace, but with a welcoming smile on his face.

Alex's girlfriend stopped as soon as Alex got out. She stared at him. "You look really different," she said.

Alex suddenly felt self-conscious about his haircut. "Gem did it. You don't like it?"

Siale ran her hand through his hair. "It's a lot shorter than I've ever seen you wear it," she said.

Alex fought back the urge to close his eyes at the tingles that ran through his skin from her touch.

She nodded. "I really like it." She looked up into his eyes. "You look really handsome."

"See," Cassie said from behind him. "I told you Siale would like it."

She and Siale hugged. Alex fought back a smile at the thought that the pair would soon be sisters-in-law. It was obvious both of them would be happy about the relationship.

"Good to see you again," Red said. He shook Alex's hand. "And you as well," he told Tennison. "We have your rooms ready." He tipped his head to indicate the warehouse and told Alex, "We've been busy since you were last here. I think you'll like what we've done with the place."

Siale looped her arm through Alex's and led them inside. To Alex's amazement, it had undergone a lot of changes since his last visit with Boris. The inside of the building had been changed from a regular warehouse to a huge common room with individual rooms branching away for living quarters. More werewolves than he remembered occupied the area. They passed children playing ball and board games in the main room, families in the smaller television room, and others working on a few more improvements at the end of the hallway.

Siale greeted those they passed. It touched Alex that she knew all of their names. She led them to three bedrooms at the end of a branching hallway.

"It's a little quieter over here," she said. "You might sleep better than by the families. Sometimes the kids like to stay up and play."

"This is amazing," Alex told her. "Your dad's really done a lot with the place."

"Yeah," Cassie agreed. "How many families stay here?"

Siale thought about it for a moment. "Four of the families are still here from before I went to the Academy, but Dad's welcomed a few more. He says they come and go depending on their circumstances."

"It's great that you're able to help them here," Tennison said. "I'm sure they appreciate it."

"It's nice to be safe," Siale replied.

The words matched exactly how Alex felt. They had taken great care to ensure that Drogan knew he was no longer at the Academy. Tracks, the car, and flight tickets wouldn't be hard for the Extremist to follow, and then to all appearances, the teenage werewolves disappeared off the face of the earth. Thanks to Red's connections, they were able to sneak through the airport's food delivery entrance and leave in one of the cargo trucks. They then met the car outside the airport.

As stressful as it had been to get away, Alex felt like he could breathe again without looking over his shoulder. The thought that Drogan watched his every step had vanished. He smiled back at Siale.

"I really like it here," he said. The words brought an answering smile and a kiss from her.

After Alex, Cassie, and Tennison had settled their stuff in three of the spare rooms, Siale led them to where Red waited in the dining room. Alex's first visit to the warehouse with Boris had revealed a werewolf safe haven. Now, Red had turned it into so much more. He could hear werewolves cooking in the kitchen, and the huge tables in the dining room let him know just how many depended on the warehouse for food and shelter.

"This is an incredible place," Cassie told Red.

Siale's father smiled. "We're proud of it." He gave his daughter a warm look. "It's better now that I have family to share it with."

Siale nodded. "When I found out what my dad was doing here, I told him I needed to be a part of it. It's so neat to give werewolves a place of safety."

"Jaze Carso has done it to such a greater extent, but it's nice to do my share. It's home," Red replied. He motioned for them to take a seat at the nearest table. "By the smell of things, Jassa will have dinner ready. You don't want to miss her home cooking."

Soon, nearly twenty-five werewolves joined them around the tables. There was still room left for three times that many.

"We're prepared," Red told Alex, noticing the direction of his gaze. "We've almost filled it up a time or two. It helps to be ready in case the space is needed."

"I'm sure they appreciate it," Alex replied. "It's amazing what you do here."

"It really is," Tennison agreed. "I didn't know there were places like this."

"They're all across the country," Red told them. "We keep in contact, carefully of course so the Extremists don't find our locations. We help each other when we can."

"Are the other safe houses this big?" Cassie asked.

Red nodded. "There's a huge one in New York. Bigger than this, I think. There was another in New Orleans, but the General found them." Pain touched his voice. He shook his head. "I lost some good friends that day." He looked at Alex. "You did our race a big favor when you took him out."

Alex nodded without speaking. He took down his father because the General had killed Kalia pointblank with a pistol to the head. The consequences hadn't mattered. Only revenge for Kalia's death had occupied his thoughts at the time. Now he was in the same city where her family lived and her grave was. He hadn't thought that far when he accepted Red's invitation to stay for the summer.

Cassie caught his expression and changed the subject. "So what do you need us to do here?"

Red nodded toward the other werewolves. "I have plenty of help. I have a feeling you guys will find enough to occupy your summer."

"Doing what?" Tennison asked.

Siale jumped in. "I'll show you. Are you guys full?"

At their nods, she led the way to the kitchen. Everyone washed their own bowls and helped Jassa put away the remaining sauce and noodles.

"Don't worry," she reassured them, her thick Jamaican accent making the words musical. "There's plenty left if any of the youngsters come back tonight with empty stomachs."

Siale gave Jassa a hug. "Thanks for taking care of Dad while I was at school."

"He takes care of everyone else; I make sure he eats enough not to waste away. It's a win-win for us all." Jassa waved them away. "Now go have some fun. We'll take care of the rest."

Siale led the way outside.

"Where are we going?" Cassie asked.

"You'll see," Siale replied, her gray eyes sparkling. "I'll show you what the nightlife is like by the ocean."

Alex could hear the push of the waves against the sand from blocks away as they walked down the street. Instead of emptying out at night like he was used to with Greyton, night brought more and more people outside. The heat of the day dissipated as the moon rose, and the stars glowing from above shone on teens and adults alike filling the streets with entertainment and fun.

"This is crazy," Cassie exclaimed. She turned sideways so she could skirt past a group of teenagers kicking a small hacky sack around in a circle. "Everyone's out on the streets!"

"I can't believe all the stores are still open," Tennison replied.

"There's an ice cream shop," Cassie pointed out.

"Come on," Tennison said, holding out his hand. "I know how much you like rocky road."

Cassie smiled at him. "You know me so well." She slipped her hand into his.

"Girls and chocolate ice cream." Tennison winked at Alex. "Don't stand in their way."

"Have fun, you two," Alex told them.

It made him happy to see his sister so enraptured with Tennison. She appeared so much more carefree than she had ever been before the werewolf came into their lives. Tennison definitely made her life better by being a part of it. The tall werewolf opened the door to the ice cream shop across the street and waved Cassie inside with a flourish.

Siale and Alex continued down the sidewalk. It overwhelmed his senses to see so many people crowding the streets. Laughter and shouting filled the air along with the smells of hundreds of people from every walk of life. Vendors sold snow cones, smoothies, and various fried foods from small carts, the clothes from the small shops cluttered the sidewalk in an effort to draw in customers, and all around him, people bartered, joked, and jostled each other.

Teenagers came rushing out of a store with drinks, chips, and hot dogs. "Last one to the beach gets to find the wood," a boy called over his shoulder. They took off running toward the sound of the waves. Alex watched their progress through the crowd and lost them amid the hustle of city life.

A shoulder slammed into Alex's. It took all of his self-control to keep from attacking the guy who continued on his way as though nothing had happened. While the others had appeared excited at the buzzing atmosphere of the packed city, Alex's nerves were on edge. His muscles were so tense they ached, and he had to fight back the impulse to phase in order to protect Siale even though she appeared to be perfectly comfortable in the rowdy crowd. He thought his time in Greyton would have prepared him for such things, but there was so much more going on that his senses were on overload.

"Siale!" a voice called.

Alex turned in time to see a boy close to their age rushing through the crowd toward her with several other teenagers behind him. Alex's instincts to protect Siale flared. Just before the boy reached Siale, Alex grabbed him by the throat and slammed him onto his back on the ground.

"Alex, no!" Siale cried.

Alex glared down at the boy whose eyes were wide as he looked from Alex to Siale. His hand itched to tighten around the human's throat, ending the threat.

"Alex, Jerry's a friend," Siale pleaded. She dropped to her knees next to him and set a hand on his shoulder. "Alex, please!"

Alex looked at her. There was true fear in Siale's gaze. He

realized it wasn't fear of the human, it was fear for him. She was afraid Alex was going to kill him.

Alex fought his instincts, caught in an internal battle. He didn't know what to do. His instincts had screamed danger, and so he had reacted. The wolf had fought to defend Siale, to keep her safe from the mad rush of a boy who might have meant her harm.

The human side of Alex said he had acted rashly. He couldn't attack people; he was acting like the animal they feared him to be. The teenager had done nothing wrong. He couldn't just attack strangers on the sidewalk.

The fight or flight instincts thrummed through him, telling him that everywhere he looked there was danger. There were too many humans, too much potential for Siale to get hurt. He couldn't protect her in such a crowd. But he shouldn't have to protect her. They were supposed to be safe. He had it all wrong.

Alex felt like he was going crazy. He blinked, unable to come to terms with what was happening.

"Alex, you need to let him up," Siale said quietly, her voice calm and steady. She set a hand on his arm.

Her touch broke through the confusing haze that filled Alex's mind. He locked on her gaze.

"You're okay?" he asked softly.

She nodded. "I'm fine, Alex. Please don't hurt Jerry."

Alex realized he was still holding the teenager down. He let go of the boy's throat and rose. His senses thrummed, charged by the crowd who had gathered to watch them, by the other humans who had come with the boy and were now pulling him to his feet, by the angry red fingermarks on the boy's throat, and by the way Siale was watching him as if uncertain what his actions would be.

"I'm sorry," Alex said. He turned and ducked into the

crowd.

"Alex!" Siale called.

He ran through the mass of bodies. Everywhere he turned, the crowds were thick with every manner of individual, teenagers, homeless men and women, parents with children, couples, street entertainers, and vendors hawking their wares. He ducked past buildings and between shops. He avoided salesmen on the streets and men and women dancing and singing to crowds who threw them coins. Alex couldn't get away from the panic that filled him. His heart didn't skip, but it thundered in his ears with the force of a raging storm.

The scent of popcorn, hotdogs, fish, French fries, and cotton candy tangled in his nose along with the unfamiliar seaweed and salt smell of the ocean. His sneakers fell on the asphalt with resounding thuds of desperation. The brush of bodies against his arms, chest, and back filled him with terror. He didn't want to hurt them, but he couldn't push down the thought that they wanted to cause him pain, to betray him, to end him.

The thud of his sneakers turned to soft shushes when the asphalt gave way to the sand of the long beach and the ocean Alex had never seen before. His steps faltered. Alex stared past the mass of people laughing and playing along the shoreline to the water beyond.

The fall of moonlight on the ocean danced magically to his wolven eyes. The trickle of light played along the midnight depths as though they were one and the same, light upon darkness and dark upon light. He couldn't tell where one ended and the other began. It was as if he could walk along the ocean to the point where it met the sky, a mirror that reflected itself in the rise and fall of the never-ending waves.

His troubled soul calmed slightly. Alex turned away from the crowds and began to jog down the beach. The sound and the masses died away as he left the light of the city behind. The beach became darker, welcoming.

His footsteps slowed at the mouth of an empty wooden pier reaching out into the water. The crowd was gone, and with it, the chaos of indecision. Alex walked along the pier, following it to the end. His footfalls sounded lonely; the only answer to their echo was the slow push of the ocean onto the sand below.

Alex reached the end of the pier and sat down, letting his feet dangle. Leaning on the wooden crossbeams, he stared out at the ocean that looked as though it traveled on forever, ebbing and flowing in a soothing, numbing rhythm as steady as his newly repaired heart.

His soul connected with the ocean. He felt like it was a part of him even though he had never seen it before. It called to him like the moon. He took a deep breath and let it out. His tension eased, but the guilt that filled him refused to go away.

He had almost hurt someone Siale cared about. He thought had been protecting her, but away from the pandemonium, he could think clearly. He realized he had acted rashly and almost cost a human his life. Jerry didn't deserve that; nobody did.

About an hour later, footsteps sounded down the pier. Alex didn't have to look back to know who was there.

"How did you find me?"

"I could find you anywhere," Siale replied. She sat down next to him and looked out at the ocean. After a moment of silence, she said, "Did you know that you smell like cedar and clover?"

Alex glanced at her, bemused. "Clover? That's not very manly."

Siale smiled. "When I was little, Mom and Dad took me

on a trip once to my grandmother's farm. They had fields upon fields of clover." Her gaze took on a wistful look. "The sun was so warm and the clover filled the air with a rich scent I had never smelled before." She looked at him. "I thought it was one of the most wonderful things I had ever smelled, until I met you. Now you're it."

Alex watched her, the way her eyes twinkled like the moonlight on the waves as she spoke, how her cheeks flushed with a touch of embarrassment when she smiled.

"I guess that's a strange thing to say to someone," she admitted, ducking her head.

Alex shook his head. "Not really." He was silent for a moment, then said, "You smell like sage with lavender."

Siale looked at him in surprise. "Is that a good thing?"

Alex nodded, failing to keep back a small smile. "Have you ever crushed sage between your fingers? It's vibrant and alive, and awakens the senses. Add a hint of lavender to it and it is definitely my favorite scent in the whole world."

Siale gave a little thoughtful huff. "And here I thought I smelled like vanilla."

Alex shook his head. "Nothing so normal for you. It would never fit."

Siale smiled and looked back at the ocean. "So, when are you coming back to hang with my friends?"

Alex stared at her. She kept her gaze on the dark expanse that stretched before them. "Siale, I can't. There's no way."

She glanced at him out of the corner of her eye. "Of course there is."

Alex shook his head. "Did you see me? I almost killed your friend."

"But you didn't," she pointed out.

Alex let out a breath. "Only because you stopped me," he admitted. He felt Siale's silence as much as heard it. He kept talking to fill the void he was afraid would settle between them. "It's not them, it's me." He spoke quietly. "I was filled with panic with all those humans around. I wanted to run or fight, or I don't know what. I felt like they were dangerous, but I'm the dangerous one." His voice dropped quieter. "I can't trust myself anymore."

Siale touched his arm. He lowered his gaze. "You were betrayed by a human, Alex. It's understandable."

Alex shook his head. "It's not Officer Dune, or Drogan, or the General. It's nobody but me. I'm broken, Siale, and there's no way to fix it."

He rested his head against the wood. The faint scent of pine touched his nose, memories of forest meadows and grass waving in the wind. He wanted to go there, to be as far away from civilization as he could possibly get.

"You can't run away," Siale said, her voice just above a whisper. "You're here, Alex. Be here."

"What if I can't?" Alex asked. He turned his head toward the ocean so she wouldn't see the pain in his gaze. He had become the beast they feared. Perhaps humans were justified to keep werewolves away from their society. Maybe everything he fought for was wrong.

"I told them who you are."

Alex's heart slowed. He stared at her. "Do you think that's a good idea? It might be dangerous for them. I'm not sure—"

Siale stopped him with a kiss. When they parted, Alex's breath caught in his throat. He blinked, trying to remember what they had been talking about. "What was that for?"

Her eyebrows pulled together as she watched him. "Alex, I need you to trust me. You've been betrayed by so many people, but not me, never me. I love you because I see everything that is inside you, the love, and the demons. I know what drives you and why you try so hard to protect everyone else, but you forget about yourself. That's my job. Let me take care of you. Put your trust in me, all of your trust, and I'll never let you down. I promise. Can you do that?"

Silence hung between them. Alex blinked back tears, his chest so full of loss, guilt, anger, and heartache that he could barely breathe. He had to do something or he felt like he would jump off the pier into the unknown depths below. He took a shuddering breath and turned to her.

When he nodded, the love and care in her eyes was so great that the tears he had fought to keep at bay broke free and trailed down his cheeks.

Siale leaned against him, holding him, her silky brown hair brushing against his wet cheeks. "I love you, Alex," she said in a voice that left no doubt about the truth to her words.

Alex held her close. "I love you too, Siale."

They sat in silence until Alex was able to gather himself. He watched the flow of the ocean until they were just a boy and a girl at the end of a pier, in love with each other and the way the moonlight danced beneath their feet on the waves.

Alex pushed away the guilt and fear that he wouldn't fit into society, and he placed his trust entirely in the girl at his side. She held his heart, and so he gave her his soul, too. Whatever his fate, he had chosen for her to be the one with him. For some reason he couldn't fathom, she had chosen him as well. He would trust her, no matter what she asked.

Siale rose to her feet and held out her hand. He took it and stood beside her. The steady rhythm of the waves filled him with peace as he walked with his one to the shore.

Chapter Fourteen

When they reached the crowded beach, something caught Alex's eye. He turned in time to see a seven on the sleeve of a black hoodie.

"Did you see..." Alex's voice died away as two more teenagers passed them, one in a green hoodie and another in a red one, both with sevens on the sleeves. "I must be going crazy."

"Not really," Siale said. "Look."

He followed her finger to the sight of two girls in the crowd wearing matching blue shirts. Each had the seven on the shoulder, and when they turned, the word 'Werewolf' was emblazoned across the back like a sports jersey.

"You've got to be kidding me," Alex said.

Siale grinned at him. "You have a few supporters. Well, the Demon does, at least."

"I wore the hoodie Terith made me when I was in the Saa," Alex said, remembering. "It got destroyed when I phased during one of the fights."

"It was on the news," Siale reminded him. "You were wearing it when you saved those girls."

"So they want to be werewolves?" Alex asked, trying to understand.

"People emulate those they look up to," Siale replied. "You just happened to do a few things that were hero worthy."

Alex shook his head. "That's ridiculous."

"Is it?" his girlfriend asked, her gaze on the teenagers.

Alex followed Siale through the streets. He saw two more hoodies with the seven on the shoulder. Instead of 'Werewolf' on the back, they both said, 'Demon'.

"This city's crazy," Alex whispered.

Siale glanced at him with a warm smile. "It's not limited to this city, Alex. Werewolf acceptance is growing. You started something when you went to Greyton, and it's not stopping."

Alex hesitated at the sight of Siale's friends hanging out on the edge of the block where he had left them. A few others had joined the group. Cassie and Tennison conversed with the humans as though they fit right in. Alex felt a pang of jealousy when Cassie said something and the girls around her laughed. He shook the feeling away. It was good that his sister felt comfortable with the humans. She deserved to have more friends.

Alex, on the other hand, had to force down his own feelings of panic. He owed it to Siale to give her his trust, but crossing the street felt like climbing a mountain.

Siale spoke softly. "My friends have known I'm a werewolf since we were little. We grew up together on the beach and on these streets, and we were in the same classes at school until things got too dangerous. They're trustworthy." She looked up at him, her gaze saying how important it was to her.

"Okay," Alex replied, pushing down his uncertainty. "I'll give it a shot."

Siale led him to the waiting group.

"Derek said you were back," one of the girls said, crossing to give Siale a hug. "It's been way too long!" She glanced at Alex, then did a double-take. "Who's the hottie?"

Siale smiled, taking the question in stride. "Sam, this is Alex. He's my boyfriend."

The rest of the girls hurried to join them. Alex felt all of their eyes on him. He gave what he hoped was a confident smile. The girls immediately smiled back.

The first girl twirled a strand of her long red hair and

smiled at him. "Hi, Alex."

"Chill, Sam," another girl said. "Siale said 'boyfriend', remember?"

Sam shrugged, batting her eyes flirtatiously. "It doesn't hurt to get to know someone else's boyfriend, right? I mean, what if it doesn't work out? He'll want other options."

"Sam!" Siale exclaimed, but she didn't appear the least bit offended. She slipped her arm through Alex's and smiled at her friend. "Flirt all you want, but he's mine."

"Yet again, all the cute ones are taken," a girl with curly black hair said with a dramatic sigh.

"I heard that," one of the boys called from the group.

"Oh, Raven, you'll find a guy someday," Siale reassured her.

Alex found Jerry, the boy he had pinned, standing near the street corner. Several other teenagers waited with him. Alex left the girls talking about cute boys. He forced himself to keep calm, reminding himself that he was far stronger than the teenagers around him, but the detached part of him said that was what he should be worried about.

He felt all of the boys' eyes on him when he stopped a few feet from Jerry.

The teenager smiled. "Hey."

"Hey," Alex replied. "I'm sorry for reacting the way I did. Are you okay?"

Jerry nodded. There were still red marks on his neck, but he acted as though nothing had happened. "It's okay, bro. You needed an outlet."

Alex was caught off guard. "An outlet?"

"Yeah, man. You needed to vent, to rage, you needed an aperture for your emotional escape. I understand the necessity of diffusing a burgeoning fury before it turns into an explosion of epic magnitude. I'm happy I could be the focal point for your necessary dissipation of fervent wrath."

Alex stared at him. Jerry smiled back, shoving a strand of dreadlocked hair behind his shoulder.

One of the other boys laughed, taking pity on Alex. "Don't worry. Jerry's got a college vocabulary with a surfer mindset."

"A surfer mindset?" Alex repeated.

Another boy nodded. "You know, the waves contain the secrets of life and all that."

"If you don't live on a board, you don't live," a boy with a Mohawk said.

"Hang ten until the world ends," another crowed.

The first boy jostled him. "A bad day surfing beats a good day working."

Mohawk grinned at the challenge. "When in doubt, paddle out."

His friend replied, "The board is mightier than the sword."

Mohawk laughed and said, ""A wave is better than a rave."

"Toes to the throes," a girl called.

"The thrill is worth the spill," another said.

Alex fought back a smile at their enthusiasm. He had no idea what they were talking about, but the fact that Jerry seemed to forgive him gave him room to breathe.

"You got it all wrong," Jerry said. The entire group fell silent; even the girls stopped their conversation near the sidewalk. Everyone listened to what Jerry wanted to say.

The teenager didn't appear to realize or care that he had such an attentive audience. Instead, he looked toward the ocean as though he saw it despite the blocks of buildings in the way. His voice was almost musical when he said, "It's not that the ocean wants the surfer to descend to the depths of its ebony waves, or that the surfer is compelled to struggle to stay upon the fluctuating surface. Instead, the ocean and the surfer share a symbiotic soul, the ocean to be ridden and the surfer to throw his life upon a polished tree to ride the breaking tides of the moon's compulsory pull. Together, they create a beauty unmatched by the swell of dawn or the scintillating sound of the seagull before a storm. The surfer and the sea, heart and heartbeat, each seeking the perfect ride where the soul becomes the wave and the water becomes the blood."

Silence fell after Jerry was finished. Someone clapped from the back of the group. Jerry blinked and he focused on his friends, his expression showing his surprise at seeing them there.

"Good words, Jer," a teen with long black hair braided in beads said.

"Come on, Preacher," another told him. "Let's grab some grub and get down to the beach."

"Sustenance for my stomach would be most appreciated," Jerry replied, allowing himself to be led away.

Alex watched them go.

"Don't worry about it," the boy with the beaded hair told him. "Jerry forgave you the second you slammed him. He doesn't have a vindictive bone in his body."

"Vindictive, Brooks, really?" Sam asked.

He laughed. "I've been hanging out with Jerry for too long." His smile faded and his expression became serious. "But honestly, Alex, when Siale told us who you were, we understood."

"You shouldn't have to understand," Alex replied.

"What's not to understand?" Brooks asked. "Werewolves have had it bad for years. You fight for your life and spend your time with Jaze Carso freeing others of your race from fates worse than death. The rest of us are riding waves and chillin' on the beach. You're bound to be on edge, especially with the whole officer betrayal thing."

"She told you that?" Alex asked, glancing at Siale.

The girls had gone back to their conversation, but Siale met his gaze with her warm smile before turning to answer one of her friends.

"If someone I trusted turned me over to someone else intent on killing me, I think I'd have issues, too," Brooks said. "I'd probably want to hit every human I saw." His eyes lit up and he glanced at one of the other boys. "That gives me an idea. Hey Reko?"

"Yeah?" a teen with spacers in his ears answered.

"Are the Wharfers playing tonight?"

Reko nodded. "I saw Flynn by Docker's. They're probably already warming up."

Brooks glanced up at the waning moon hanging within the stars above. "Plenty of light. Let's give them a game."

"You sure that's a good idea?" Reko asked, glancing meaningfully at Alex.

Brooks nodded. "Our boy needs to hit someone. Let's give him someone to hit."

"I don't know if that's a good idea," Alex said.

Reko's face lit up and he nodded with enthusiasm as if Alex hadn't spoken. "I'll spread the word."

Alex watched the boy run to the rest of the group. "Is there something I need to know?"

Brooks shrugged. "Only that we play the Wharfers every couple of days down at the beach. We're pretty well matched except for Flynn, their quarterback."

"You mean football?" Alex asked, grateful to finally be on familiar footing.

"Yeah, you play?" Brooks replied.

Alex nodded. "I'm the quarterback for my school." He caught himself and said, "We have just a school league is all, nothing serious." If word got out that a werewolf football team was making the rounds through school tournaments, Alex didn't want to imagine the investigations that would follow.

"Great," Brooks said. "Let's go."

Alex threw Siale a questioning look. She laughed. "Oh, no. Don't look at me. The girls aren't getting involved in this one. You guys have fun and we'll cheer from the sidelines."

"Yeah," girl named Sariah said to Cassie. "The boys are crazy."

"Crazy for a good time," Mohawk replied.

"That was super lame," Sariah told him.

Mohawk laughed and took her hand. "You like it when I'm lame."

"I like you," Sariah said. "The lameness, not so much."

She laughed when Mohawk picked her up and carried her across the street toward the ocean. "As long as you say you like me, that's all that matters," Alex heard him say.

Everyone made their way to the beach. Alex followed Brooks and the others north when they hit the sand. Siale's friends jumped around and jostled each other, their excitement contagious. Alex couldn't help getting caught up in it when Brooks grabbed the ball Reko had brought from who knows where and motioned to him.

"Go long!"

Alex took off running up the beach. Brooks threw the ball and he grabbed it, spinning at the last minute to dodge around a group of girls cooking hotdogs over a driftwood fire. He took several steps back and threw the ball in a tight spiral. It zipped past Brooks and two other boys right into Tennison's ready hands.

Brooks looked from Tennison to Alex. "I think we know who's playing quarterback."

Tennison nodded. "Just wait. He's got skills."

Alex smiled at his friend's compliment. "Only because my receivers are awesome."

Brooks grinned. "Flynn's not gonna know what hit him." He nodded over Alex's shoulder. "Looks like they're ready for us."

Alex glanced back to see a group of boys tossing a football a short distance away. Soda bottles filled with sand marked the end zones. The moonlight overhead was bright enough to light the beach without a problem. Spectators already lined the makeshift field.

A tall boy with long blonde hair eyed him down when Alex and the others met them in the middle of the sandy field.

"Who's the newbie?" Flynn asked.

"This is Al...uh, Al," Brooks replied. He turned slightly and winked at Alex. "Al's from inland."

"Living without the depthless oceans is unfathomable," Jerry said with a hint of worried confusion. "Without the knowledge of the perceptive waves, how is one to know the actuality of existence?"

"No one knows," Flynn replied with good humor as if he was used to Jerry's ways. He tossed the football in the air and caught it again. "Ready for a game?"

"Are you ready?" Reko asked in challenge.

Flynn grinned. "Born ready."

Mohawk pulled a coin from his pocket. "Call it in the air."

"Heads," Flynn replied.

When the coin landed with the tails side up, Brooks called, "Our ball." He motioned for his friends to join him in a huddle.

Chapter Fifteen

"What's the plan, coach?" Reko asked.

Brooks nodded at Alex. "Alex is the plan. Catch the ball when he throws it at you and score."

"Got it," Reko said. He grinned as they made their way to the center. "Best plan ever."

"That's what you think," a member of the other team said from across the line.

"It's what I know," Reko shot back.

Alex waited until everyone was set, then called, "Hike."

Mohawk tossed him the ball. He fell back a few steps and kept his gaze on Brooks who was double-covered, all the while watching Tennison out of the corner of his eye. The werewolf juked left, faking out his coverage before running for the end zone. Alex let the ball fly. Tennison caught it with ease and let himself get tackled halfway to the other side.

"So that's how it's going to be?" Flynn asked, eyeing Alex as they settled on the new line.

"That's how it's going to be," Brooks replied with a grin.

"Hike," Alex called. He caught the ball and checked both sides. Tennison was covered. Brooks and Reko were held up by blockers, as were the other members of their team. There was a shot to the end zone if Alex cut left and spun around Mohawk and his defender.

Alex tucked the ball and ran. He spun, then the way was free. Two steps later, a force slammed into him so hard he hit the ground in a puff of sand.

Alex stared at Flynn. The quarterback of the other team gaped back in realization. Flynn gave his head a slight shake. Alex nodded and rose to his feet, his instincts suddenly on edge.

"Keep it cool," Flynn whispered when Alex passed him

on his way back to the line.

Alex turned the ball in his hand, caught off guard but curious as to why a werewolf was hiding out playing football on the beach instead of at the Academy where it was safe. The voice in the back of his mind noted that safe was a loose term of late, but he pushed the thought away.

"Hike," he called.

Brooks made it past his defender and ran for the end zone. Alex threw a tight spiral that hit the human in the chest just before he crossed the line made by the soda bottles.

"Touchdown!" Reko yelled. Several of the team high-fived each other.

"Take that," Mohawk said.

The other team shot them dirty looks and gathered on the line.

Brooks motioned for his team to huddle. "Who's got Flynn?"

"I do," Alex said.

The others stared at him. "The dude's like hitting a brick wall," Reko warned, shoving his sun-bleached hair out of his eyes.

"Yeah," Mohawk seconded. "It's like you're the bug and he's the windshield."

"More like you're an insignificant speck of sputum colliding with an unyielding pane of glass," Jerry said, his gaze distant as if he wasn't thinking of the football game at all.

"That's exactly what I said," Mohawk replied, following them back to the line.

"Ready for the reply?" Flynn asked. He raised his eyebrows at Alex.

Alex grinned at the challenge. "Ready."

"Hike."

Flynn backpedaled a few steps. His gaze flicked from one

receiver to the next. Alex counted to ten. As soon as the seconds were up, he rushed the quarterback.

In the space of a heartbeat, they were both in the sand. Stunned silence came from both the players and those who watched the game.

"Dude," Reko said, his voice carrying over the beach. "Nobody's ever sacked Flynn!"

Alex sat up and eyed the werewolf next to him. Flynn grinned. "There's always a first."

Alex climbed to his feet and held out his hand. The werewolf took it and rose.

"That'll be the last time, though," Flynn said in challenge.

"We'll see about that," Alex replied.

When he reached the line, Brooks slapped him on the back. "That was the awesomest thing I've ever seen!" the human exclaimed.

Alex shrugged. "Beginner's luck."

"Whatever," a boy with blue hair called. "You hit him like a boss! Do it again."

"I'll try," Alex told him, fighting back a laugh at his team's enthusiasm.

"Hike," Flynn called. He released the ball before Alex reached ten. The tight spiral hit one of his receivers in the arms and he was tackled close to the end zone.

"Come on, Al," the quarterback said. "How you gonna stop that?"

Alex smiled as he made his way to the new line. "You'll see."

This time, instead of waiting to rush, Alex fell back. Flynn's eyes flickered to the right before he let go of the ball. Alex darted in that direction and caught the ball before it reached Flynn's receiver.

Alex took off running. His team and the onlookers

cheered as he made his way toward the opposite end zone. He was almost there when the force of a battering ram slammed him to the ground. He couldn't stop smiling when Flynn held out a hand and helped him back to his feet.

"Nice hit," he said with a chuckle.

"Yeah, would've killed the others," Flynn replied as they waited for the humans to fall in at the line.

"Good thing I'm tough," Alex said.

Brooks took the spot next to Alex. "Got that right! Let's score and end this thing."

"End it?" Alex asked. "We just started."

Brooks answered, "We started playing late. The girls have the barbecue going. We don't want to miss the hotdogs."

"Life is best when given a slaughtered carcass that has been mutilated and mashed, pressed into an edible cylindrical form, cooked to perfection by scorching in flames while skewered on a tree limb, laid between a creased piece of toasted dough, and slathered in mutilated tomatoes," Jerry said.

Mohawk rolled his eyes. "You have a way of describing food that makes it sound a bit less appealing, Preacher."

Jerry gave him a confused look as if he didn't know what the boy was talking about. "Descriptions are merely words framed around the subject of which the descriptor is describing."

Mohawk stared at him. "Uh, you lost me."

"Let's get this party over with," Flynn said.

"Gladly," Brooks replied.

When Alex called hike, everyone ran for the end zone. Alex knew it was only a matter of seconds before Flynn flattened him to the ground. He counted in his head as he searched for an open teammate, but everyone was occupied. Tennison could have used his werewolf skills to lose his coverage, but it would have been obvious. Alex was glad his soon to be brother-in-law knew to keep a low profile.

"Ten," Flynn called.

Alex watched the charge out of the corner of his eye. The werewolf came in with the force of a bull, intending to smash Alex to the ground hard enough that he would remember it.

Instinct took over. Alex waited until just before the werewolf hit him and ducked his right shoulder. He caught Flynn low in the chest and forced himself back up. The werewolf's momentum combined with Alex's movement threw him up and over Alex in a flip that landed him on his back on the ground.

"Run!" Siale called from the sidelines.

Alex could hear Cassie and the other girls cheering him on as he tucked the football and ran past Flynn's teammates to the end zone. His team closed in on him, yelling and laughing. The boys slapped him on the back.

"Dude!" Mohawk yelled. "It's been forever since we beat the Wharfers! It's about time someone like you came along!"

"Great job, dude," Reko said.

"Yeah, let's grab some dogs and enjoy the victory," Brooks told them, leading the way to where the girls waited next to the welcoming fire.

The other team fell in with them. Apparently, being enemies on the field didn't cross over to food. They eagerly accepted sticks and began roasting hot dogs over the flames.

Siale held out a stick to Alex. "Good game," she said.

"It was a bit more of a challenge than I expected," Alex admitted quietly.

"Why's that?" Siale asked.

Alex glanced over his shoulder. "Their quarterback's a werewolf."

"Seriously?" Siale replied in surprise.

Alex nodded. "I'm going to have a chat with him. Will you save that for me?"

Siale smiled. "Of course."

Alex made his way to where Flynn sat on the sea wall looking out at the ocean.

"You put on quite the show out there," the werewolf said without looking around.

Alex chuckled and sat down. "I could say the same about you. You're quite the legend out here."

The big werewolf smiled. "King of the beach and all that."

"It's a good place to be," Alex admitted. He couldn't explain the way he was drawn to the sound of the ocean. The ebb and flow of the waves soothed something deep inside of him. He let out a slow breath. "You should come to the Academy."

Flynn glanced at him. "That's a real place?" At Alex's nod, he smiled. "I've heard about it, a school where werewolf kids can grow up unafraid. It sounds pretty inviting."

"But?" Alex asked, hearing the unspoken word in the werewolf's voice.

Flynn opened his hand to indicate the beach. "But I've got this." He looked at Alex. "Also, playing football for the city school has given me more opportunities than you can imagine. I have scholarship offers coming in from every direction. I could go to whatever college I want to and play football. It's amazing!"

"Do they know you're a werewolf?" Alex asked.

Flynn lifted his shoulders in a small shrug. "It's not exactly a question on the application, you know. Why make it a big deal."

Alex stared at him. "What if they find out?"

"They won't," Flynn stated.

155

Surprised at how certain he sounded, Alex asked, "How can you be sure?"

Flynn lifted an eyebrow. "I've been in public school my entire life, even when other werewolves went into hiding and were getting killed off. I figured I was safer acting normal than running."

"How did your parents feel about that?"

Flynn threw a small rock off the wall. It hit the sand a few feet below and a tiny puff of dirt rose. "They weren't thrilled," he admitted. "But eventually they stopped asking me to leave. I had friends, I was happy, and I didn't want to give it up." He gave Alex a straight look. "I didn't accept that I was different, and so I wasn't."

"It was that easy?" Alex asked with doubt in his voice.

Flynn nodded. "Sometimes we're the ones who separate ourselves from the world. We forget that to the sun, we all walk, talk, and live. The moon might make us different, but the animal we become at night doesn't have to change who we are during the day."

Alex thought about the werewolf's words. "Sometimes I think I don't fit into the human world," he admitted.

Flynn rose and crossed his arms. "Who says the world is for humans?"

"There are dangerous werewolves out there."

Flynn accepted that. "And dangerous humans. It's not race that makes someone dangerous. It comes from some twisted place inside." He looked at Alex. "Maybe you sell yourself short."

Alex pushed off from the wall and made his way across the beach. He stopped just before the waves lapped at his sneakers. With the ocean in front of him, it was easy to forget that the world lay at his back. Several lights from boats showed on the dark waves, blinking in the darkness like stars fallen to the earth.

"It's not always so simple," he said at the sound of Flynn's footsteps.

Flynn studied the waves a moment before he said, "You've had to sacrifice a lot more than me to keep the peace, that's for sure."

Alex didn't know what to say. He pushed a toe into the water, shoving up a mound of wet sand. "You know who I am."

Flynn threw him a smile. "It wasn't too hard to figure out, *Al*," he said, emphasizing the name. "You're a bit of a loose cannon."

Alex chuckled. "I've been told that before."

Flynn glanced at him. "For what it's worth, I'm honored to play football with you."

"It's not over," Alex replied. "I'm here the whole summer."

"Bring it," Flynn said with a grin.

Chapter Sixteen

"How can we help?" Alex heard Cassie say as he made his way to the warehouse kitchen the next morning. Even at the early hour, kids ran through the corridors and adult were getting ready for the day.

"Have you ever made French toast?" a woman asked.

"No," Cassie replied. "But I'm happy to learn!"

Alex leaned against the door frame and watched his sister attempt to crack eggs on the side of a plastic bowl. The first egg smashed completely. Egg yolk mixed with shells dripped down the side. Her second egg cracked and half of it landed on the floor.

Jassa, an older werewolf with kind eyes, walked over. "Oh dear," she said with a smile. "Let me help you."

She showed Cassie how to crack the egg gently and open the shell so that everything landed inside the bowl without shell pieces.

"Werewolves are strong," Jassa said. "But when we channel our strength, we can do great things."

"Like crack eggs?" Cassie asked with a hint of doubt.

Jassa winked. "Just wait and see what we come up with." She looked up and noticed Alex. "Come in, come in. More hands are always welcome."

She motioned for him to join another person at a counter slicing bananas and apples. The werewolf had blond hair in dreadlocks that were escaping the hairnet he wore.

"Mick, help him out," she instructed.

"Yes, Jassa," Mick replied. He handed Alex a knife. "Know how to use one of these?"

Alex bit back a grin. "I think I can handle it."

Mick chuckled. "I'll bet you can."

Alex cut up the apples and removed the seeds. He put

them in the jar Mick pointed to.

"Jassa's teaching the kids about trees later and she wants to help them plant the seeds outside around the garden," he explained.

"There's a garden?" Alex asked in surprise.

Mick nodded. "If you're lucky, she'll make you pull the weeds," he said in a wry tone. He lowered his voice. "My suggestion is to help out for breakfast, then amscray before she thinks of something else for you to do. Otherwise, you'll be stuck here all day."

At that moment, Siale came walking in with a basket of ripe tomatoes. Alex felt the room brighten just by the smile she gave everyone. Her eyes lingered on Alex.

"We can wash those over here," Jassa instructed.

Alex felt the loss when their gaze broke and Siale followed Jassa to the huge sinks in the corner.

"Or maybe you're okay with staying here all day," Mick said, nudging Alex with his elbow meaningfully.

Alex chuckled and turned back to his apples. "I can't help it. She's my girl."

"And she knows it," Mick replied. "Good for you. Incoming!" The werewolf ducked.

Alex turned to see what he was talking about and a glob of dough hit him square in the face. Alex grinned at the sight of Tennison kneading more dough in the corner as if nothing had happened.

"Dude, for a survivalist, you really need to work on your survival skills," Mick said with a laugh. He tossed Alex a rag.

"What's going on here?" Jassa asked, stopping near their station.

Alex quickly wiped off the dough. "Uh, just an accident. Sorry."

Jassa studied him a moment as if she didn't believe what

he said. She finally shook her head and wiped her hands on her apron. "Werewolves," she muttered when she walked away.

"Here," Mick said.

Alex looked down to see a mushy, overripe banana in the werewolf's hand. He accepted the slimy fruit and held it low beside the table so Jassa wouldn't see it. Tennison was busy rolling the dough he had made into small balls and setting them on a pan. Alex glanced at Jassa. The cook was helping two female werewolves at another counter cut up potatoes for a big pot.

Alex gave a low whistle. When Tennison looked up, he let the banana fly. It hit the side of his friend's face and slid with a plop to the table.

Mick and Alex burst out laughing.

Tennison grinned as he wiped the slimy substance from his cheek.

"What is going on here?" Jassa demanded, storming over to Alex's table again.

At that exact moment, Tennison chose to let another glob of dough fly.

"In my kitchen, we don't— ahh!" Jassa's gasp of dismay could be heard across the kitchen. Silence filled the room. She stomped away with dough on her face and in her hair, and a look Alex didn't dare interpret.

Alex sliced apples quickly, afraid he and Tennison had ruined their chance to stay at the warehouse. He didn't want to go back to the Academy and admit to Jaze that their immaturity had cost them a summer break. He let out a breath of regret and grabbed another apple.

Two eggs hit him. One took up residence on his chest and the other splattered in his hair. Shocked, Alex looked up to find Jassa and Cassie crouched behind their table armed with more eggs.

"Take cover!" Mick yelled.

Food soared through the air. Tomatoes and potato peels hit the table above Alex. He and Mick answered with smashed bananas and apple cores.

"Take that, you mongrels," Jassa yelled, sending more eggs in their direction.

"Never!" Mick replied, answering with a handful of noodles that had taken up residence on the floor by his foot.

"Hey, Alex," Siale called.

Alex poked his head out, only to have a huge helping of chocolate pudding splatter across his face. He laughed and grabbed a nearby heap of gelatin. It caught Siale on the cheek and hair as she turned away, coloring her brown hair purple.

She and two other girls picked up the huge pot of pudding.

"Wait!" Jassa shouted. She stood with her hands up.

Everyone paused.

The cook shook her head, wiping dough, apple seeds, and noodles from her apron. "This has gotten out of hand. We do have werewolves to feed, you know."

"Truce?" Mick called from beneath the table.

"Truce," Jassa replied.

Mick and Alex rose.

"It's one thing to have a little food fight; it's another to waste food hungry mouths are waiting for," Jassa explained. She tried to keep her expression serious as she carefully wiped pudding from between her fingers, but her mouth pulled up in a half smile as her gaze flitted behind Alex and Mick.

Two buckets of cold water were dumped on them. Alex and Mick gasped at the sudden shock. Alex glanced back to see Cassie and Siale holding the buckets. His girlfriend gave him a little shrug.

"That's what you get," she said.

Alex caught her around the waist. As he pulled her close, his sneakers slipped on a patch of gelatin and water. They both fell backwards and landed on the floor with a splash. Everyone around them laughed.

"Come on, dude," Mick said, holding out a hand.

He pulled Alex to his feet and Alex helped Siale. The werewolves in the kitchen all stared at each other; everyone was covered in all manner of food.

"At least we got to wash off," Alex said.

"There's more where that came from," Cassie replied.

"Let's get back to work," Jassa told them. "Or you're going to miss the waves."

At Alex's questioning look, Siale said, "Trust me."

"Look where trusting you got me," he replied. He slid a handful of pudding from his hair and wiped it across her face before she could back away.

She laughed and buried her head against him, smearing it across his chin. "At least it's chocolate."

Mick shook his head, staying away from them to avoid getting any on him. "Girls and their chocolate," he replied, shaking his head.

***

After breakfast, they found Siale's friends waiting just outside the main door to the warehouse.

"We thought you guys would never be ready," Brooks said.

"The sun's just coming up," Tennison pointed out.

"Exactly," Travis, the boy with blue hair, said. "Perfect timing."

"For what?" Cassie asked.

"The waves," Jerry replied. "The waves wait for no mortal."

Brooks handed Alex the extra surfboard he was holding. "Let's go, Demon. I brought you my lucky board so you won't kill yourself out there."

"What if I told you I can't swim?" Alex asked.

Everyone around them froze as if Alex had said the worst thing in the entire world.

"You can't swim?" Reko asked in horror.

"Not even a little?" Clarice, a girl with blonde pigtails, asked.

Alex shook his head, but he couldn't hold the laughter in any longer. The way they were looking at him was worse than anyone had even looked at the Demon. It was as if not being able to swim was far more awful than turning into a creature out of a nightmare.

"I'm kidding," Alex said. "I can swim."

Brooks slapped him on the back. "You almost put a jinx on our whole friendship."

Siale grabbed three more surfboards from a shed on the side of the warehouse. Cassie and Tennison accepted theirs with concerned expressions.

"You know we've never done this before," Cassie said.

"Don't worry," Siale told them. "We'll take it easy on you.

It'll be fun."

They followed the group down the street. The early morning sunlight was just cresting behind them, casting long shadows along the pavement.

Alex caught Siale's hand and walked slower, letting the others go on ahead of them.

"So you've been surfing your whole life?" Alex asked.

"Most of it," Siale replied. "Why?"

Alex watched her closely. "I remember teaching you how to swim in the lake in Rafe's forest. Do you remember that?"

Red colored Siale's cheeks. "Um, slightly."

Alex's eyebrows rose. "Slightly? You were terrified! You nearly crawled on top of me when we jumped off the cliff together."

Siale gave an embarrassed smile. "What if I told you I was falling hard for you?"

Alex tried to grasp what she was saying. "So you lied?"

Siale shook her head. "I may have stretched the truth a bit. There was a time when I couldn't swim."

Alex stared at her incredulously. "How old were you?"

"Four?" she said as more of a question than an answer. She put a hand on Alex's arm. "Alex, you gave me something important that day. You gave me peace from the nightmares that haunted me even when I was awake. Being in your arms was the most wonderful thing I had ever experienced. Everything I did was to prolong that moment."

Something about the innocence in her words made Alex smile. "You're telling me that you faked not being able to swim so that I wouldn't let you go."

Siale smiled up at him, batting her eyelashes flirtatiously. "It worked, didn't it?"

Alex thought about the way he had felt holding her in the water. He had given her his heart fully at that moment. "Yes, it definitely worked," he admitted, adding, "Even though you *lied*."

"Stretched the truth," she corrected.

Alex laughed again and pulled her to him. Something about the fact that she had faked not being able to swim just so that he would hold her and make her feel safe made him love her even more. After all she had been through, he didn't know what it had cost her to put so much trust in him, but she had. Unable to stop himself, he kissed her on the forehead. "It's a good thing you're so beautiful when you lie."

She smiled up at him. "It's a good thing you're so handsome when you get upset."

"Why?" he asked. "Would you leave me if I wasn't?"

"Most definitely," she replied, winking at him.

"You guys coming?" Cassie called.

Grinning, Alex and Siale ran to catch up to the others.

"Look!" Vanessa said, holding her surfboard to the side to show its shadow with the fins from the bottom. "It looks like a shark!" She moved her hand so that it looked like the shark's mouth opening and closing.

"Sweet," Jerry said with a low laugh. "A land shark. Now the predators of the waves can become slayers of the sand. No pedestrian will be safe from serrated teeth and impassive eyes."

"Thanks, Jer," Brooks said dryly. "Just what the newbies need, worrying about sharks."

"What do we do if we come across a shark?" Cassie asked, her forced smile not hiding her worry.

"They shouldn't bother us," Mohawk told her. "Sharks mostly keep to themselves."

"Mostly?" Tennison repeated.

Reko grinned. "Don't worry. If they bite you, you'll know."

"That's reassuring," Cassie replied.

Chapter Seventeen

Alex was amazed at how many surfers were already riding the waves. The water rolled, twisting and turning with more force than he had seen the night before. Whitecaps touched the tops of the waves, throwing spray on the surfers who waited for the perfect moment.

"Here goes nothing," Cassie said. She took off her shirt and shorts like the other girls so she could go out in the swimsuit she had worn beneath.

"We put everything under the umbrella," Vanessa told her, pointing to the rainbow-colored one Travis was busy burying in the ground.

Siale set a stack of towels beneath the umbrella with her shorts and tank top. Cassie and Tennison followed.

Alex pulled off his shirt and tossed it with the rest of the clothes. Silence settled over the group. Alex turned slowly, suddenly aware that everyone was staring at him, at his scars. He wondered if surfing had been the wrong decision. Siale was wearing a black swimming suit that covered up most of her scars. Her friends acted as though they were used to the others that showed on her arms and legs. With his shirt off, though, most of Alex's could be seen.

"Dude," Reko said quietly.

Alex reached for his shirt. Jerry's voice stopped him.

"It's okay," the human told the others. "He's a samurai."

"A samurai?" Brooks asked; he glanced away from Alex's scars as if just looking at them hurt.

"Yeah," Jerry continued. "Alex is a warrior fighting for the peace of the past, the old ways when one's worth was judged by his or her character, not race. The world would be a superior place if the population as a whole could embrace the unparalleled ways of Alex's samurai."

The crash of the waves filled Alex's ears. He looked at the ocean, unable to meet the expressions on his new friends' faces.

A hand touched his shoulder. "If we don't head out now, we'll miss the best of them," Brooks said. The boy handed Alex the surfboard he had carried over. "Let's get out there."

"Come on!" Mohawk said. "To the waves!"

Excitement flooded the group. Surfboards were picked up, the awkward silence forgotten. Siale's arm slipped through Alex's as they made their way to the water. Alex smiled at her and held her close with his free hand.

"I love you," she said.

"I love you, too," he replied. She tipped her face up and he kissed her.

"Come on, love birds," Reko called. "Afraid to get your feet wet?"

Siale laughed. "I can out surf you any day, Reko. You know that!"

He grinned. "Prove it, Wolfie!"

Alex stared at her as the others ran into the waves. "Wolfie?"

"Yeah," Siale said with a big smile. "It's what they used to call me before it became against the law to be a werewolf." She shrugged. "I've kind-of missed it."

Alex chuckled. "It's cute, Wolfie." He kissed the tip of her nose before they both stepped into the ocean.

"This is amazing," Cassie said from a short distance in front of them. She and Tennison were already on their boards paddling to reach the deeper water.

Alex wasn't sure how he felt about being out in the depths where he couldn't see what was below the waves. At the lake back in the forest, he knew there weren't things like sharks and jellyfish. The ocean was different, something vast and unknown. His instincts were quiet, not giving him direction either way.

"Come on," Siale said, climbing onto her board before her feet couldn't touch. "You'll love it."

Alex followed her example. He used his hands to pull through the water, propelling him after the others. They dove beneath the breaking waves, maneuvering the noses of the boards under the water and diving down so that the waves washed over them instead of forcing them back toward shore. It took Alex a few tries to get the hang of pushing the back of his board down when the wave passed so that the board would angle him up again, but soon he was keeping up with the others without a problem.

Once they were past the breakers, the fun began. For a while, Alex just rode the ocean sitting on his board. It was amazing to watch his friends paddle for the big waves, guessing which would break. Jerry and Mohawk caught the first one, disappearing from view as the water pushed them along. The smiles on their faces when the wave broke and vanished toward the shore was enough to tell Alex how it felt.

"Come on," Reko said to Siale.

Up to the challenge, Siale paddled out behind him, intent on a rolling wave that pushed Alex back as he watched from the top of his board. He laughed when Reko's footing slipped and he plunged into the wave instead of riding it. The human came up grinning as if he guessed the ribbing he would get when Siale came back.

Alex's vantage point gave him a great view of Siale. She pushed up and centered herself on the board with her knees bent and arms out for balance. His breath caught when the wave pushed her forward, catching her board along the water and propelling her forward as though she glided on glass. It was perfection and grace in a single frame, an image he wished he could hold onto forever.

Siale held out a hand and let it trail in the wave that towered beside her. Alex swore he could make out the familiar melody of her laughter, but knew such a sound would be swallowed up by the crash of the waves around them. With her hair swept back and her body swaying with the force of the water, she looked as though she belonged to the ocean, a part of it instead of detached and floating above. The smile on her face when the wave finally broke was enough to make Alex's heart skip a beat.

He put a hand to his chest, realizing that though the feeling was there, his heartbeat was still steady. The fact that he owed his healed heart to Drogan drove the happiness from his mind. He didn't know how to stop the man responsible for all of the pain in his life. The fact that Drogan shared his blood as his half-brother made his stomach twist in a knot.

"Hey, Alex, the next one's yours," Brooks called.

Jolted from the dark direction of his thoughts, Alex stared at the human. Brooks paddled his board closer. The beads in his long black hair clacked together when he sat up. "You don't hide your thoughts very well."

Alex fought back a wry smile. "You mean I don't look cheerful?"

Brooks chuckled in return. "Only if cheerful means you look like you wished a shark would swallow you up. In that case, you're doing great."

"Sorry," Alex told him. "Don't worry about me. Go enjoy surfing."

Brooks shook his head. "Look, man, the ocean is a place to forget about everything else." He waved an arm to indicate their surroundings. "You're away from the land. The worries of that world don't exist out here. It's one of the reasons so many people are drawn to the ocean." He gave Alex a knowing look. "You can't surf the waves if you're concentrating on anything else. You have to get free of your thoughts and let your mind be clear. Focus on the heartbeat of the ocean, the swell, the fall. Let it work its magic."

At that moment, Mohawk fell off his board with a dramatic scream.

"Magic?" Alex repeated, failing to hold onto his dark mood.

Brooks laughed. "Hitting a note that high *is* magic." He tipped his head in the direction of the waves. "Come on. Let's give it a try. Do what I do."

Alex followed Brooks. He saw Cassie and Tennison paddling after a wave. They fell short of catching it, but both of them were smiling as though they were having a great time anyway.

"Go, Alex!" Siale called.

Alex lifted a hand in reply, then grabbed his board again when he almost fell off. He paddled harder to catch up to Brooks.

"Okay," the human yelled over his shoulder. "Get ready! Feel the roll of the ocean. Two more waves and it'll be ours."

Alex followed the boy's eyes to the ocean behind him. The water was pushing up a swell.

"That's the one," Brooks called. "Follow my lead. Paddle toward shore until you feel the wave catch your board. When you feel yourself sliding, pop-up and stand." His voice rose as he shouted over the rushing wave. "Try to stay in front of the break. Good luck!"

Alex paddled as hard as he could after Brooks until he felt the wave grab his board the way the human had described. The swell began to fold and Alex's board slid down its face. He put his hands on the board as he had seen the other

171

surfers do and pushed up to a standing position.

It wasn't hard to balance. With all the years of training in combat, Alex felt comfortable standing on the board with his knees bent and arms out. What alarmed him was the feeling of the wave behind him, ready at any second to swallow him board and all into the murky depths below. Instinct kicked in and Alex leaned back, giving more weight to the power of the wave. The nose of his board rose as he steered his board.

Exhilaration filled him, forcing out any other thought. He realized the truth of Brooks' words. Riding the wave, there was nothing but the wave. He reached out a hand like Siale had done, and his board shot out from under him, plunging him into the water.

It took a moment for Alex to figure out which way was up. He felt the pull of his board on the cord around his ankle, drawing him toward the surface. He kicked out and his head broke to the fresh open air. He took a deep breath and looked around.

Brooks was sitting up on his board close by. "You did it!" he exclaimed.

Alex laughed as he paddled next to the human. "For half a second."

"Trust me, Alex," Brooks replied. "Most people don't get half a second on a wave their first try, or a dozen after. You did great."

The feeling of peace that had filled Alex during the wave stayed with him as they made their way back to the others. They went after more waves, rode the ocean, and talked about what lay beneath the surface.

"I'm telling you," Reko insisted. "There's a shipwreck around the reef. I saw it on television. We should go there sometime!"

Brooks nodded. "We will, sometime."

"You always say that," Reko protested.

Brooks motioned toward the waves. "That's because I like it out here more than chasing shipwrecks. You keep your treasure. I've already got mine."

"Brooks, you're such a romantic," Clarice said, pushing her wet blonde braids behind her shoulders.

Brooks' eyes widened when he realized she thought he had been talking about her. "I'm, uh, I meant, I just..."

His voice died away when she leaned over and planted a kiss on his cheek. Unsettled, both of their boards flipped, dunking them in the water.

Brooks came up sputtering and Clarice laughing.

"I'm kidding," she said, splashing him. "Everyone knows your love is the ocean. A girl would only ever be second, and I deserve much more than second place in someone's heart."

She climbed back on her board and paddled toward the waves. Brooks clambered back onto his surfboard with much less grace. He stared after her, his expression a bit lost.

"Girls, am I right?" Reko asked, bumping Brooks' board with his foot.

"Yeah, girls," Brooks repeated, but he sounded a little less sure.

Mohawk nudged Vanessa and they both smiled knowingly at each other.

"Should we call it a celestial dawning?" Jerry asked.

"A morning," Brooks explained at Cassie's confused look.

Tennison nodded. "Definitely. I'm about to fall off this board my muscles are so tired. How do you guys do that every day?"

Brooks chuckled. "It takes practice, and don't pretend you couldn't continue for hours. I know how you werewolves are."

Tennison grinned. "You got me."

"All the same, I could definitely take a break," Cassie said. "I think I fell off every wave in the ocean."

"The waves are never-ending in their response to the beck of the moon and the kiss of the waiting shore," Jerry replied.

"I think she was being ironic," Brooks told him. The human shook his head. "Irony's lost on him entirely."

Cassie smiled at Jerry. "I think it's wonderful. I could definitely surf every morning, or attempt it at least."

"We'll keep practicing," Tennison promised. "You'll eventually get it."

"Either way," Cassie replied. "I'm just happy to be out here."

"Welcome to surfing," Reko told her. "Now it's in your soul forever."

They paddled to shore, riding the waves and letting them push the boards forward. When his feet touched the sand, Alex picked up his surfboard with a feeling of accomplishment. He pulled on his shirt with the others and followed them inland.

"You're sure quiet," Siale said.

Alex gave her an embarrassed smile. "Sorry about that."

"What are you thinking about?"

He shook his head. "For once, nothing. Nothing at all."

She nodded. "I understand that completely. I've missed it." She waved her hand to indicate the city in front and the ocean behind them. "All of it. It's a part of me."

Alex ran a hand down her back, smoothing her hair. "It might be hard to leave."

"Let's just stay forever," she said with a hint of longing in her voice.

"Maybe we can surf for the rest of our lives," Alex replied, feeling the same draw for such a simple life.

"It wouldn't be a life poorly spent," Jerry said from behind them.

Both of them looked back, surprised to see him following them.

Alex winked at Siale. "No, it wouldn't."

Chapter Eighteen

That night, they helped Jassa prepare spaghetti and garlic bread for dinner.

"I think I know why they say vampires are allergic to garlic," Tennison said, holding the potent-smelling herb as far away from him as he could.

"You'll notice that we don't have a problem with vampires here," Mick replied.

"You have a point," Alex told him. "Maybe we should use more of it."

"No, thank you," Tennison said with a grimace. He put the lid on the container and set it into the refrigerator, shutting the door with a bang.

Behind his back, Cassie took a bite of one of the pieces he had just spread. When he turned around, she gave him a big kiss. Tennison kissed her back for a second, then his face twisted. He pulled back and stared at her.

Cassie laughed. "Like my new lipstick?"

Tennison shook his head. "At least I won't have to worry about you getting attacked by vampires, either."

Cassie giggled and wrapped her arms around him. "I love you, my garlic-sensitive boyfriend."

Tennison laughed and hugged her back. "And I love you, my stinky little girlfriend."

"Aw, what a cute couple," Mick replied. He rolled his eyes with a grin.

"Let's get this food out there before the troops mutiny," Jassa told them.

The other werewolves in the kitchen picked up the pots of spaghetti, sauce, salad, and garlic bread. Alex followed behind with two jugs of red juice and a container of parmesan cheese under each arm.

The tables were already two-thirds full of werewolves. Jassa said that with the full moon coming in the next few days, the warehouse would fill up even more. The fact that the warehouse was a safe place to phase away from the dangers of Extremists or hostile humans appealed to families as far as a few hours away. Alex was grateful Red had created such a place.

"I can't have butter," a woman with red hair and a green sweater said. "It doesn't mesh well with my figure."

"I would stay away from the bread," Siale recommended with a warm smile as though she was familiar with the woman's needs, "But Jassa used coconut oil and salt in the spaghetti, so you should be fine."

"Thank goodness," the woman replied.

Alex was in the middle of pouring her a generous helping of punch when a bellow rang through the warehouse.

"Alex Davies!"

Alex took a steeling breath. He set the cup back down, careful not to drip any punch on the woman's khaki-colored pants. He turned slowly.

"How dare you?" Boris demanded from the steps that led to the warehouse floor. He stormed down them with the fury of an entire wolf pack. "This is my city. You have no right—"

Red stood in Boris' path, barring his way to the tables and Alex.

"Boris, you know the rules. There's no fighting here. If you have a dispute, you can take it outside. It's up to Alex whether he chooses to follow," Red said, his voice level and firm.

"But he shouldn't..."

Five other Alphas left their places at the tables and stood behind Red. Even angry, there was no way Boris could reach Alex.

His blue eyes, the same color Kalia's had been, flashed with rage. "I'll be waiting in the alley," he growled, his gaze locked on Alex. "You better follow."

Boris stormed back outside and slammed the door shut behind him.

Everyone looked at Alex. The carefree atmosphere of the warehouse had vanished, leaving only discomfort. The scent of Boris' wrath lingered above the aromas of tomatoes and pasta. The children who had been playing found their mothers and fathers, climbing onto their laps with the confused worry of the young confronted with an unknown situation.

Alex handed Tennison the jug of punch. "Take over, will you?"

"Alex, you don't have to do this," Siale said, touching Alex's arm.

"I do," Alex replied. "I understand what he's gone through. Please don't follow me out."

Siale shook her head. "You can't ask that of me."

Aware that everyone was watching them, Alex put his hand over hers. "Siale, I need you to trust me. If I don't take care of this now, Boris can cause problems here for the rest of the summer. It's better not to draw it out, and he's easier to work with if he doesn't have an audience."

"We've got your back, Alex," one of the Alphas said.

The others who had stood with Red nodded.

"One word and we'll take care of him," another called.

Words of agreement rose from the other werewolves.

The thought that so many of them cared touched Alex. He smiled, calming the room. "Thank you, but I'll be fine. Please eat the amazing food Jassa's prepared. I'll probably be back before you're finished."

Alex's forced confidence and nonchalant attitude did the

trick. The werewolves around the room relaxed and went back to their meals. At Alex's nod, Cassie and Tennison resumed serving food with the others.

"Alex?" Siale asked, her voice quiet beneath the regular commotion of so many people eating in one place.

"I'll be back," Alex told her. When she continued to watch him with her worried expression, Alex gestured to the little boy who held up a bowl for the spaghetti she had been dishing out. "Luke's starving. We don't want him to waste away," Alex said, winking at the boy. Luke grinned at him.

Siale let out an accepting breath and spooned spaghetti into his bowl. Jassa followed close behind with a scoop of sauce.

Alex was aware of eyes following him as he made his way to back to the kitchen. He was prepared to meet Boris, but he wasn't going to be stupid about the situation. Heading out the side door would give him the advantage of where to confront the angry werewolf instead of being bombarded the instant he stepped into the alley from the stairs.

"Alex," Red said from the door to the kitchen. Alex paused and Siale's father closed the distance between them. "You don't owe Boris anything."

"His sister died because of me," Alex replied. He kept his voice neutral, forcing himself to focus on the matter at hand instead of the pain of the past. "He has a right to be upset."

Red nodded. Alex wasn't surprised he knew about what had happened. He was a good father and Siale loved him very much. It was only right that she would tell him the things that affected them at the Academy.

"Fighting you isn't going to help him get over it," Red said. He paused, then continued, "Neither is killing you."

"Knowing I'm here and doing nothing about it won't help him either," Alex replied. "There's got to be some place in the middle where we can both live our lives." He put a hand on the door that led from the back of the kitchen to outside, but opposite from the alley where Boris waited.

"What if there's not?"

Red's question hung in the air.

Alex finally looked back at him. "Then Boris is right. This is his city. I have no right to take whatever peace he has left from him."

Alex slipped out and made his way around the warehouse. A glance in the alley showed Boris leaning against the wall next to the door. His arms were folded and the anger on his face showed clearly in the light of the waxing moon. Alex spotted a huge two-by-four next to the Alpha. He shook his head, glad he had chosen to go around instead of waiting for the werewolf to clobber him.

Alex moved to the mouth of the alley. "Hey."

Boris rose immediately and grabbed the board. He stalked down the alley toward Alex.

"What are you doing?" Alex demanded.

Boris' steps slowed only slightly at Alex's steady tone. "What I should have done a long time ago," the werewolf said.

"Murder?" Alex replied, backing away to keep the werewolf from closing too much space. "There're prisons for actions like that."

"Then you should be there," Boris shouted.

To Alex's surprise, tears showed on the werewolf's face when he turned toward the moonlight.

Boris threw the two-by-four. The wood flew past Alex and slammed into the building across the street, splintering in the pieces. The Alpha's breath heaved and he stared at the sidewalk in front of him with his teeth clenched and lips pulled back in a grimace.

"I can't do this anymore," Boris growled.

Alex watched him in silence, unsure of what to do.

After a moment, Boris glanced up at him. There was something in the Alpha's gaze that took Alex by surprise. Within the anger and hatred, he was shocked to see acceptance.

"I need to show you something," Boris said, his voice quiet. "Wolf up."

The huge werewolf pulled off his shirt.

"Uh, wolf up?" Alex asked. "Is that a thing?"

Boris nodded with what looked like the ghost of a reluctant smile. "Yeah, it is. Now wolf up before I leave you behind."

Alex pulled off his own shirt and phased. He glanced back at the warehouse, knowing Siale would be concerned if he disappeared.

Boris gave an impatient bark. Alex answered with a snort and followed close behind.

It felt strange following the Alpha through the streets. The last time he had done so was when Boris had led him to the warehouse his first time. So much had changed since then. The only reason he followed the Alpha was because he felt like he owed Kalia's brother at least that much. Where they would end up, he had no idea.

Boris led the way around the back of their huge mansion and through a crack in the gate. The security guards who patrolled the perimeter didn't bat an eye at the two wolves who crossed the lawn and entered the back door that had also been left open. Boris padded upstairs. Alex followed him to a room down the hall on the right side.

Kalia's honey and clover scent lingered in the carpet fibers and in the wood that framed the doors. Alex's heart ached. He shoved the feeling away, reminding himself to stay on guard. At Boris' low bark, Alex followed him into the bedroom.

Boris phased in the walk-in closet. Alex waited near the door, ready to bolt if the werewolf was crazy enough to come out with a gun or silver weapon.

Boris left the closet clothed in jeans and a black tee-shirt.

"Grab something," the Alpha said shortly. "I'll meet you in the hallway."

Alex stepped into the closet with a surreal feeling. If anyone had told him that day that he would be in the house of the student who hated him the most, putting on the said student's pants and a shirt that portrayed a heavy metal band, he would have said they were crazy.

He glanced around the werewolf's room. Boris' walls were lined with framed and signed concert posters, sports memorabilia, several autographed guitars, and lights that made the ceiling glow orange and green. Everything was signed and no doubt extremely expensive. There was a picture of Mr. Dickson near the door, and one of Kalia and her mother on the nightstand. Kalia looked much younger and was missing her two front teeth. Even Mrs. Dickson smiled, something Alex wasn't used to seeing.

"Are you coming?" Boris called from the hallway.

Alex jumped as though he had been caught doing something wrong. He stepped out the door and pulled it shut behind him.

Boris looked at his shirt. "Fitting," he said wryly.

Alex glanced down. The name of the band was 'Wolfsbane'. When he looked up again, Boris was already halfway down the hall.

"Are you going to tell me why you brought me here?" Alex asked, hurrying to catch up.

"You mean instead of tearing your head off?" Boris

glanced back at him, his expression unreadable.

Alex nodded. "I would have put up a fight, but yeah."

Boris paused with his hand on a doorknob. "I wanted to kill you. Since Kalia's death, I wanted to end you in every way I possibly could. I dreamed about it, imagining different scenarios."

The Alpha let that sit for a few moments as he led the way down the hall. He stopped by a door and let out a breath. "I avoided Kalia's room because it hurt too much. I couldn't stand to be reminded of its staleness because it meant she wasn't coming back, so I never went in." He hesitated, then said, "Until I sleepwalked and woke up in here the other night."

"You sleepwalk?" Alex asked, keeping his tone carefully neutral.

Boris shook his head. "Never. I haven't ever sleepwalked. But I kept having nightmares about Kalia." He glared at the door as if it took an effort to keep his emotions away. "I kept seeing her die and I couldn't save her." He let out a shuddering breath. "The other night it was the worst. She kept calling my name, and I ran down this hallway that got longer and longer. Every doorway I checked was empty. She finally said, 'Wake up', and when I did, I was in her room."

He pushed the door open.

Kalia's scent was stronger this time, flooding out and wrapping around them like a memory that wanted to be so much more because as Boris had described, the scent was stale, old, lingering, reminding them that she was truly gone. Alex's feet felt glued to the ground. He couldn't will himself to step forward.

Chapter Nineteen

When he didn't follow Boris into Kalia's bedroom, the werewolf grabbed the front of his shirt and pulled him inside. "Like a band-aid," Boris said, his voice a low growl. "Just rip it off."

Dust covered the huge four poster bed, the vanity and couches, the beanbags, and the recliners that were all positioned just the way Alex remembered them from when he had stayed with Kalia during one of her headaches. Despite the lack of care the rest of the room had received, a fire crackled in the fireplace.

At Alex's questioning look, Boris gave a sad smile. "Mom won't let the maids touch anything in here, but she insists that the fire be built every night because Kalia liked it."

Sadness filled Alex at the thought of Mrs. Dickson showing love in such a way. She hadn't been the most expressive toward Kalia, but the untouched room and roaring fire said more than words.

"When I woke up in here, I couldn't understand it," Boris said, his voice quiet. He walked across the floor, motioning for Alex to follow him to Kalia's vanity. "Then I saw these."

Alex's heart slowed at the pictures taped around the mirror. They were mostly pictures from the Academy, and he was in every one, sitting at the table in the Great Hall, running through the forest in wolf form, talking in front of Professor Mouse's class, asleep on the couch in Pack Jericho's quarters. Alex didn't know when she had taken the pictures, but it was obvious she cherished them.

The picture in the middle of the mirror kept his attention. It was of him and Kalia sitting on the top step in the courtyard. Their faces were close together as if they were in a serious discussion, and the smile on Kalia's face showed how much she was enjoying it.

"She loved you," Boris said.

Alex's heart tightened as if gripped in a fist. He tried to speak, but the knot in his throat refused to release his voice.

"I know," Boris cut him off before he could work any words free. "I know you love Siale and you can't help it. These pictures just made me mad, do you know why?"

Alex shook his head.

Boris' eyes narrowed. "Because I couldn't fathom that someone Kalia loved so much would skip her funeral. She deserved that much. It made me think you were lying to her about everything, leading her on. She deserved better." Boris held up a hand when Alex tried to speak. "So I decided to find out for myself. I hacked into the security footage from the funeral."

He left without saying anything else, leaving Alex to follow him out of Kalia's room. Alex pulled the door shut behind him with reverence. The thought of the pictures covered in dust tore at him. He knew she had loved him. He had hoped she would be able to turn those feelings toward Torin, but the pictures proved he had been wrong.

He found Boris back in his room sitting at the computer. The Alpha spoke without preamble, "I searched for hours that night. Why do they have to take so many stupid pictures?" Boris muttered, more to himself then to Alex. He clicked on something and let out a breath. "Then I found this."

Boris turned the screen. Alex felt as though he had been punched in the stomach.

It was a picture of him at the graveyard while Kalia was being buried. The rain was falling. He stood amid tall tombstones and marble angels that hid him from view of the other students and family members around the grave. Alex's head was bowed and his hand squeezed his closed eyes. Tears trailed down his cheeks and his tightly pressed lips showed obvious agony.

"I knew it then," Boris said, his voice cracking. "I knew you loved her. I was wrong. I was very wrong."

To Alex's surprise, the huge werewolf stood and grabbed him in a tight hug. The Alpha's shoulders shook with silent sobs. Alex blinked back tears of his own and patted Boris' back.

"I knew you loved her," Boris said again, repeating the words as if they mattered the world to him. "You didn't lead her on. Her feelings weren't thrown away, and she didn't die for nothing."

"It's my fault she's gone," Alex said as a sob of his own escaped.

Boris pushed him back, giving him a stern look. "I've blamed you ever since her death, ever since the day Jaze called us and told us what happened." He shook his head. "But someone who loved her that much," he gestured to the image on the screen, "Wouldn't put her in harm's way if he could help it. Since the moment I saw that picture, I haven't had another nightmare." He rubbed his face, wiping away the tears. "I don't hate you anymore, Alex." He took a shuddering breath. "In my heart, you'll always be my brother."

Alex stared at him, stunned.

Boris held out a hand.

Alex numbly held out his own and Boris shook it. "Brothers, then," the Alpha concluded with a satisfied nod.

Footsteps sounded on the stairs. Boris hurried to the door and pushed it shut. After a moment, he glanced out, then gestured to Alex. "It's probably time for you to go. Dad's home and he's not as accepting as I am. We better sneak you out of here."

The thought of Mr. Dickson's armed security guards being sent on a werewolf hunt made Alex more than willing to follow Boris back outside and through the gate.

"I'm truly sorry," Boris said when they paused near the road from the mansion.

"You had a right to hate me," Alex replied, still trying to come to terms with what had just happened.

"Not now that I know the truth," the Alpha replied.

At Alex's uncertainty, Boris waved his hand. "You better get going. I think I terrified everyone at the warehouse, but it was the only way I could think of to get you alone."

"You could have just asked me," Alex pointed out.

Boris paused. "Well, maybe I'll try that next time. Tell Red I'm sorry and I hope he lets me back in."

"He will," Alex assured the Alpha. "Especially if I come back alive."

Boris chuckled. "Better wolf up and get going then."

Alex pulled off the heavy metal band shirt and jeans and phased. He trotted out into the night with a feeling of complete shock. When Boris stormed into the warehouse, Alex had never imagined such an outcome. He paced through the streets feeling lighter than he had in a long time. He hadn't realized how much Boris' anger and hatred had weighed on him. Though he still carried the guilt of Kalia's death, the fact that her brother was no longer one of his mortal enemies made him able to breathe easier.

Alex's steps slowed when he neared the warehouse. A figure waited in the shadows where he had left his clothes. A slight breeze pushed at his back, sending whoever's scent it was away from him. Thoughts of Drogan or the curs made him wary. If an enemy was outside, he wondered if the werewolves inside the warehouse were safe.

All hesitant emotions fled the second Siale stepped out of the shadows in wolf form. Her light gray coat contrasted beautifully with the white marks on her shoulders. Her eyes danced, teasing him as if she guessed what he had been thinking when he saw someone in the dark alley.

Surprised to see her in wolf form waiting for him, Alex gave a wolfish grin and trotted toward her. Siale whirled around and took off running down the street. She paused a block away and gave a challenging bark before taking off again. Alex barked in answer and ran after her.

Siale wound her way through streets, beneath wooden walkways, around trees with reaching, spreading roots, and around, and even over, parked vehicles. Her knowledge of the city let Alex know just how much she had explored on her own. By the time he caught up to her, she was in the ocean, prancing through the waves. Alex jumped in, splashing and biting at the water as though he was a puppy. Siale pouncing against his side, rolling him in the water. He came up sputtering and dove at her, but she danced out of the way. He made of show of falling face-first into the water again. She gave a huff of laughter and followed.

By the time they made their way to the shore, Alex was exhausted but happy. He let his tongue hang out and gave a dramatic sigh, falling into the sand at her side. Siale replied with a huff of laughter and settled down next to him. Her head turned and Alex followed her gaze, paying true attention to his surroundings for the first time.

The moonlit beach was beauty itself. The waves pushed at the sand with a sound much more full and beckoning than it had been when he was in his human form. Tones similar to those of the calling pack filled his ears, answering why so many were drawn to the sea. The salty seaweed and fish smell of the water drifted with the breeze that also carried the lingering smoke and hotdog scent of the barbecues that were held on the beach at sundown.

The almost full moon reflected on the water, broken into a million pirouetting pieces that ebbed and flowed, nearly connecting but shattering again with each sigh of the waves. The stars above filled their own ebony sea, a darkness that flowed and encompassed all around it. It was so perfect and complete, a scene that resonated with Alex's soul. He let out a sigh without knowing it.

Siale's shoulder bumped his. He caught her understanding gaze. She leaned against him, filling him with her scent and the comfort of her presence. She had helped him through so much, and knew so much of him, yet he still saw respect in her eyes along with love and adoration.

Alex rose and tipped his head, asking her to follow him. She stood unquestioningly and padded beside him back to the warehouse. Alex phased in the shadows and pulled on his clothes. Siale stepped from the warehouse wearing a simple white and light blue stripped summer dress that wrapped around her calves in the breeze.

"Care for a walk back to the beach with me?" Alex asked, holding out his hand.

Siale slipped her fingers into his with a smile. "Definitely."

Alex pulled her close. "You keep smiling like that and I'm going to forget what I'm doing."

She looked up at him with another smile. "So there's a purpose to this walk?"

"Perhaps," Alex replied vaguely.

His answer seemed to satisfy her. Siale walked at his side with her hand on his arm and her gaze on the night sky.

"There's something so reassuring about the stars," she said. "Even when it's cloudy, I know they're out there."

"Do you like them more than the moon?" Alex asked.

Siale nodded. "I do, actually." She gave a smile that held a hint of embarrassment. "I know werewolves love the moon, and I do, too, but it's ever-changing. The stars are the same, holding their constellations forever even as the earth rotates. It's beautiful, you know?"

Her voice held a hint of a need for reassurance. When Alex nodded, relief showed in her gaze. "It is beautiful. I've never thought of them quite in that way." He looked up at the sparkling sky. "But I understand what you mean. Life changes so fast sometimes it's nice to have something that will always be the same."

She squeezed his hand. "Thank you for not laughing."

"I could never laugh at you," he replied.

The way she looked at him was almost too much. He meant to lead her to the pier, but he felt that the time was right, standing on the moonlit beach with the ocean giving its song to the moment. The stars she loved so much blanketed their shoulders, and the ocean breeze danced through her long brown hair, brushing it across her back.

The moment was hers as much as his heart, and he wanted to make it last forever.

"Siale, I love you," he said. He found the velvet ring box in his pocket and slipped it out without her noticing.

"I love you, too, Alex," she replied.

He shook his head. "I don't think you understand. From the moment I looked into your eyes, my heart was yours completely. You're the first thing I think about when I wake up, and the last image in my mind when I fall asleep. I may fight like I have nothing to lose, but in truth, I have everything to lose. You are my stars in the night sky, Siale, you are my constant, my true north, my every hope and dream."

"Oh, Alex," Siale said.

Alex dropped to one knee in the sand and opened the velvet box. When he held it up to her, Siale's hand flew to her mouth. Tears filled her eyes.

"Siale Leanna Andrews, will you make me the luckiest werewolf in the world by becoming my wife?" Alex asked with tears in his own eyes.

"Yes, absolutely yes," Siale replied. She threw her arms around his neck, laughing and crying at the same time. "Oh, Alex, I'm so happy!"

Alex picked her up by the waist and spun her around. "Me, too," he said, smiling up at her. He brought her down and kissed her. "I couldn't imagine my life without you in it," he said. "You are everything that's wonderful."

She set a hand on his cheek. "You gave me so much to live for when I wanted to just die," she told him, her voice breaking. "You gave me the chance to start over, you believed in me, and you let me be myself. The 'me' I see in your eyes is someone I try to attain. You bring out my laughter and happiness whenever you walk into a room. Holding your hand is the greatest thing I could ever ask for, because it means I'm yours." The tears in her eyes spilled over when she looked at the ring Alex held. "And now this."

With shaking fingers, Alex slid the ring on her hand. The seven purple stones glittered in the starlight while the diamond glowed like a star of its own.

"It's beautiful," Siale breathed. "I've never seen anything like it."

"I knew the moment I saw it that it was meant to be yours," Alex told her; relief that she liked it made him happier than he could express.

She threw her arms around his neck again and hugged him. "You've made me the happiest girl in the universe," she said.

Chapter Twenty

When they reached the warehouse, Alex asked Siale to let him talk to Red before she told him the news. He didn't know how the werewolf would react to the engagement of his seventeen year old daughter. He made his way nervously through the warehouse to the room where Red usually tinkered with the things that had been broken by either rambunctious young werewolves or normal wear and tear.

To Alex's surprise, Siale's father was up despite the very early hour. Part of him had hoped for the remaining few hours until dawn to come up with what to say to the werewolf, and so he crossed the room feeling quite unprepared to talk to Red about Siale.

"Problems with the toaster?" Alex asked, coming up to the table Red worked on.

"One of them," Red replied, glancing up. "Glad to see you're still alive. I wasn't sure if I'd have to head out there swinging."

A power cord wrapped in electrical tape, a bicycle chain, and a hair dryer lay on Red's other side. Alex realized with a start that the head werewolf of the warehouse had stayed up doing odd jobs in case Alex needed him.

"Um, thanks," he said. "It went better than I expected."

Red nodded, keeping his eyes on the toaster as he removed the fasteners.

Alex picked up the power cord. Red glanced at him and he set it back down.

"Something you need?" the werewolf asked.

"You might want to sit down," Alex said.

Red set his screwdriver on the table and gave Alex a straight look. "I'm already sitting."

Alex wanted to kick himself. "Oh. Right." He took a

breath to calm his thundering heartbeat. "I proposed to your daughter."

Instead of the shock Alex expected to see on Red's face, Siale's father merely nodded. "It's about time." He picked up the screwdriver again and used it to lever the shell off the toaster chassis.

"So you're not mad?" Alex asked, thrown off guard.

Red chuckled and looked up at him. "I knew you were going to propose when you got here at the beginning of summer. You had that look about you, in love yet totally unsure about yourself. You are both so besotted with each other I don't know how you function on your own. You two need each other like the surfer needs the ocean. Now that you've been out there, you know what I'm talking about."

Alex nodded. "I really do." He hesitated. Red began to fiddle with a latch near one end of the toaster. "Thank you, sir," he finally said.

Red glanced at him, his mismatched eyes creased at the corners with humor. "I expect you to call me Dad."

Alex's chest tightened. He blinked quickly and nodded. "Thank you, Dad."

Alex collapsed into bed thinking of his own parents. It had been ten years since he had called anyone dad. Watching his parents die at Drogan's hand and holding Cassie with the knowledge that they were next had taken away his youth. Jaze and Nikki's patient guidance had given them both structure and loving values, yet they had little William, and they were expecting again. He had been entirely prepared to keep a respectful relationship with Siale's father; Red's insistence that he be called Dad had changed things.

Alex rose and unplugged the cell phone Trent had sent with him. He ascended the stairs to the top landing, then climbed the ladder that led to the roof. Pushing up the trap door, Alex stepped out. He hit the speed dial, smiling at the fact that Trent had already programmed his number in.

"You do realize that most people are asleep at this hour," Trent said, sounding more amused than annoyed.

"Only normal people, Trent," Alex replied.

"Oh, that's right," his friend answered. "We're anything but normal."

"Exactly." Alex fell silent for a moment, then said, "I proposed to Siale today."

"I'm sorry she rejected you," Trent said with mock sadness. "Do you need a shoulder to cry on?"

Alex chuckled. "She accepted, idiot."

"Well, congratulations!" Trent exclaimed. "How'd you trick her into it? Chocolate? Promises of riches?"

Alex sat back against the roof with a smile. "She happens to love me."

Trent gave a snort of disbelief. "Great. How am I supposed to trick Jordan into that one?"

"Oh, come on. I've seen the way she looks at you. She's probably already accepted in her head a million times."

Trent sounded like he was smiling when he replied, "You think so?"

"You just have to work up the courage to ask. I believe in you, Trent."

"Well, that makes one of us, but since it's you, I guess it'll be enough," Trent told him.

"Good," Alex said. He turned the conversation to the subject that was bothering him. "So what did you find at the location?"

Trent knew Alex was talking about the place where he was tortured. "You're not going to like this," he said, his tone solemn.

"I'm sure of it. Shoot."

Trent sighed. "It was burned to the ground before we got there. Jaze thinks Drogan did it by the scents still lingering around the place." He was silent, then said, "Drogan's gone, and so are his curs. They vanished, and now they're attacking cities, hurting humans by the hundreds, then they disappear again without a trace."

Alex let out a slow breath, thinking things through. After a moment, he said, "I need to talk to Jaze."

Trent patched him through to the dean's room. Despite the early hour, Jaze sounded wide awake. "Hi, Alex. Trent said he told you what we found."

"Yeah, it doesn't sound good," Alex replied.

"Drogan took revenge against the Extremists who captured him. We shouldn't be too surprised, except that he also burned the records, computers, cell phones, and anything else we could have used to track down the rest of their group. Drogan and his curs were thorough."

"Too bad we didn't catch them in the act," Alex said quietly. "We could have killed two birds with one stone."

"Now I'm afraid Drogan's gone lone wolf on us."

"Is that a bad thing?" Alex asked, catching the dean's tone. "Isn't he more vulnerable alone?"

"It's the opposite," Jaze replied. "Lone wolves are dangerous. They don't have anyone to hold them accountable or to protect. A werewolf without a pack is a loose cannon because it's unnatural. Our instincts keep us together. Pack hierarchy is important because not only does it give those of lower rank someone to watch over them, it gives the Alpha purpose." The dean's voice lowered. "It worries me to think what Drogan's doing with his curs. People are being hurt and no matter what we do, my team can't locate them."

The thought made Alex's stomach twist. Fighting the curs had let him know just how powerful they were. The thought of Drogan sending them against unarmed humans or werewolves made him feel sick.

"We have to find them."

"We're trying," Jaze reassured him.

Alex shook his head as he thought. "They came to the Academy to find me. What if he sends them there again?"

"It's protected," the dean replied. "Mouse has gone over security with the Black Team and the GPA. There aren't any more holes. If they try to bulldoze their way through with brute force like last time, we now have countermeasures in place."

"Has he tried?"

"No, he hasn't." Jaze paused, then said, "I know that worries you as much as it does me. If he attacked the Academy, at least we could attempt to take the curs out there. As it is, we keep searching, but we have no idea where he is. We have to wait until he surfaces again."

"Then let's flush him out."

Jaze was quiet for a moment, then said, "I'm listening."

Alex scuffed his toes across the top of the roof, feeling the rough surface as he said, "Use me as bait. We know he wants me, so if we set it up—"

"Absolutely not. Alex, I'm not going to—"

Alex cut him off. "Jaze, Drogan's out for blood. I left him at that Extremist facility. Now he's turning his hatred against those who can't defend themselves. Do you want to wait until he hurts more humans?"

"No," Jaze replied, his voice tight. "But I also don't want him to turn the full force of his cur army on you."

"I've accepted that it needs to happen." Alex paused and let out a breath, willing his voice to calm. "Jaze, we can do it safely. We'll set a trap. If the curs come after me, great. We'll be able to capture them or kill them before they hurt anyone else. If Drogan surfaces, even better. Maybe we can kill two birds with one stone after all."

"I don't like it," Jaze said. "I don't like it at all. You're finally getting the chance to just be a teenager. Are you sure you want to jump back into all of this?"

"If it means protecting others from Drogan? Yes, without a doubt," Alex told him.

"Where?"

Alex heard the resignation in the dean's voice. He rubbed his forehead, thinking. "It'll have to be somewhere believable, or else he'll know it's a trap."

"The Academy's out," Jaze said.

"Definitely," Alex agreed.

"Let me think on it," the dean told him. "You should probably get some sleep. You sound tired."

Alex smiled when he remembered what had kept him from sleeping in the first place. "I proposed to Siale."

"Good for you!" the enthusiasm in Jaze's voice erased the solemnity of their previous conversation. "I'm so happy for you."

"Siale's incredible," Alex replied. "I can't believe we're actually engaged. It's like I'm dreaming."

Jaze chuckled. "Then you chose the right one, otherwise it'd be a nightmare."

Alex laughed. "Definitely a dream, the best dream ever. I never knew anyone like Siale existed until we went in that warehouse." A smile lifted his lips. "Who knew jumping in that body pit would end up being the best action of my life?"

"You're lucky Cassie didn't kill you after that one."

"I know," Alex said with another laugh.

"Does she know?"

Alex stood. "Not yet. I'm planning to tell her in the morning." He glanced at the faint line of gray on the horizon.

"Which isn't too far away."

"You'd better get some sleep," Jaze told him. "Knowing the way girls react to such things, you're going to have a long day ahead of you."

"You don't think she'll be happy about it?" Alex asked in surprise.

"The opposite," the dean corrected with another chuckle. "They'll start planning the wedding."

"What have I done?" Alex said with a dramatic sigh.

"I'll let Nikki know the good news," Jaze replied. "Keep us posted."

"Will do," Alex promised.

He hung up the phone. Instead of going back to his room, Alex stayed on the roof and watched the sun rise above the distant mountains. It felt surreal to hear the rush of the ocean at his back and watch the way the fingers of sunlight stretched across the land as though reaching for the waves.

The door behind him opened.

"Dad told me I could find you up here," Siale said.

Alex turned at the sound of the smile in her voice. "I figured I'd make the happiest day of my life stretch as long as I can."

Siale stepped into Alex's arms. "You realize it's a new day already, right?"

Alex shrugged and smiled down at her. "As long as you're in it, every day is going to be perfect."

She batted her eyelashes up at him. "You sure you won't get bored of all this perfection?"

He laughed at her teasing expression. "If I do, I'm sure I can find some trouble to keep it interesting."

Siale's smile spread. "Of that, I have no doubt." She turned in his arms to watch the sunrise, linking her fingers through his. "Brooks asked if we'd like to go surfing this morning."

"Definitely," Alex answered. He glanced at her. "What about inviting them for breakfast?"

"At the warehouse?" Siale replied. When he nodded, doubt touched her voice. "We'd have to clear it with Dad. I don't know it if would be a good idea."

"You know you can trust them," Alex said. "And they know we're werewolves. They haven't turned us in yet. What's there to be afraid of?"

Siale lifted her shoulders. "Sometimes you don't know who you can really trust."

"Yeah, but it's Brooks and Jerry." Alex smiled at her. "And Clarice and Reko. I trust them."

"You trusted Officer Dune," Siale said, her voice gentle. "Sometimes, you have to be careful rather than take unnecessary risks."

A thought struck Alex. He stared at her.

At his expression, she said, "Alex, I'm sorry I brought it up."

Alex shook his head quickly. "Siale, you're brilliant!" He kissed her. "Officer Dune is exactly who we need!"

"For what?" she asked, confused as she watched him press the call button on the cell phone.

"You'll see," Alex answered. As soon as he was patched through to Jaze, he said, "We have to do it in Greyton."

"Don't you think they've been through enough?" the dean asked with touch of surprise in his voice.

"Hear me out," Alex replied. "Officer Dune owes me, big time. You said there were tracks from the curs around the school at the prom, so we know the last one drew them there. And after Drogan's attack on the hospital, I don't think the citizens of Greyton would balk at the chance to get a little payback of their own. The world knows what Drogan can do. He's already following in his father's footsteps. I have a feeling that any citizen who has the chance to help put an end to his reign of terror would willingly jump at it."

"If we can ensure their safety," Jaze replied.

"Exactly," Alex answered.

"Let me think about it." The dean's voice was more musing than denying. "I'll get back to you."

Alex hung up the phone with a feeling of relief. That relief immediately faded at the look of worry on Siale's face. He realized his short conversation with Jaze left little doubt what he was up to.

"You're going after him."

Alex forced a smile. "Actually, I'm doing the opposite. I'm letting him come after me."

"Alex..."

He touched her cheek. "Drogan's vendetta against me almost got you killed. I can't let that happen again." He nodded toward the warehouse. "Your dad let me into both of your lives and trusts me." His throat tightened and he swallowed. "If I'm going to be a part of this family, I have some responsibility to help take care of it."

Siale nodded, surprising him. "Yes, you do. And I do, too."

Alex realized what she was getting at. "Siale, you can't come with me."

Her gray eyes flashed. "You can't stop me, Alex. We're in this together."

He shook his head. "There's no way—"

She lifted up her shirt, revealing the scars across her stomach. "You're not the only one who wants some payback, Alex. I want this world to be safe from Drogan and his curs, too. I'll do whatever it takes."

Alex closed his eyes, afraid of the pain that ran through him at the memory of almost losing her. He opened his eyes and set his hand gently on her cheek again, watching her. "That's exactly what I'm afraid of," he said quietly.

She covered his hand with hers. Warmth ran up his arm from her fingers. "We do this together," she said.

He hesitated, but there was no give in her expression. If he left to go after Drogan and the curs without her, she would never forgive him. Maybe together they would be strong enough to take the werewolf down.

"Okay," he finally let in.

She smiled up at him. "We can do this."

He nodded, but couldn't quite push away the worry that filled him at the thought of the love of his life even in the same proximity as Drogan.

He asked the question that made his chest tighten. "What if I can't protect you?"

Siale's smile faded. Emotions filled the depths of her eyes. "Then you'll know how I feel."

The comment made the corners of Alex's mouth twitch in a small smile. "You're afraid you can't keep me safe?"

Siale nodded. "You've been hurt too many times," she whispered.

He opened his arms and she leaned against his chest. His heart beat strong and steady, reminding him of the werewolf who had saved his life by starting it again.

"We'll stop him together," he whispered.

Siale nodded, her soft hair brushing against his chin. Alex's arms tightened around her and they watched the sun slowly rise above the horizon.

***

They crossed through the television room on their way to help make breakfast. Alex paused at the sight of many of the adult werewolves gathered around the TV.

"Can you believe this?" one werewolf asked, her tone one of disbelief.

"It's horrible," her husband replied. He had an arm around her shoulders and held her close to him.

"Someone needs to stop him," another said.

Alex crossed the room and Siale followed at his side. One werewolf glanced back and saw them. He nudged his neighbor. The adults cleared away to give them room to see the screen.

"Drogan has taken up where his father, The General, left off. Clearly vengeance is his motive as he storms cities with brutal efficiency. Hundreds were injured and at least twenty-five dead in his most recent attack," the reporter said.

The screen changed to a video of Drogan's curs tearing through a shopping center. Humans ran in every direction. Mothers and fathers carried their children, their eyes wide with terror. Even though the audio had been cut out, Alex could imagine the screams of terror.

A cur spotted whoever was taking the video. The beast charged, and the screen froze.

"Due to the video's graphic nature, we are unable to show more of what happened, but the massacre is just one of several. Where will Drogan hit next? Terror fills to nation as our citizens wonder whether it is even safe to go outside. Homeland Security is investigating, but the mutants disappear without a trace. Drogan Carso is at the top of the Most Wanted list. If anyone has word as to his whereabouts, please call this number."

"What do we do?" the female werewolf who had spoken

before asked.

Alex realized she was talking to him. "I've got a plan," he told them.

"We want to help," her husband said.

The adults around them nodded.

"Thank you," Alex said with gratitude. "We can definitely use it."

Chapter Twenty-one

"It almost feels real," Siale said.

"Close enough," Cherish replied, twirling back into Jericho's arms. "I'd take a fake summer dance over night shifts at the hospital any time."

Jericho smiled at her. "Me, too." He winked. "It got me out of working at Mom's shop."

"What? You don't like selling wedding dresses and tuxedos?" Siale teased.

"I do look great in white," Jericho answered.

Alex grinned when he brought Siale back. She smiled up at him. "Too bad it's not real," she said. "Our last dance got interrupted."

Alex had been forcing down feelings of foreboding since they stepped into Greyton High School. He didn't know if it was because of Officer Dune's betrayal at the last dance, or worry about when the curs would show up. Either way, it felt like his instincts were on overload. His gaze kept straying to the doors where Cherish's classmates waited, guarded in the lunchroom by members of the Black Team.

When they had announced the plan to the mayor, it surprised Alex how quickly the man had jumped onboard. Apparently more than just the werewolves were anxious to exact revenge against Drogan.

"My mother was in the hospital the day he took it over," Mayor Hendricks had told him. "Nobody should have to wait in fear wondering if their loved ones are suffering at the hands of a madman."

The mayor and as many of the students as they could safely protect had entered the school dressed in tuxedos and prom dresses, laughing and talking as if they were truly carefree teenagers on their way to an impromptu summer dance. Even the news team had taken up the story, anxious to do their part to bring Drogan to justice.

"It's going to be okay." Alex focused on Siale again. She gave him a soft smile. "We're in this together."

"That's what worries me," he admitted.

She lifted up the edge of where her purple dress top met the elegant black skirt. Jericho's mother had cunningly fashioned a hidden pocket there and the butt of her gun showed.

"I knew I loved you," Alex said with relief.

"You mean it's not for my dancing skills?" she asked.

At that moment, Cassie tripped on Tennison's shoe and fell against Siale. Both girls grabbed onto Alex and he ended up on the ground with them sprawled on top of him.

He and Siale burst out laughing.

"We squash you and you laugh?" Cassie said. "What is wrong with you?"

"That may be the best timing ever," Alex replied, grinning as Tennison and Jericho helped everyone to their feet.

"Are you alright?" Tennison asked Cassie. "I've got to watch my clumsy feet."

She shook her head and gave him a warm smile. "I'm the one with the grace of a rhinoceros."

"I think you're amazing," Tennison told her, leading her away.

Alex held out his hand to Siale, and when she took it, he said, "I definitely love your dancing skills."

Siale laughed and slapped Alex lightly on the shoulder. "Maybe I need to up my combat training. I should have been able to dodge that."

"It's hard to be prepared in such a beautiful environment," Alex replied.

He looked around at the gymnasium. It had been

decorated in purple and black with silver stars hanging from the ceiling and a moon backlit in one corner for the theme of dancing the summer night away. He could almost let himself pretend that it was real and that he finally got the chance to enjoy a real dance with Siale, but instinct kept his muscles tense and gaze wandering.

The news team had done a story on the werewolf and human students renewing their friendships created at the last dance. Alex was grateful Jaze had kept the news of his disappearance secret; it would have put a bad spin on the last gathering. Any positive publicity toward werewolves would help his efforts in their acceptance. If Drogan and the curs could be stopped, perhaps the negative news would end altogether.

"It's the perfect place for a proposal," Siale replied.

Confused by her train of thought given the fact that he had already proposed, Alex followed the direction of her gaze. His heart skipped a beat at the sight of Tennison on one knee in the middle of the dance floor. He was holding the little ring box up to Cassie, and she looked like she didn't know whether to laugh or cry.

"Yes!" she said with a mixture of both emotions. Tears showed in her eyes and she couldn't stop smiling when Tennison picked her up and spun her around in a circle.

Alex and Siale rushed over to them. Cassie was grinning from ear to ear when she showed them her ring.

"Can you believe it?" she asked. "It's absolutely beautiful!"

"I'm so happy for you," Alex told her. He gave her a hug and looked at Tennison who was beaming with happiness. "Good job."

"Did you tell her yet?" the tall werewolf asked.

"Tell me what?" Cassie replied. She looked from Alex to

Siale and her eyes widened. "You, too?"

Alex nodded.

Cassie let out a shriek and hugged Siale. "I'm so glad you're going to be my sister!" She turned a surprised gaze on Alex. "When did you propose?"

Alex grinned. "It was a few days ago. We wanted to keep it a secret so your day would be special." He smiled at Siale. "It was Siale's idea. She didn't want to take away any of your surprise."

"You are so sweet," Cassie told Alex's fiancé. "We're going to make great sisters."

"Yes, we are," Siale agreed, her eyes twinkling. "And we can plan our weddings together."

Cassie gasped. "You're right! We can choose colors and go cake sampling. We can even shop for dresses together! Of course, since Jericho's mom owns the shop, we can find something super special. It's going to be so much fun!" She linked her arm through Siale's. "We should start planning now. There's so much to do!"

The girls wandered away already deep in their plans.

"Look what we've started," Alex said.

Tennison couldn't stop smiling. "Yeah, isn't it wonderful?"

"Congratulations," Trent said, coming over with Jordan. "I'm happy for you as long as I get to help sample cake flavors."

Jordan smiled from his side. "I hope a lot of them are chocolate."

"I hope all of them are chocolate," Trent agreed. "I could live on cake for the rest of my life." He paused, then said, "I'm starting to sound like Brock."

"That's okay," Jordan told him. "I'm pretty good at making cakes."

"Then we'll never starve," Trent said happily.

"I guess that means we'll have to wear more tuxedoes," Tennison said to Alex with a self-suffering sigh and a tug at the collar of his shirt.

"Do you think we could just keep the same ones?" Alex asked hopefully.

Jericho and Cherish reached them. Cherish shook her head at Alex's question. "You'll want something that goes along with their colors. Lavender or light yellow is in right now."

Jericho smiled at Cherish. "I'm sure my mom would love the help finding the girls dresses. Are you up to the challenge?"

"Definitely," Cherish replied. She waved a hand to indicate her green dress. "I may be a tomboy, but at heart, every girl loves to play dress up. Maybe I'll even find my own dress," she said with a wink at Jericho.

His eyes widened. "I thought you said you wouldn't even consider getting married until you got your degree."

She shrugged and grinned at him. "Maybe somebody's changing my mind."

Jericho's face lit up. "This may be the best day of my life."

Cherish linked her fingers through his. "I was going to say the same thing."

Girls shrieked in a corner of the gymnasium. Alex spun, convinced they were under attack from Drogan or his curs. Instead, he spotted Siale and Cassie showing off their rings to the other werewolves who had come with them. Alex was glad Siale didn't have to hide her ring in her little purse anymore. Warmth ran through him at the sight of it on her finger.

Trent set a hand on Alex's tense shoulder. "Hard to

forget why we're here, right?"

"It'd be nice if everyone could just enjoy themselves," Alex replied, glancing around the gymnasium to confirm there weren't curs hiding in the corners. "I'm not sure a tuxedo was the best choice for the evening." He tugged at the collar. "It's hard to breathe."

"Relax," Jericho told him. "You're not taking them on alone. We're all here for a reason."

"Yeah," Tennison said even though the smile wouldn't leave his face. "We're ready for this."

A roar bellowed so deep, guttural, and angry that everyone inside the gymnasium turned to stare at the back doors.

The doors exploded inward, sending splintered wood, twisted metal, and chunks of brick onto the dance floor. The curs stormed inside with a ferocious rage and spread out in a half circle.

Lucian appeared in the doorway. The misshapen cur's steely gaze searched the dance floor. When he saw Alex, his good eye narrowed and his tattered ears flattened against his skull. The creature stalked into the room, his claws gouging chunks out of the gymnasium floor with each step.

Alex took a calming breath. This is what he wanted, he reminded himself. This is what they had prepared for.

"Back away," he said quietly without looking at his friends.

Trent, Jericho, and Tennison fell back from either side. Out of the corner of his eye, he saw Jericho's hands tighten into fists. The Alpha wanted to fight for him. Alex glanced at the older boy and gave a small shake of his head. Jericho nodded, but reluctantly.

Alex turned his full attention to the advancing cur. Lucian was bigger than he remembered. The creature's misshapen body lurched forward with each step instead of the smooth pace of well-fitting bones and muscles. Lucian's knobby head and patchy fur gave the cur the appearance of something not-quite complete. The deep scar along his face that severed his eye looked painful and poorly-healed.

Alex remembered the cur standing above Siale on the Academy steps, his fangs laced with bloody drool and a look of anticipation in his good eye as he lowered his head to end her life. If it wasn't for Siale's strength and her speed with the knife, she would have died. The creature wanted to kill.

Alex changed his mind. As he stared into the cur's face and read the expectation in Lucian's leer, he knew it wasn't want, but need. The cur needed to kill. He needed to maim and destroy. He had been made for that one purpose, and now his purpose was focused on Alex.

The cur's legs bent. His muscles bunched, tight like a tiger's as he locked his deadly gaze on Alex's chest. He leaped into the air.

Alex pulled the syringe of concentrated sliver from behind his belt and slammed it into the cur's chest. The creature's impact barreled them both to the floor and screams filled the air. Alex stared up at the cur. The dose he had given the beast was the most silver they could fit into the small vial and was enough to lay out four Alpha werewolves, but the cur's hide was thick and his kind seemed to have a very high tolerance for pain. Alex didn't know when the silver would kick in.

Lucian lunged for his throat. Alex shoved his arm in the beast's mouth to keep him from reaching his target. The cur ground down and Alex let out a yell of pain.

"Alex!" Siale shouted. Shots sounded and Alex heard the impact of her bullets slamming into the cur's side.

The cur's head jerked up. He glared at Siale and a snarl

tore from his throat. Lucian's good eye narrowed and he looked at those watching them as if he had just remembered they were not alone in their fight. The cur leader gave a deep bark of command.

The curs attacked. Instead of a controlled fight like Alex had expected, the curs appeared riled up. They tore through tables and their claws gouged the floor. The werewolves pulled their weapons from the stacked bleachers and fought back. Windows shattered. The Black Team descended from the roof. The adults from Red's warehouse pulled guns from their clothes. Above them, GPA agents shot curs with silver bullets. A few collapsed, but many continued fighting as though the silver didn't affect them.

Pinned beneath the huge cur, Alex realized his friends would be torn apart before the creatures fell. The silver didn't slow the curs fast enough. They needed help.

Alex channeled his rage. Blue tinted everything as he allowed his body to morph into the Demon. His arms and legs elongated and his muscles thickened. The force of morphing threw Lucian away from him. The cur leader disappeared from Alex's sight. Alex rose to his full height and a roar of anger bellowed from his fanged mouth.

The curs scattered around the room stared at him. Alex looked at the cornered and bleeding werewolves they fought. The carnage looked like the shopping center on the news, only this time, he could hear the screams. His heart slowed when he realized they were coming from the cafeteria where Cherish's classmates hid.

Alex attacked. His first swipe sent two curs flying against the far wall. They hit the bricks and slid to the ground where they lay motionless. Alex slammed his claws into the stomach of another before the creature could finish the werewolf he had pinned down. A cur latched onto his back. Alex spun and drove his elbow into the beast's head. Weakened by the silver bullets, it slumped to the floor.

Two more curs attacked him. Alex barely felt their teeth and claws. He grabbed the one that had its jaws around his shoulder and threw it to the ground. He then grabbed the one on his other side and slammed it into the first. The Black Team closed in and shot them full of silver.

Chapter Twenty-two

"Alex!"

He spotted Siale near the doors. Two curs lay at her feet. Vance and Dray slid new clips into their guns.

"They're trying to get the students," Siale said as soon as he met her gaze. She gestured down the hall.

Alex took off running. His claws gouged deep into the floor, propelling him forward. He ran past her in a blur and reached the doors to the cafeteria in time to see three curs advancing on the students.

Jaze, two members from the Black Team, and Siale's father stood in their way. They shot the curs, but the creatures didn't appear to feel the bullets. Alex remembered diving into the lake. Mouse had said that the curs didn't show any instinct for self-preservation. The way they advanced despite the flood of bullets echoed that statement. They wouldn't stop until the students and werewolves were dead.

Alex let out a snarl of defiance. The curs paused in their tracks and stared back at him. The beasts exchanged glances. Alex bared his fangs and gave another guttural growl. The curs charged.

Alex leaped onto the back of the middle cur. The beast reared up, clawing at him. Alex sunk his claws into its shoulders and jerked backwards. Off-balance, it fell. As soon as Alex's back touched the ground, he kicked with his clawed feet. The cur crashed into the wall and collapsed on the ground.

The other two attacked while he was still on his back. Alex grabbed the throat of the first one and used its head to block the second's attempt to bash in his skull with a table. Alex threw the unconscious cur to the side and leaped to his feet. The cur holding the table threw it through a window.

The glass shattered, revealing the pouring rain outside. Thunder crackled and the wind howled as if to match the threat inside the school.

The cur ran at Alex. He dodged its sweeping claws with a spin Coach Vance would have been proud of and caught it around the neck. Driving a knee into its back, he pinned it to the ground. Jaze ran up and fired four bullets into its skull. At the fourth, the beast finally stopped moving.

"The door," Red called.

Alex glanced that way. Three more curs stalked toward them. His stomach tightened at the sight of Lucian in the middle of them. The cur leader gave a bark of command.

The curs separated, pacing to either side of Alex and Jaze. He turned his head back and forth in an attempt to watch them both. He couldn't let them get to Jaze or the students. A yell sounded in the hallway. He couldn't protect them all. The curs were out of control.

That wasn't true. The realization hit him when Lucian gave another bark and the two curs advanced. They were under their leader's control. They had been created using wolf DNA, and so they followed pack hierarchy. Drogan, as the lead Alpha, hadn't shown his face. If Alex could kill Lucian, the rest of the curs would be leaderless. In the ensuing chaos, they would be easier to pick off.

Glass rained down from above and bullets flew through the air. A glance up showed more members of the GPA clothed in black and peppering the curs with silver. Rain poured through the broken windows. Thunder rumbled, much louder this time. Two seconds later, the lights went out.

Screams of terror filled the cafeteria. Alex's werewolf eyesight made it easy to see the curs, but the students behind him weren't as lucky. They had willingly risked their lives so he could end the curs. Alex wouldn't let them regret their bravery.

He rushed at the cur on his left and swiped, lashing through its eyes with his claws. Before the roar of pain escaped its mouth, Alex was already attacking the second. He leaped and drove both his front and back claws into the cur, barreling it against the wall so hard the bricks cracked. He hit the ground on his back and turned, throwing the cur away from him with such force it slammed into Lucian.

The cur leader silenced the yelping cur with one swipe of his black claws. Alex rose to his feet, his chest heaving and his gaze locked on Lucian.

"There's more of them!" someone shouted in the gymnasium. An answering volley of bullets echoed down the hallway.

"Time to end this," Alex growled, his voice deep and guttural.

He stalked toward the lone cur left in the room. Lucian glared at him, his good eye narrowed and filled with hatred. Alex wanted to make him pay for what he had done to Siale. He saw the steps covered in her blood and the answering leering smile that crossed the cur's face. Siale hadn't deserved pain or fear, and the cur had brought her both.

"You're finished, coward," Alex growled.

To his surprise, Lucian dove out of the nearest window. The glass fell to the lunchroom floor, its sound lost within another crack of thunder.

Alex didn't dare leave the school. They had promised the safety of the students. He could hear more bullets in the gymnasium. The curs would be under control if he could just finish Lucian.

"Go after Lucian!" Jaze shouted over the roar of the storm. "We've got this!"

When Alex glanced at him, the dean gave an encouraging

nod. "Go, Alex. End this."

Alex leaped out the window after Lucian. The cur's dark form disappeared around the end of an alley. As soon as his paws hit the ground, Alex phased into wolf form. Dark fur, much darker than the last time he had phased, ran along his body. His muscles thinned and lengthened. Instinct called for Alex to run and the thrill of the chase pulled at him. He ducked his head against the pouring rain and followed.

Lucian took one alley, then another. Alex pushed himself faster, leaping garbage cans and ducking beneath tattered fences. The cur's twisted wolf and human scent filled his nose despite the storm. Lightning crackled and Alex saw the cur turn at the end of the next alley.

Alex drove forward, pushing all of his strength into the run. He slid around the corner. Something slammed into his side with the force of a semi-truck. Alex hit the wooden fence that lined the other end of the alley so hard he could barely breathe. He pushed up to his paws and saw the wooden stake protruding from his chest.

The cur leader grinned triumphantly from the street corner. He held another broken chair leg in his claws and looked eager to use it.

Alex willed the Demon to come. The blue light filled his senses. He bit back a gasp at the pain as his chest deepened, pulling at the wood sticking out of it. His body couldn't heal with the wood in the wound. He leaned against the fence and grabbed it in both sets of claws. A snarl of pain tore from him when he pulled it free. Blood ran down his torso, mixing with the rain.

A deep chuckle sounded. "Got a little too far from your friends," Drogan said.

Ice ran through Alex's veins. He looked up and saw the Extremist leader standing on a fire escape above them. The hatred that glittered in his half-brother's eyes was enough to let Alex know he had done exactly what the Alpha wanted.

"You're finished, Alex," Drogan said. "You took my bait and you're alone. Haven't you learned anything about being in a pack?" His eyes sparked when he concluded, "Lucian, finish him."

Lucian stalked across the street toward him. Alex pushed away from the fence and stood. He longed for the healing moonlight, but the dark thunderheads shut out all light from above. With the power outage, the only light was the glitter of Lucian's eyes.

Alex's knees bent. He twirled the stake, damp with his blood, and gripped it like a knife. If he was going to die, he would take Lucian with him.

A shot echoed through the alley. Above him, Alex saw Drogan jerk back and grab his shoulder.

"You're the one's who's finished," Siale shouted from the corner of the alley. She fired her gun again. Drogan let out a growl of pain and grabbed the ladder of the fire escape.

Lucian lunged at Alex. He dove to the side at the last second and drove the stake into the cur's back. A yowl of pain sounded and Lucian spun. Alex swiped at the beast's good eye, but Lucian's claws knocked him back. The creature caught him by the throat and pinned him against the fence. Alex struggled to pull Lucian's claws free. He fought to draw in a breath and glanced behind the cur.

At the sight, a smile crossed his face.

Lucian's eyes narrowed. He opened his mouth and a guttural growl sounded as he bent his head to rip out Alex's throat. His fangs glittered in the dim light an instant before Siale's knife shoved through the back of his head.

The growl died away to a sputter. Lucian's claws opened and Alex fell to the ground. The cur stumbled backwards, turned, and collapsed at Siale's feet.

Alex pulled in a breath through his bruised throat as he stared from Lucian's still body to Siale.

"I owed him," she said.

Alex searched the fire escape and rooftops for any sign of Drogan. "He's gone," he said, his voice low.

Siale nodded. "Let's get back to the school. They might still need us."

Alex sunk his claws into Lucian's shoulder and pulled the cur with them. His ribs ached and he pressed a clawed hand to the hole where the stake had gone in. Luckily, even though the moon was hidden, his body was already healing thanks to the fact that the object had been wood instead of silver.

The sound of bullets had lessened, though a few shots were still being fired from the direction of the gymnasium. With Siale at his side and Lucian's body in his claws, Alex kicked open the closest door.

The rain stormed in around them. The humans and werewolves closest to the doors stumbled back and the few curs who were still alive stared. Alex threw Lucian's body to the ground.

"It's over," he growled.

The curs had lost their Alpha. Their drive and reason to attack the students in the school vanished with him. Their will to fight fled. The beasts closest to Alex sunk to the ground as the silver finally took over their systems. Blood covered the dance floor where less than an hour ago werewolves and humans had danced and Cassie had gotten engaged to Tennison. The two images merged in Alex's mind, creating a confusing scene of smiling students, silver stars, and dance music upon the carcass-strewn, broken gymnasium floor.

"We're done," Siale said gently. She set a hand on Alex's

arm. "Come on."

He was grateful when she led him back into the night. The rain had lessened to a soft patter that brought with it the asphalt and mineral scent of the clean city. Alex allowed the Demon to fade, and he accepted the tattered pants Siale found beneath the window where he had phased into wolf form.

"Those pants are definitely going to take all of Jericho's mother's skills to piece back together," she said.

A tired smile touched Alex's lips. "Should we just burn them and tell her our dog ate them?"

Siale smiled back. She looked so beautiful with rain dripping down her cheeks and her gray eyes sparkling.

"If by dog, you mean a werewolf mutant intent on destroying all humans and werewolves."

"I do," Alex replied.

Her answering laugh was filled with relief. They had survived, the students had survived, and the curs were dead.

"We didn't catch Drogan." The Alpha's disappearance hung heavily in Alex's mind.

"The bullets should slow him down," Siale replied. "If we're lucky, the two slugs of liquid silver might kill him."

"He's tougher than that," Alex told her. He watched the dark alley behind them, expecting the Extremist to appear at any moment.

"At least he won't be a threat for a while," Siale said reassuringly. "Let's head inside. There's a lot of cleanup to do."

Despite Jaze's urging that he sit and rest, Alex helped haul the bodies of the slain curs from Greyton High School. Siale, Gem, Nikki, Meredith, and others from Red's warehouse cleaned up the gymnasium and cafeteria.

Alex found Nikki in one corner trying not to throw up as

she scrubbed a patch of blood from the floor.

"You really don't have to do that," he told her.

"They need the help," she replied. She gave him a motherly smile. "You're the one who should be resting. Did you have your mom look at that?"

Alex glanced down at his chest where the blood had leaked through the shirt Cherish had found for him. It was dark and crusty.

"I'm pretty sure there's not much she can do. It was just wood," Alex told her.

Nikki gave a little, wry laugh. "Most people who get stabbed in the chest wouldn't be so nonchalant about it."

Alex grinned. "I guess that's what happens when you've been stabbed enough you're just grateful it's not silver."

"Just the same," Nikki said. "Promise me you'll have Meredith check it. If there are splinters, it won't heal well."

"I will," Alex promised, touched by her concern.

She bent down to clean more of the blood, then quickly grabbed her nose and mouth.

"Seriously, Nikki. You shouldn't be doing this in your condition. Gem, either. We can take care of it."

Nikki's eyes widened. "You know?"

Alex nodded with a warm smile. "I overheard the others talking when we went shopping for rings. My new little cousin doesn't seem to like the smell of that stuff." He wrinkled his nose at the odor that wafted from the thick mess. "Me neither. Let me take care of it." He took the stack of paper towels from her without waiting for her to reply.

"Alex, you don't have to do that," she protested.

He nodded. "It's the least I can do." He gave her a straight look. "You were the best mother to me and Cassie two orphans could have asked for. Even with Mom here now, I'll never forget that. Let me be an appreciative son and

221

give you a break."

Nikki caught him up in a hug. When she let him go, she was unsuccessfully blinking back tears.

His chest tightened. "Did I say something wrong?"

She shook her head quickly. "Pregnancy comes with a heightened sense of smell as well as an exciting array of sporadic emotions. I never know when they're going to hit." She wiped her eyes and gave him a watery smile. "I'm just proud of you, Alex. You're an amazing person."

"Thank you," he replied, giving her another hug.

Chapter Twenty-three

After everything was cleaned up, Meredith, along with Cherish's mother, Mrs. Summers, came back with enough sandwiches and sodas for all who had helped.

"Thanks for giving us the chance to do this," Alex told Officer Dune as they waited outside near the doors of the school.

The officer nodded. "It doesn't make up for what I did, but I'm happy I could help." He indicated the officers talking with parents near the cars. "I'll go make sure everyone's alright."

Most of the students besides Cherish's little group had left. Though there were a few who had been tended to by Meredith and Nyra's ministrations, the rest went home only a bit shaken and more excited about their part in the night.

"Did you see their teeth?" Alex heard one student in a blood-spattered tuxedo exclaim as they walked out the front doors. "I swear they were as long as my arm!"

"I'm pretty sure you call those fangs," the girl at his side answered, "And you can ask Jesse about how long they are. He got bit by them."

"Did you see Gentry?" another girl asked. She held up the hem of her dress; it had dark red stains along the bottom. "She screamed so loud I think she scared one of them!"

"I was screaming, too," a boy with dyed green hair admitted. "That was scary."

The girl holding his arm nodded in emphatic agreement. "Let's hope we don't have to do that again," she said, glancing at the tarped pile of bodies that were being loaded into the back of a black, unmarked moving truck.

"The werewolves said we got them all. How cool is that?" Josh, Cherish's friend, told Jen.

She worried a strand of her bright red hair around her finger nervously. "It's cool as long as they stay dead."

"They're not going to come alive again," Tanner, Sarah's boyfriend said. He gave Alex a worried look. "Are they?"

Alex shook his head. "They're dead. All of them." He smiled. "We couldn't have done it without you guys. Thank you."

"Thank you," Principal Dalton replied from where he and Mayor Hendricks waited by the row of cars that left with the students. "You gave us the opportunity to fight back."

Alex walked over and shook both of their hands. "You gave us the same thing," he told the men. "I don't know how else we could have pulled it off. Thanks to the bravery of your students and staff, a threat to the nation was stopped today."

"Anything we can do to help defeat Drogan, you let us know," the mayor replied.

"I doubt he'll fall for something like this again, but we've taken away his army. Drogan's alone." For some reason, the thought didn't reassure Alex the way it seemed to with the others.

"Let him rot," Josh said as he opened the car door for Jen and helped her inside.

Tanner did the same for Sarah.

Before taking her seat, Sarah gave Alex a quick hug. "Thanks again, Alex," she said. She kissed him on the cheek. "You were great."

Alex smiled as Tanner shut the door. The human turned to Alex.

"Thanks again, man. Come play soccer with us sometime," Tanner told him.

"I will," Alex promised. He watched them go.

"You're welcome here, you know," Principal Dalton said.

At Alex's questioning look, the mayor nodded in agreement. "We've been working on the legislation. If we can get the government to recognize werewolves as citizens, it won't be a problem."

"Are you serious?" Alex asked in shock. "You would let werewolves come to this school?"

Principal Dalton opened his hand to indicate the building behind them. "You've already been at the school. There would just be classes involved instead of only dancing."

"Do you think the students would accept us?" The thought of attending the school as an actual part of the student body sent a thrum of excitement through Alex.

"I do," the principal replied. "There will be some controversy at first for sure, but people will get used to the idea."

Mayor Hendricks set a hand on Alex's shoulder. "Give us time, Alex. We can remove prejudice if we can erase fear, and I think you've taken many steps towards doing just that." The mayor nodded behind Alex.

He turned to see a reporter talking in front of a news camera. A smile crossed his face when he recognized Cooper Peterson, the reporter who had been captive in the hospital with him when Drogan held everyone hostage, and the same man who had made the first national plea for werewolves to be given the chance to live as equals among humans.

"As you can see," Cooper was saying. "They are loading the bodies of the slain mutants while I speak. Chief Harrington confirmed just moments ago that all of the mutants have been killed. Thanks to the efforts of Jaze Carso and his werewolf task force working in conjunction with Greyton City and our brave men and women of the police department, as well as," he looked over his shoulder to confirm that the agents of the GPA were still there,

"Members of several other unidentified departments that I assume to be government related, Greyton High School will be cleared of the remnants of this battle and life will continue much safer than before."

Cooper's gaze locked on Alex. His smile deepened and he motioned to the werewolf.

"Excuse me, please," Alex told the mayor and principal.

He walked to Cooper's side. "I can't believe our luck," Cooper said into the camera. "Here is Alex Davies, the werewolf we have been told helped to instigate the anti-mutant attack. Alex has become a familiar face in the efforts to improve werewolf-human relations. I'm not surprised to find Mr. Davies at the forefront of the efforts to relieve the nation of the threat brought about by Drogan Carso. Alex, do you have anything to say?"

Alex let out a slow breath to center himself and smiled. "It's good to see you again, Cooper."

"Same to you," the reporter replied with true gratitude. "Things are improving."

"Very much so," Alex said. He motioned behind him to where the back doors of the truck were being closed. "The curs, I mean mutants," he corrected himself, "are gone. Families can breathe easier knowing that they don't have to be afraid to shop or spend time outside their homes. I am so grateful to have been involved in this confrontation. The citizens of Greyton have again shown amazing bravery, and their willingness to accommodate our needs in this attack has allowed us to destroy the threat entirely." He thought of Drogan. The Extremist had escaped yet again. The threat wasn't quite over.

Alex faced the camera. If Drogan was watching, he wanted to leave a message that would hit home hard. "Drogan, you're finished. If you're smart, you'll go hide in a corner somewhere and leave werewolves and humans to live in peace. The world is changing. Peace is attainable, and the families of this nation deserve to live unafraid no matter what their race." He swallowed and took a risk. "Brother, let it go. Please. I'm begging you to let peace have a chance. Stop hurting the innocent. Nobody should have to live in fear, and you have the choice. Just let it go. Please." He turned back to Cooper. "I'd better get back and help with the cleanup. Thank you for what you do. I appreciate it."

"We're happy to do our part," the reporter replied, shaking Alex's hand. "Thank you for your time."

Alex saw Siale out of the corner of his eye. A smile spread across his face. "Can I introduce you to someone?"

"Anyone," Cooper replied with a hint of surprise.

"Siale?" Alex called.

She came over with a questioning look at the camera. Alex introduced her to Cooper. "Cooper Peterson, this is Siale Andrews, my fiancé."

Cooper's answering smile was huge when he shook Siale's hand. "I am so glad to meet you. I didn't know Alex was engaged. Are you a werewolf, too?"

Siale looked at Alex. He left it up to her to choose what she wanted to say.

She nodded and gave the camera a warm smile. "I am a werewolf, and I'm so happy. Alex proposed to me at sunset on the beach a few weeks back, and I couldn't be happier. He's a romantic at heart."

Cooper chuckled and spoke into the microphone. "I apologize to all of you ladies who had your hearts set on our dashing Alex, but he's been taken by this beautiful young woman. I wish them all the happiness in the world, and," he turned back to Alex and Siale, "Maybe I can get an invitation to the wedding?"

He left the question hanging. Alex made a split-second decision. "Who knows," he replied. "Maybe everyone will."

"What do you mean?" Cooper asked.

Alex looked at Siale. "What do you think about having a public wedding?"

Siale looked a bit taken back, but she nodded. "I think that would be wonderful."

"There you have it," Cooper said. The fact that he had the biggest story in the nation in regards to both the mutant elimination and Alex's wedding was evident by his grin.

When the camera turned off, Cooper gave Alex an apologetic smile. "Sorry for putting you on the spot there. That was amazing!"

Alex looked at Siale. "Are you sure that's okay? I should have talked to you first."

Siale shook her head. "Everyone knows you. If our wedding will help people feel better about werewolves, then I think we really should."

Alex kissed her. "You are amazing."

She smiled up at him. "That's why I'm marrying you."

Alex chuckled. He glanced up and realized Cooper was still standing there. "Uh, sorry. Sometimes we get a bit carried away."

"That's alright," Cooper replied. "That's how it's supposed to be when you're young and in love." He smiled at Siale. "Ever since we first aired what happened in the hospital, we've gotten more letters about Alex than any other single event. Having a young person who has been so brave acting as the forefront of the werewolf movement has been a wonderful thing. Everyone loves a wedding. I can guarantee that letting the nation watch is going to do wonders for easing prejudices."

"I'm happy it'll help," Siale said.

Alex could see the effect she had on the reporter. Siale's soft smile and sincere gray eyes could win anyone over.

"It's great to meet you, Siale," Cooper was telling her. "I look forward to spending more time with you both as the wedding draws near."

"Thank you very much," she replied. She met Alex's gaze. "I'm going to go see if your mother or Nyra needs help with the food." She gave a little wave to Cooper and the cameraman. "It's nice meeting you."

"How'd you pull off that one?" Cooper asked as they watched Siale enter the school.

"Flat out luck," Alex replied.

That brought a chuckle from Cooper. "I need some more luck," he said.

When Alex reached the mayor and Principal Dalton again, he found Jaze talking to both men.

"Your student has become quite the public speaker," Mayor Hendricks noted with an approving nod at Alex.

"He's taught me a thing or two, that's for sure," Jaze replied. He gave Alex a searching look. "Did you really just invite the entire nation to your wedding?"

Alex fought back a surge of embarrassment. "That may have been rash."

"I think it was brilliant," Mayor Hendricks said. "In fact, let us host your wedding here." He paused, then quickly told Alex, "If, of course, you'd like that. I don't want to rush you into things or make decisions for you, just know that Greyton City is more than happy to open its doors for such an event." He winked. "It's been nice to give Greyton the chance for positive media. We're rising as a recommended place to live. Being the city responsible for taking down Drogan's mutant army will definitely help."

"You don't think the fact that it was a target will make

people more wary to come here?" Principal Dalton asked.

"I don't think so," the mayor replied. They wandered away discussing the prospects.

"You do whatever you'd like," Jaze told Alex quietly. The dean's gave Alex's shoulder a fatherly squeeze. "If you want to get married in front of four people or thousands, you let me know." He paused, then said, "I say four because your mother, Nikki, Red, and I insist on being there. Of course, then there is Cassie and Tennison, and Trent and Jordan, and well, maybe a few more than four."

Alex laughed. "Of course. I couldn't imagine it any other way."

"Jaze, guess what!"

Both werewolves turned expectantly at the sound of Brock's voice. The human with the spikey brown hair who was the head of security at the Academy grinned. "They actually know what Jarlsberg cheese is, and they put it on a sandwich! It's the best thing ever!"

"I thought you were supposed to be running DNA checks on the curs," Jaze said, giving his friend a quizzical look.

Brock waved his sandwich and a piece of tomato fell onto the sidewalk. "Mouse and I already did that. There are nineteen vials in the SUV waiting to go home with us." The skinny human shrugged. "Can't do more than that, so I thought I'd grab a bite to eat before I waste away."

"I don't think that's possible," Jaze said.

Brock nodded. He glanced over Jaze's shoulder and his eyes widened. Alex and Jaze turned.

"See, Ashley, Jarlsberg is the perfect cheese to pair with honey baked ham and spicy mustard," a woman with curly blonde hair was telling Mrs. Summers.

Alex recognized Jennifer Stauffer as Cherish's mother's

best friend from high school. Since Jaze reunited them, the werewolf had moved to Greyton to be closer to her friend. They both worked together at the diner where Mrs. Summers supported her and Cherish.

"Maybe we should suggest it to Bernard," Mrs. Summers replied. "He's always looking for new recipes to spice things up."

"Who. Is. That?" Brock asked. He gulped down the bite of sandwich in his mouth and wiped his face on his sleeve. "I need to meet her."

"Go ahead," Jaze told him. "That's Jennifer. You helped us find her, remember? Her name used to be Jacey."

"What do I say?" Brock looked truly afraid at the thought of talking to her.

"Say hello," Jaze replied encouragingly. "You've spoken to girls before."

Brock gave him a straight look. "Jaze, since we met in high school, have you ever seen me speak to a girl willingly?"

The dean thought about it for a moment. "I guess not," he admitted.

Brock nodded. "Exactly."

Alex made his way over to the table. He could still hear the pair arguing.

"It's not that hard," Jaze encouraged. "She's not going to bite."

"Didn't you say she was a werewolf?" Brock shot back.

"Jennifer?"

She turned at the sound of Alex's voice. "Alex!" she exclaimed. She gave him a hug. "It's so good to see you again! It's amazing what you've helped accomplish here."

"Thanks," Alex replied. He looked back at where Brock was now waving his arms and the sandwich and arguing adamantly with Jaze. "Uh, could you do me a favor?"

"Anything," she said with a warm smile.

Alex didn't know how to start, so he rushed in. "One of Jaze's pack mates thinks you're beautiful and would like to come talk to you, but he doesn't know what to say. Could I introduce you?"

She followed Alex's gaze. "Do you mean the one talking with Jaze Carso?" At his nod, she studied Brock. "Well, he is cute, and he's eating the same sandwich I am. Maybe he has good taste."

Alex grinned. "That's actually what caught his eye. He said something about yars or yards..."

"Jarlsberg?" she finished.

Alex nodded. "Yes, thank you. Brock is sort of a..." He thought of a polite way to say it. "A food fan."

"Me, too!" she said with interest. "Except they call it food connoisseurs. I wonder what he thinks about the mustard."

"You should go ask," Mrs. Summers said encouragingly.

Jennifer gave a sharp nod. "I think I will." She took her sandwich and walked over to the pair.

"And I don't think cheese is a good basis for—"

"For what?" Jennifer asked.

Brock turned and his eyes widened. "Uh, for...for...for beginning a relationship."

"I agree," she replied.

Brock's face fell.

"Unless it's a good Jarlsberg," Jennifer continued. "How is it?"

Brock stared at her. He seemed to realize she had asked him a question because his head jerked down and he looked at his sandwich. "Divine, actually."

"That's the word I was going to use," Jennifer said with a satisfactory nod. "It has an amazing nutty flavor and melts on the tongue."

"Not too soft," Brock said.

"With just the right amount of holes," Jennifer concluded.

Both of them laughed.

"I'm going to excuse myself," Jaze said. The expression on his face said he didn't know what had just happened, but he wasn't going to press his luck. He snuck away without them even appearing to notice. "What did you do?" the dean asked when he reached Alex and Mrs. Summers.

Alex shrugged. "I mentioned cheese. Apparently that was the selling point."

Mrs. Summers gave Alex a grateful smile. "I'm happy for her. She's needed someone, and she's a bit shy."

"So is he," Jaze told her. "I can never get him to actually leave the Academy and socialize. Who knew his love of food would actually lead to a woman?"

"We'll cross our fingers," Mrs. Summers replied.

A familiar hand touched Alex's shoulder. He took a deep breath of the sage and lavender scent that washed over him.

"Ready to go home?" Siale asked.

He turned and wrapped his arms around her. "Home is wherever you are."

She smiled up at him. "I like it when you're cheesy."

Mrs. Summers, Jaze, and Alex burst out laughing.

"What did I say?" Siale asked.

Alex shook his head. "Just the perfect thing. Let's go, love."

She smiled and took his hand.

Chapter Twenty-four

Alex leaned his head back against the headrest. The curs were gone, the nation was safe, at least from Drogan's most recent threat, and they were on their way back to Red's warehouse that had begun to feel like his home away from the Academy. Alex's chest gave a slight throb, reminding him that rest helped the healing process. He closed his eyes and willed the smooth ride of the jet to lull him to sleep.

He was almost there when Cassie shouted, "He what?"

Alex's eyes flew open. He knew what was coming. Dread tightened in his stomach. He heard the storm of his sister's footsteps coming up the alley between the seats. In that moment, he wished could be back at Greyton High School fighting curs.

"Alex Davies, did you just tell that reporter that we would get married on national television?"

Alex took a steeling breath and glanced at her. His sister's dark blue eyes, the exact same color Jet's had been, were filled with anger, horror, and tears.

Alex hated to see any girl cry. The fact that he was responsible for such an expression from his twin sister tore at him. He swallowed and went with, "To be fair, I only told Cooper about Siale and me."

"But Alex," Cassie said, her voice tight as if she barely kept back sobs. "The four of us are supposed to get married together. It was going to be special!"

The magnitude of what he had promised struck Alex hard. It may have been the worst thing he had ever done to his sister. He turned to face her completely and set a hand on her arm. "I'm sorry. I messed up." He let out a slow breath. "I forgot how much you don't like crowds."

"You just set our wedding in front of the biggest crowd

possible," Cassie replied, her tone revealing how hurt she was.

Alex glanced toward the back of the jet. Siale gave him an apologetic look. He couldn't blame her. He was the one who had spoken to Cooper without clearing the idea with both the girls and Tennison. He had messed up his sister's wedding, and he didn't know how to fix it.

"Cass, I really didn't mean for it to happen this way. Cooper was asking me about Siale and the wedding came up." He sighed and shook his head. "I wasn't even thinking about crowds or cameras or anything."

"What were you thinking about?" She didn't ask it accusingly. Her voice was quieter and her expression searching as if she was trying to understand despite her own hurt.

Alex loved her for that. "I was thinking about Drogan," he said honestly. She shook her head as though disappointed, but Alex kept speaking, "I was thinking about the fact that he has tried everything possible within his means to destroy all of the happiness in our lives. He killed our parents, he's hounded our every step, and he has hurt those we care about." Alex's eyes burned. He blinked quickly. "He almost killed Siale. Kalia's dead because of him and the General, and everyone's had to live in fear because of the monster he's become."

A pop sounded. Alex realized he was gripping the arm of the chair separating them so hard that it cracked. He swallowed and let go. "Cassie, I didn't expect to live this long." The admission took a lot from him. "When Jet saved us from Drogan, I told myself I would live for you, and for the memory of Mom and Dad. When you and Tennison hit it off and I found Siale, I started to dream about a real life. Then the General killed Kalia."

He shook his head. "I lost something that day. Call it my sanity, my hope, my dreams, but it was really my belief that we could live a normal life away from fear and pain. Drogan has seen to that." Alex gritted his teeth. "I have fought and fought, but I can't keep everyone I care about safe." He motioned with a hand at the city they had left behind. "But killing the curs changed that. Drogan may be a threat, but I don't have to be afraid. You're strong and you have Tennison. I saw Siale kill the beast that almost took her life, and I watched humans and werewolves working together to make this world a safer place to live in."

He sat up, willing her to understand. "Cassie, if we're going to live a normal life, we need this peace. We need humans not to be afraid of us. The professors should be able to live in homes of their own, not in a school trying to shelter werewolf students from the dangers of the world. Living in fear brought the fear to us, and I'm done with being afraid."

"So the wedding..." Cassie let the words hang.

Alex nodded. "The wedding was my way of welcoming the nation into my life. They made me their werewolf poster child, even with the Demon, so I wanted to turn that back at them. I want to show them that werewolves can love and dream, that we can hope and live with the belief that tomorrow is a better day. I invited them to the wedding because marrying Siale is something I never would have dreamed possible, and now it is. I have been given a gift, and I want to share it with the world in the hopes that it will make a difference. Mom and Dad taught us that love is real, and I want to show the nation that love can really be enough."

Cassie was quiet for a few minutes. Alex watched her, unsure what she would say.

"Do you really think it'll help?"

Surprised at her question, Alex replied, "You mean with

humans and werewolves?" When she nodded, he answered honestly, "Jaze tried to get humans to accept werewolves, and it backfired because humans and werewolves were both coming from a place of fear. The werewolves had to reveal themselves in order to survive, and the humans were afraid of how strong the werewolves could be. If I can show the nation that werewolves are just like them, that we can fall in love and work to build a life together, maybe, just maybe, they'll let it happen. If the generations who fought Jaze's werewolves realized that we're just kids who deserve a chance at life, perhaps they'll see us differently."

"Our wedding can do all that?" Cassie asked skeptically.

Alex lifted his shoulders in a small shrug. "Honestly, I'm not sure. You know me. I'm kind of the jump first and ask questions later type."

"Kind of?" Cassie repeated with the ghost of a smile. "I think you invented it."

Alex smiled back. "Exactly. Jump with me, Cass. Throw fear, caution, and prejudice away. We've learned to be just as afraid of them as they are of us, but in truth, we're all the same. We all want to live our lives in peace. Perhaps showing them werewolves trying to do just that will help all of us realize that there isn't so much to be afraid of."

Cassie's forehead furrowed. "It could be dangerous."

"Yeah," Alex agreed. "We could get shot on the spot." The wound in his chest gave a small throb and he rubbed it. "I'm a bit tired of scars, but I can take a few more."

"I'm not so sure about that."

Alex smiled at his sister. "At this point, if they weren't holding me together, I'd fall completely apart. It the scars that remind me of where I've been and why I'm so crazy sometimes."

The look Cassie gave him said she knew exactly what he

was talking about. "The deeper scars are the ones that don't show."

Alex nodded. He took a chance. "Cassie, will you get married with me."

A little laugh escaped her as if she couldn't help it. "Are you proposing to your sister?"

Alex laughed in return. "Yeah. That does sound completely wrong."

She gave him a true smile. "I will get married with you, Alex. I've watched you sacrifice so much to try and make this peace happen. I can be courageous and have my wedding with the whole world watching, because I'm marrying the werewolf of my dreams. If sharing that can lead to even the slightest possibility that we might be able to raise our family in peace someday, it's completely worth being a little brave."

Alex gave her a hug. "You've made me the happiest brother in the whole world."

She laughed and pushed him away. "Now you're just being weird."

He grinned. "That's what I do." He paused, then said, "Thank you, Cassie. It means more to me than you know."

"I'm happy to do my part," she replied.

When Cassie walked to the back of the jet, Siale came up and took her seat.

"I should have asked you instead of putting you on the spot like that," Alex told her.

Siale shook her head. "We both want the same thing. As long as I get to marry you, we can do it in an abandoned warehouse or in front of the world. It doesn't matter to me."

"I wouldn't have to wear a tuxedo in an abandoned warehouse," Alex said musingly.

"That's true," Siale agreed. "We could get married in camo gear and face paint."

"You know just how to win your fiancé's heart," Alex replied with a chuckle.

A yawn escaped her. "Are you as exhausted as I am?"

"Definitely," Alex answered. "Want me to be your pillow?"

She gave him her special, sweet smile. "Only if you'll be my pillow forever."

"Deal," he agreed.

Siale leaned her head on his shoulder and he rested his head on top of hers. His last thought was of how lucky he was that he had such an amazing sister and fiancé. He had messed things up, but both of them were so understanding toward what he was trying to accomplish, and they made it work. With them in his life, he felt truly unstoppable.

Chapter Twenty-five

"Just forget about everything else," Brooks told Alex as they rode the waves. "Nothing exists but you and the ocean."

"It's a perfectly symbiotic relationship between two parts hydrogen, one part oxygen, and a werewolf who wants to fly across the surface of the world." Jerry trailed his fingers through the water. "Be free, brother wolf. Channel your ancestors of the forest. They didn't own the trees, they were a part of them. The wolf didn't exist without the trees, and the trees without the wolf. Together, they made the forest. Become a wave rider, Alex of the wolven way. Become one with the ocean."

"Thanks, Preacher," Alex told him. "I'll try."

"To try is the first step toward achieving," Jerry replied with a vacant smile and his eyes on the endless stretch of water in front of them. "Try, believe, and succeed. You will fly."

Alex nodded. He watched the waves, counting the ebb and flow the way Brooks had taught him. The pattern became evident. Two small waves led to a bigger one; two more after that led to the biggest. He pushed everything away, thoughts of the wedding, of the summer drawing to a close, of returning to the Academy. He watched the way Siale and the others rode the waves as if they truly were a part of them. Even Cassie and Tennison had gotten good at staying on their boards for a few seconds.

Though Alex had ridden waves many times during their summer break at Red's, he felt as though he wasn't quite able to capture the feeling of the first time. With their departure in a few hours, he was running out of time. He didn't know if he could go back with something like that gnawing at him. The waves beckoned and teased, pulling at his legs and feet, urging him to join in the fun his friends were having.

"This is it," Alex whispered.

He counted the waves. Two little ones, one big one.

Mohawk and Reko took the wave and rode for a few seconds before Reko fell and Mohawk clipped his board, tumbling down as well.

One little one. Alex began to paddle. The next small wave pushed him forward toward the shore. He could feel the swell as the wave pulled behind him, drawing the water beneath his board in a swirling eddy. He paddled harder, keeping his board in front of the wave. Out of the corner of his eye, he could see it building. The water crested, white spray foaming at the top.

Alex felt the moment. He pushed up on his board and balanced on the balls of his feet. He bent his knees and let his body sway the way his combat training had drilled into his muscle memory. He wasn't going to fall off the board, not this time.

The wave rose bigger than any of the others he had seen that morning. It towered above him, driving him forward. Alex rocked back slightly on his board, repositioning his weight to give the wave more force. It propelled him forward.

The water curled above him in a perfect circle, rushing up one side and falling down the other. The wind pushed at his hair that had begun to grow out again. The spray from the wave splashed across his scarred chest, the newest wound healed and another symbol of his survival. A normal person wouldn't have made it through such things, but he wasn't normal.

The thought brought a smile to Alex's lips. He bent his knees just a bit more. The roar of the wave filled his ears, all-encompassing and demanding to be heard. The rush of the water, the wind, and the shadows of the wave he rode took away all thought except for one, just to be.

Alex reached out a hand and let it trail in the water at his side. The spray hit his face with the salty sting of the ocean he had come to love with all of his heart. In that moment, he was one with that love, that power, and that peace. He was the ocean. He flew across the surface of the world.

The wave crashed on top of him, driving him down. His board tugged at his ankle as he tried to figure out which way was up. His lungs burned, telling him he hadn't taken in a big enough breath when he went down. He kicked hard and attempted to follow the pull of the board.

Alex's head broke the surface of the water and he took in a huge gulp of air. The cry of an impassive seagull met his ears as the animal flew so high above it looked like a mere speck in the rising sunlight. He pulled his board close and climbed on top.

"Alex, are you okay?" Siale asked anxiously.

Alex turned to see her and Brooks padding up.

He gave them both a big smile. "That was amazing."

Brooks nodded with an answering smile. "You got it."

Alex ran a hand down his face to wipe the water away. "I finally did," he said. "All the practice paid off."

"People can stay out here for a lifetime and not ride a wave like that," Brooks said. His beaded hair clacked together when he turned his head to look at the others. "They'll be talking about that one for a long time. The wave was yours."

Alex nodded. Before he had attempted to surf at the beginning of the summer, such a statement would have sounded crazy to him. The ocean was so vast and impersonal, a giant expanse of water without the ability to care or think or act. It was merely the ocean.

But now, after living for months on its surface, Alex knew better. To him, the ocean had changed from expressionless to having such a variety of emotions and moods that one never knew what to expect, and the moment you thought you did, the ocean would remind you that you were wrong. He had grown to love the fickle beauty of the surface that could be glassy smooth at one moment and the next be filled with waves so high and dangerous that even the most experienced of the surfers wouldn't go out. The ocean didn't care about plans or schedules; instead, it reminded Alex of his own smallness and the fact that there were some things he just couldn't control.

At the very bottom of it all, in that one moment riding the perfect wave, his wave, Alex had found something. He had realized that all the planning in the world, all the training, all the effort put into timing, couldn't account for the beauty of a single wave, a board beneath his feet, and the feeling of the water running through his fingers.

He had found that life, in all its vast significance, was a compilation of moments of living, not fighting to survive, not planning for tomorrow, but of living in the same moment in which he breathed, of grasping the moment when it came, and of allowing himself to accept that he was a part of something beautiful instead of just watching from the sidelines. He didn't own the ocean, but for that moment, he had been one with the wave. The wave had truly been his.

"Should we head in?" Siale asked.

It was easy to lose track of time on the ocean. Trent was probably already waiting for them at the little airport.

"Let's go," Alex replied.

"You guys take care," Brooks said. "We'll be looking forward to surfing with you again!"

"Next summer," Siale promised.

The human nodded. "We'll be waiting."

Chapter Twenty-six

Students began to arrive shortly after Alex and the others landed at the Academy.

"I'm so excited that this is our last year!" Cassie exclaimed.

"Are you tired of it here?" Tennison asked her.

She shook her head quickly, her curly brown hair swishing around her shoulders. "Not at all, but because it's our final term, Professor Colleen told me that we get to be teacher aids. We can help teach the other students!"

"That's only if you learned anything worth teaching," Terith said, catching up to them.

"Any chance we can teach the new kids how to build internal-combustion engines?" Trent asked his sister.

"I don't think it counts if you taught it to yourself," she replied. "They didn't exactly teach that in our classes."

"Maybe they should," Alex said. "It would be nice to focus on more practical stuff to prepare the students for the world and help them get jobs."

"I've heard some of the human high schools have shop classes," Siale pointed out.

Trent grinned. "That's perfect!"

"What's perfect?" Jordan asked, meeting them in the hallway.

"You," Trent told her. He kissed her on the nose.

The sight of the ring on Jordan's finger made Alex smile.

"No public displays of affection," Terith told her brother.

"You're just upset Von's helping Professor Mouse set up the biology classroom," Trent shot back.

"I could help," she replied. "But they have a snake in there." She gave a visible shudder. "Disgusting."

"Maybe you'll be the biology assistant and your job will

be to feed it," Trent suggested.

Terith paled at the thought. "I'd rather free the mice. They could go to the forest. I'm sure they'd be happy there."

"Everyone should have the chance to live where they're meant to," Alex said. He looked up and realized everyone was looking at him. "I guess I said that aloud."

"You did." Siale slipped her arm through his. "You seem like you have a lot on your mind."

Alex forced a smile. "Just thinking about the Choosing Ceremony."

Jericho spotted them from the doorway to the Great Hall. The tall, brown-haired Alpha smiled. "Good to see you guys again. Did you have a good summer?"

"It was amazing," Cassie told him. "We spent it surfing." She exchanged a smile with Tennison. "For the most part."

Tennison gave Alex a knowing look. "Yeah, for the most part."

Alex smiled. "It was pretty relaxing."

Jericho chuckled. "So now pretty relaxing means killing a horde of murderous mutants and announcing the wedding of the decade? My mom hasn't stopped asking me when you guys are coming to the shop. I think she's already set aside fifty dresses for you girls."

"Oh, good!" Cassie exclaimed. "Mom's going to take us next weekend. Siale, are you thinking the empire, an A-line, or something more like a ball gown? I've been thinking about getting gloves. Something lacey or silk would go just wonderfully with a sweetheart neckline and a mermaid cut, although I'm definitely in love with a few of the newer chiffon styles."

Alex stared at his sister. She had grown up mostly as a tom-boy because of their situation. Learning how to fight and take care of herself had turned her into a tough, albeit shy, sister. Watching her delve into the world of fashion and wedding planning was revealing a whole new side he had never experienced before.

"What?" she asked, catching his look. "Mom got a bunch of magazines. I've gone through every page and cut out the dresses I like. It'll give Jericho's mom a better idea of what we want." She smiled at Siale. "We could even match if you wanted, or do opposites. You'd look good in anything."

"Thank you," Siale replied with a smile, though Alex could tell she felt almost as overwhelmed at the wedding planning as he did.

He leaned close to her ear. "Is the abandoned warehouse still on the table?"

She nodded. "Let's go right now."

"Done," Alex replied with a grin.

"Everyone gather for the Choosing Ceremony!" Nikki called from the stage at one end of the Great Hall.

A thrum of adrenaline rushed through Alex at the sight of the werewolf students sitting in the Great Hall waiting for Dean Jaze's address.

"Go on ahead," Alex told Siale and the others. "I'll catch up."

He grabbed Jericho's arm when the Alpha walked past.

"What's up?" the tall werewolf asked. "If you're worried about the Choosing Ceremony, don't be. It sounds like we'll probably be able to choose whoever we want again. If that's the case, you're back as my Second without question."

Alex made sure everyone was out of sight and was careful to keep his voice low when he said, "I need you to do me a favor."

"Whatever you need," Jericho replied, his gaze curious.

Alex took a steeling breath. "I need you to choose Siale as your Second again."

Jericho watched him closely. "Why?"

Alex looked past him at the students. "I've messed with the hierarchy in too many packs last term. I don't need to do it again."

Jericho ran a hand through his brown hair. "I'm not sure what you're getting at."

Alex set a hand on the Alpha's shoulder. "Trust me. Please."

Jericho finally nodded. "Alright, Alex, but you better know what you're doing."

"I do," Alex said. It wouldn't be easy, but he knew for sure what he needed to do.

They joined the others in the Great Hall. Alex avoided Jericho's gaze.

"Welcome, students!" Dean Jaze said. He looked around the hall. "We're growing in size every year. I'd like to extend a special welcome to our new first term students. I guarantee you'll have an exciting experience at the Academy!"

Many of the older students exchanged smiles and knowing glances.

Jaze smiled. "For some of you, this will be your last term at the Academy. For the first time since Vicki Carso's Preparatory Academy was established, we have a graduating class! We've established a new curriculum that includes student teaching and teacher aid opportunities. Allowing you older students to help out with our younger groups will be a great new opportunity." He glanced behind him. "Professor Colleen has graciously accepted the responsibility of being the liaison between our Senior Class and the teachers, so there will be separate meetings with her when the term is under way."

Anticipation for the Choosing Ceremony was building. Students whispered back and forth, and Alex could see the

Alphas looking around to make sure they hadn't missed anyone in their mental tallies. Alex's stomach twisted.

"As you know," Jaze continued, "We shook things up last term by having the Alphas choose only those werewolves they haven't had in their packs before." He paused and nervous anticipation filled the air. "This term, those restrictions have been lifted."

The sighs of relief that filled the room made a few of the professors chuckle.

The dean smiled. "I know it was difficult, but I feel we taught significant lessons about learning to work with anyone in your environment, not just those you prefer to have around you. However, there were a few complications." He met Alex's gaze and smiled. "So we'll allow the Alphas to do things their way once more." He raised his arms. "Let the Choosing begin!"

A cheer went up from the students.

Jaze said, "Torin, please take the stage."

Alex listened to Torin choose Sid Hathaway and Boris select Parker Luis. There were no surprises. Everyone seemed just as relieved as the professors that the packs were going back to their regular hierarchies. The rest of the Alphas took turns choosing their Seconds by order of the number of terms they had spent at the Academy. Eventually, only Jericho remained.

The Termer Alpha walked to the front of the room. Alex felt expectant gazes fall on him. He kept his eyes firmly on the back of the seat in front of him.

"Are you okay?" Siale asked quietly.

"I will be," Alex replied.

"I choose..." The Alpha fell silent.

Alex prayed that Jericho would keep his word. The students usually in Pack Jericho shifted uncomfortably in their seats. After a term apart, everyone was anxious for a normal pack life again.

"Siale Andrews," the Alpha said.

Surprised murmurs ran over the students. Alex saw Siale's shocked expression out of the corner of his eye.

"It's supposed to be you," she said.

Alex turned to her and forced a smile. "It's you. You deserve it. Take your place as Jericho's Second." When it looked like she was going to protest, Alex said, "Go ahead, Siale. It's okay."

"Are you sure?" she asked, her eyebrows pulled together in worry.

"I'm positive," he told her. "You were a great Second last term. Go on up."

Alex watched her pass through the students on her way to the dais. It was hard to ignore the questioning gazes of the werewolves around him, but Alex kept his face forward.

Torin took the stage again. "Alex Davies."

Alex's heart skipped a beat at the sound of his name. He swore it had never rung so loudly in the Great Hall. The name echoed from the corners, catching in the eaves and bouncing back at him. He didn't know why Torin would call him to his pack again after everything Alex had put him through the year before, but Alex knew what his answer had to be.

He rose from his seat, but didn't move toward the dais. His fingers gripped the back of the seat in front of him hard enough that the wood cracked.

"I deny all Choosings."

Alex's voice boomed through the sudden silence of the surprised students.

"Can he do that?" Torin asked Dean Jaze who sat behind him with the other professors.

Alex met the dean's gaze, careful to keep his face expressionless.

After a moment, Jaze nodded. "It's his right." He paused. "Not one I would recommend, but Alex is allowed to be a lone wolf if it is his desire."

All heads swiveled back to Alex.

Alex's heart pounded in his chest so hard he wondered if the students closest to him could hear it. He remembered the dean's words when they spoke about Drogan becoming a lone wolf.

"Lone wolves are dangerous. They don't have anyone to hold them accountable or to protect. A werewolf without a pack is a loose cannon because it's unnatural. Our instincts keep us together. Pack hierarchy is important because not only does it give those of lower rank someone to watch over them, it gives the Alpha purpose."

But Alex wasn't an Alpha or a Gray. He was caught somewhere in between. The Demon didn't exactly fit anywhere. Alex had defeated Alphas at the school and undermined their leadership. Why anyone would want him in their pack was baffling. Alex made the only decision he felt was right.

"It is my desire," he confirmed.

At the dean's nod, Alex sat back down. He kept his gaze on the seat in front of him until every student in the Great Hall was standing with their pack and he was the last werewolf sitting. An uncomfortable moment of silence filled the air.

Jaze clapped, breaking it up.

"That concludes the Choosing Ceremony. Please follow your Alphas to your quarters. For those who are new, your Alphas will show you the ropes here at the Academy. Class will begin tomorrow."

A groan followed the dean's announcement that was as much a tradition as the Choosing Ceremony. Alex caught a few backwards glances while the students filed out after their Alphas. He waited until the last one was gone before he rose and went outside to the statue that overlooked the courtyard.

Chapter Twenty-seven

Alex settled against the cold stone at the base of Jet's statue wondering where he fit in now that he had thrown all order out the window.

The footsteps he heard were welcome.

"Telling Jet how you managed to create chaos on the very first day of your final term?" Professor Kaynan asked.

The red-eyed professor took a seat next to Alex on the cool grass. Alex liked that he didn't ask if he could sit; Kaynan had been like an uncle to him ever since he and Cassie arrived at the Academy. The werewolf knew him almost better than he knew himself.

"Jet thinks I've outlived my welcome here," Alex answered, keeping his voice steady.

Kaynan looked up at the great black wolf statue. "I don't believe that one bit." He looked at Alex. "If anyone belongs here, it's you. You were one of the first orphans; the Academy practically belongs to you."

Alex couldn't bring himself to meet the professor's gaze. He plucked a blade of grass and twirled it between his finger and thumb. "I don't fit in here. I'm not a Gray or an Alpha, and I've beaten two of the Alphas in rank duels, something a Gray is not supposed to do. If I stay, it'll only create more trouble." His voice quieted. "But this is my home."

Kaynan was quiet for a moment before he said, "Would you like to hear what I think?"

Alex nodded silently. He heard the professor shift his back against the base of the statue in an effort to find a more comfortable position. Kaynan then tipped his head up to look at the darkening sky. "I don't fit in here either, truth be told." He glanced over and met Alex's surprised look. "Think about it. I was born a human, not a werewolf. I died in a car accident and woke up in a lab made into a werewolf. I'm the only red-coated wolf I know of." Alex could hear the depth of emotion that came with the statement the professor tried to keep light. "I fit in here less than you do."

"But you're a professor," Alex pointed out.

Kaynan grinned, his dark red eyes touched with his smile. "Jaze might have been a little desperate when he assigned positions here. We were shorthanded."

A slight answering smile touched Alex's lips at the professor's candidness. "Why are you still here then?"

Kaynan shrugged. "Let's just say that when you have your home, it's the wolf way to fight for it no matter what. Grace and I are very happy here." He gave Alex a warm smile. "In fact, she's expecting."

Alex pretended to be surprised for the professor's sake. "That's wonderful!" he said. "Congratulations!"

"Thanks," Kaynan replied. "We're very excited. Grace is going to be an excellent mother."

"And you're going to make a great father," Alex told him.

The corner of Kaynan's mouth lifted in a half-smile. "That's to be seen, I guess. In the meantime, this is your home, Alex. Being an outsider as I am, I've seen the way it works. I know how Alphas act and Grays." His gaze was serious as he studied the student. "You came here as a Gray, that's for sure. Now, though, you act more like an Alpha. Before, you were interested in protecting those closest to you, Cassie, Meredith, Kalia, and Siale. Now, though..." He gave a thoughtful smile. "The decision you made tonight was for the good of the school, for the good of the packs and the students. That was an Alpha's decision."

Professor Kaynan stood. He set a hand on Alex's shoulder and looked down at him. "Trust your heart, Alex. This is home. You have a place here and love. A wolf needs something to fight for. A werewolf needs more than that. Werewolves need the little things, smiles, hugs, knowing where you sleep in safety at night, and understanding where you fit in the scheme of things." He smiled. "You fit here, Alex. You just need to find your niche."

Alex listened to the professor walk away. He looked up at the cold metal of the statue. The seven on the wolf's shoulder shone in the moonlight. His tattoo that matched Jet's burned slightly in reminder.

"Thanks, Jet," he whispered.

A few minutes later, another set of footsteps made him rise.

"I was worried about you," Siale said. A smile touched her lips when their eyes met as if she couldn't help herself. She gave him a hug. "Jericho told me you asked him not to choose you. Do you really want to be without a pack?"

Alex kept his tone light. "It's not going to be that bad."

"You're a werewolf," Siale told him. "Pack is family."

"You're my family," he replied. He waved a hand at the Academy. "The professors are my family, Cassie and Tennison, Trent and Jordan, Terith..." He paused, then said, "I suppose I should include Von as well, but he snores."

Siale slapped his shoulder. "He's not that bad."

Alex chuckled and pulled her close. "No, he's not, and I'm glad that he and Terith seem so happy." He sighed and rested his chin gently on the top of her head. "I just can't do it anymore. Last term I spent half my time cleaning toilets just to keep Torin happy."

"You guys have resolved things," she pointed out.

Alex nodded. "Yes, but an Alpha's job is to give orders for the good of his pack, and the Grays are supposed to follow those orders to avoid chaos and maintain the discipline that keeps the pack together." He paused, then said quietly, "I don't think I can follow orders anymore."

"You never argued when Torin told you to clean the toilets," Siale said softly.

She had never mentioned anything, but Alex had always wondered how she felt about her boyfriend scrubbing toilets for hours on end at the whim of the vengeful Alpha. Though she had never looked at him differently, the humiliation of all Torin had put him through had eaten at Alex. The Demon was hard enough to control when he was on his own; Alex couldn't imagine what would happen if he continued letting others tell him what to do.

"I wanted to beat him again," Alex admitted. He felt her watching him closely, but he couldn't bring himself to meet her gaze. "I wanted to break his bones and make him wish he hadn't ordered me around." He squeezed his closed eyes. "That's not how a Gray's supposed to feel."

"It's not always easy to take orders," she said, trying to understand. "But we follow them because the Alpha's supposed to know best."

"But what if he doesn't?" Alex turned to her, his gaze troubled. "What if every time the Alpha made a decision, you were left wondering if he was right? What if the simplest orders gave the greatest frustration and you wanted to go against them just to show you can?"

Siale was silent for a moment before she said, "You don't sound like a Gray."

He sat back down at the base of Jet's statue and held up a hand. She took it and sat down beside him.

"Maybe you should be an Alpha. Your coat's been changing," Siale noted quietly. "It was almost black the last time we phased at Dad's warehouse."

Alex let out a slow breath. "I really don't know what I am anymore. I'm stuck somewhere in this strange middle where I don't want to lead, but I don't want to follow. I beat two Alphas in rank duels, but the thought of taking charge of their packs was more than I wanted to handle. I'm the most unstable of anyone I know. I don't know what to do with myself, let alone an entire pack."

Siale slipped her hand into his. She rotated their hands, studying the way their fingers linked together. "Maybe I should have chosen to be a lone wolf, too."

He shook his head. "You deserve the security of a pack. Like you said, pack is family."

She leaned her head on his shoulder. "You're my family, Alex."

Her words brought a smile to his lips. "And you're mine, Siale. I'll figure things out, I promise. I don't want you to think your fiancé is going crazy."

She looked up at him and the blue within the depths of her gray eyes was heightened in the moonlight. "You are crazy, Alex." She smiled. "And I'm crazy about you. We'll figure this out together."

So many emotions filled him that he couldn't contain them anymore. He kissed her on the lips as much to show his love as to keep sane. When his lips touched hers, everything fell away. Alex felt like he had on the wave when nothing existed but him and the ocean. He heard her heartbeat and was filled with her sage and lavender scent. He felt the brush of her hair against his hand that rested softly at the small of her back, and he was very aware of the way her hand strayed to his cheek and touched it lightly.

He pulled back and looked down at her. "Siale, I promise you this. No matter what I go through or how off the beaten path things get, I'll always be your Alex. You are my one, my love, and my everything. Seventeen might be young for someone to know what they want out of this life, but I do."

Her gaze felt bottomless when she asked, "What do you want?"

"I want you," Alex told her. "I want safety for those I care about. I want werewolves to be seen as equals with humans, and to be allowed the same opportunities. I want the professors to have their white picket fence neighborhood, I want Jaze and Nikki to be able to raise little William and his brother or sister in peace, and I want to stop looking over my shoulder for fear that my presence brings danger to those around me."

He fell silent with the realization that he had gone on a tangent.

Siale tipped her head back and looked at the stars. Alex wondered what thoughts rushed through her mind. Maybe she was starting to realize that he was too unstable to be husband material. Perhaps his goals felt too unattainable. Maybe she needed a werewolf who was willing and able to be a part of a pack. He swallowed through a tight throat, afraid he was about to lose her.

Siale's eyebrows pulled together with the little furrow in the middle when she asked, "Do you know the story of Orion?"

Confused by her line of thought, Alex shook his head. "I don't."

She kept her gaze on the stars when she said, "Orion was a great hunter who fell in love with the archer goddess, Artemis. Her twin brother, Apollo, wasn't happy with his sister's choice. One day, Orion was hunting in the ocean and only his head was visible above the waves. Apollo pointed out the black thing on the sea and bet his sister that she couldn't shoot it. Not one to pass up a challenge, Artemis drew her bow and shot the object. When Orion's body floated to shore, Artemis was so heartbroken that she placed Orion within the stars so that she could see her love every night."

"That's a sad story," Alex said; he kept his voice level despite his uncertainty as to what she as getting at.

"It's one of the versions," she replied, "But it's my favorite, do you know why?"

Alex shook his head.

She set a hand on his arm. "Because it reminds me that I could lose you. You're a lone hunter not afraid to live with your heart on your sleeve and up to your neck in adversity. Orion could best any beast, but it was his love that finally brought him down. We're different, Alex. Your love will be at your side no matter where you go."

She looked at him with an expression so honest it gripped his heart.

"Alex, just as you say I'm your one, you're my one as well. Werewolves don't love lightly." She smiled at him. "You do what you need to do. I'll be Jericho's Second in the pack to help keep the peace, and you be the lone wolf you need to be, but just know that you're never really alone. Since the moment you climbed into that body pit and saved my life, you owned my heart. No matter what you need to do, I'm with you."

Alex couldn't find the words to voice the emotions that filled him. Siale seemed to understand that. She leaned her head against his chest and listened to his heart as he held her. The moonlight strayed across the grass and snagged in the bushes along the wall, and the starlight fell on Jet's statue, covering them in his protective shadow.

"I love you, my Siale," Alex finally said.

"And I love you, my Alex," Siale whispered.

Alex rested his head back against the statue and thanked Jet from the bottom of his heart for saving his and Cassie's lives the day his parents died. The love and stability he had lost surrounded him so fully at that moment he barely dared to believe it, yet he couldn't deny the feeling of Siale's breath against his arm and the way her fingers traced patterns on his palm.

Siale sat up and looked at him. "You gave me my life, Alex. I can't wait to spend it with you."

"You've become what I live for," he replied, smiling down at her. "You are worth every breath."

Tears showed in her eyes. She leaned her head against him again. "I'm already dreading going up to Pack Jericho's quarters without you."

"Don't worry," he told her. "Everything's going to work out."

"I know." She paused, then said, "Because nobody's stupid enough to get between a werewolf and the boy she loves."

Alex chuckled and she laughed. He pulled her close and together they watched Orion travel across the sky.

Chapter Twenty-eight

When he awoke, it took Alex a minute to remember where he was. The smells were different, dust and the faintest scent of lemon lingered as though it had been a while since the place had been cleaned. The couch he slept on felt unfamiliar and lumpy. He opened his eyes and glanced around the room. A wry smile crossed his face.

All of the packs had their own quarters at the Academy. In planning for expansion, other rooms had been built so that the Academy could accommodate nearly double the number it already housed. Without a pack, Alex had found his belongings later that night moved from the bedroom in Pack Jericho's quarters where he had slept the night before and left at the end of the hallway.

Unsure what else to do, Alex had made his way to an empty hallway and taken the first set of rooms on the left. He tried all the bedrooms, but the first room was usually reserved for an Alpha, and the next for the Second. Being neither of these, Alex couldn't bring himself to settle for one of the rooms further down the hall. Instead, he fell asleep on the couch in the commons room with his stuff still in the duffle bag on the floor.

"It's not horrible," Alex said aloud. He paused, then concluded, "Except now I'm talking to myself."

Determined to make the most of the situation, Alex showered and wandered through the empty quarters, stalling until it was time for breakfast. He made his way down the hall and caught up with the throng of students hurrying downstairs toward the scent of waffles, cheesy scrambled eggs, and Cook Jerald's famous marmalade.

"Alex!" Siale called.

The sound of her familiar voice warmed Alex's heart. He

turned in time to catch her when she ran down the stairs. Laughing at her enthusiasm, he stumbled back against the banister and received a kiss.

"I've missed you," she exclaimed.

"I've missed you, too," he told her. "Seeing you made my day about a hundred percent better."

"I'm glad," she said. She slipped her hand into his. "Let's go eat."

"I'm not sure I'm allowed to eat with you," Alex replied, letting her pull him down the stairs.

Siale smiled up at him, her gray eyes bright in the morning sunlight that spilled through the windows of the entryway. "I've already cleared it with Jericho. He says you can be our pet."

"Pet?" Alex sputtered.

"Don't worry." A hand fell on his shoulder. Alex glanced back to see Jericho. "We'll make sure you have food and water like any good pet." He led the way into the Great Hall.

Alex laughed. "You guys are ridiculous."

"You can have treats," Trent said, coming up behind Jericho, his Alpha, when they stopped in the line for food. "But only if you're good."

"Then he's not going to have any," Jordan told them. She grinned at Alex, her spikey red hair skewed from the night's sleep. "Maybe we should reward you for bad behavior instead."

"That's not a bad idea," Alex replied, feeling immensely happy by the ridiculousness of their teasing. "Unless I get fat."

"I'd still love you," Siale told him. "You'd still be cute."

"So you only love me for my looks?" Alex queried.

Siale's smile deepened. "Oh no! You know my secret. It's your eyes, so dark and mysterious, like the depths of the ever-changing ocean. What are you thinking, Alex Davies?" she asked teasingly.

He took a step closer to her and lowered his voice. "That I need to kiss you so much right now it's the only thing I can think about."

Her eyes widened.

"Oh man," Trent said, stepping between them. "You'll get suspension for too much public affection in school. You know that's not allowed."

Alex blinked, Siale's hold on him broken. He smiled. "Don't worry. I have some constraint."

"I don't believe that for a moment," Trent replied.

Alex chuckled. "Maybe you know me too well."

His friend laughed. "I've been telling you that for years."

Alex took Siale's hand again and walked with her through the food line. It felt so good to have her at his side after the crazy Choosing Ceremony and the night alone in the strange quarters. He smiled at the sight of the engagement ring on her finger. He wouldn't have to last without her much longer.

"Thank you," Alex told Cook Jerald when she handed him a tray laden with waffles and cheesy eggs.

"We missed you over the summer," she replied. She winked. "We had way too much quiche after you left."

Guilt filled him at the egg and cheese pie he and Cassie had snuck before they left to Red's.

"Sorry about that," he apologized.

She shrugged and scooped a spoonful of eggs onto Siale's plate. "If you had asked, I would've told you it was a month old and should have been thrown out."

Alex sputtered. "We ate the whole thing!"

"Seriously, Alex?" Cassie said from behind him. "You've got to learn when someone's pulling your leg."

She and Cook Jerald broke out laughing.

"It was fresh," the cook amended with a grin. "And worth losing to see your expression!"

"It was the best month old quiche I've ever had," he replied with a laugh. "Thank you."

Pack Jericho insisted that he join them at their table. Feeling the glances of the other werewolves around the room, Alex took a seat between Siale and Cassie. He proceeded to pile the eggs on his waffles and took a bite of the sandwich. A glance down the table showed nearly everyone in Pack Jericho doing the same. Alex held back a smile at the thought that he had at least left a small mark on the pack.

Jaze walked through the lunchroom with Nikki beside him. Little William held his father's fingers as the dean carried a tray in his other hand. Alex focused on their conversation.

"I just don't think any college, no matter how obscure, will be open to the idea of werewolves within their student body," Professor Mouse was saying from behind them. "Every dean I've called hangs up before I say two sentences. They're afraid."

"We can't blame them," Nyra said from Mouse's side. "Tolerance is difficult to achieve, especially when fear is involved."

"But we can't let our students graduate from here with no prospects for the future," Nikki replied, setting her tray on the far table the professors used when they ate together in the lunchroom instead of in their separate quarters.

Gem smiled at little William and he scooted over to sit by the green haired werewolf.

Alex thought of his conversation with Flynn after their first game of football on the beach.

"I'll be right back," he told Siale.

He jogged over to the professors' table.

"Good morning, Alex," Jaze said with a warm smile. "Is it

good to be back?"

"It's great," Alex told him honestly. "Though a bit different."

Jaze nodded knowingly. "Being different takes courage, and you've got no shortage of that."

"That's why I'm here," Alex said. He glanced at Professor Mouse. "I overheard your conversation about colleges."

"You don't have to worry about it," Nikki told him. "We'll figure something out."

"It's already figured out," Alex replied. At their curious expressions, he said, "Someone I met while at Red's told me that college applications don't ask whether you're a werewolf or not. I feel like that's a sign. We can go to college without getting clearance for our race. We have names, addresses, and grades. As long as we can transfer our diplomas, nothing else should matter."

Nyra gave him an understanding smile. "We wish it didn't, but it does. It's too dangerous for you there if you have to hide your nature."

Alex shook his head. "Hiding what we are doesn't help anyone."

"What are you saying?" Jaze asked. There was a hint of steel in his gaze as if he had already guessed.

"We don't need to hide anymore. The best thing we can do is to let the nation know we exist just as they do, students and professors who are trying to make the world a better place in which to live. Tolerance is there, but it has to start with us."

Alex watched Jaze closely. Something flickered in the dean's eyes. Alex's chest tightened when he realized the emotion Jaze tried to suppress was fear.

"It's not safe," the dean said. "We can't protect our students beyond these walls, and if the Academy is known for what it is, they'll tear it down around us."

"They won't," Alex replied. "They can't. They've seen what we can do." He hesitated, then said, "They've seen what I can do. They know we exist. We can pretend to be ghosts, telling ourselves that wolves can live happily behind walls, or we can embrace our heritage and be strong enough to live outside of them."

Jaze shook his head. "We're not ready."

Alex met his gaze. "You might not be ready, but we are."

He realized that silence had fallen over the lunchroom.

Jaze rose to his feet. "Alex, you're in over your head. We can't protect our students if we make them a target."

"We've been targets our whole lives," Alex replied. "The only way to take the gun away is to force the world to accept that we deserve to exist."

"I've tried," Jaze replied, his tone heartbroken. "It doesn't work like that."

"It does," Alex told him firmly.

"Alex," Siale said his name quietly and touched his arm.

Alex kept his gaze on Jaze. "It's time, Jaze. We need to reveal the Academy to the world. They might not have accepted werewolves years ago, but we've shown them that we'll put our lives on the line to defend humans. We sacrificed to save Greyton and the hospital. We made ourselves targets for the curs to help end their threat. We gave the humans their lives back. Now is the time to ask the nation to return the favor."

"I won't let you risk this Academy," Jaze said, his voice laced with steel.

"Then I'll fight you for it."

Gasps spread across the Great Hall at Alex's challenge.

"What?" the dean asked.

Alex's heart thundered in his chest. He kept his focus on

Jaze. "I challenge you for the right to reveal the Academy to the world."

"It doesn't work like that," Jaze began.

Alex motioned toward the student body. "You taught us that rank duels separate those who lead from werewolves too weak to be the leader. I am ready to lead, Dean. I challenge you for that right."

Jaze's gaze traveled around the room, then back to Alex.

"Fine. I accept your challenge," he said shortly.

The dean's jaw clenched and his right knee bent slightly. With an outlet of breath, Jaze threw the first punch.

About the Author

Cheree Alsop has published 29 books, including two series through Stonehouse Ink. She is the mother of a beautiful, talented daughter and amazing twin sons who fill every day with joy and laughter. She is married to her best friend, Michael, the light of her life and her soulmate who shares her dreams and inspires her by reading the first drafts and giving much appreciated critiques. Cheree works as an independent author and mother, which is more play than work! She enjoys reading, traveling to tropical beaches, spending time with her twin boys before they start school, and going on family adventures while planning her next book

Cheree and Michael live in Utah where they rock out, practice Krav-Maga, enjoy the outdoors, and never stop dreaming.

You can find Cheree's other books at www.chereealsop.com

If you liked this book, please review it so other readers will be able to find it. Keep an eye out for Cheree's new werewolf series with some of your favorite characters from the Silver Series and the Werewolf Academy Series. The first book in The Seven will be released by the end of 2015. Cheree's next book release, Monster Asylum Book 2: The Scales of Drakenfall, is upcoming along with the Stonehouse Ink release of Shadows. To be added to Cheree's email list for notification of book releases and for sneak excerpts, updates, and giveaways, please send her an email at chereelalsop@hotmail.com

30082173R00151

Made in the USA
San Bernardino, CA
06 February 2016